Deaths of Famous
Philosophers

Deaths of Famous Philosophers

An Imaginative History of Ancient Greek Philosophy

David Roochnik

CASCADE *Books* · Eugene, Oregon

DEATHS OF FAMOUS PHILOSOPHERS
An Imaginative History of Ancient Greek Philosophy

Cascade Books
An Imprint of Wipf and Stock Publishers
199 W. 8th Ave., Suite 3
Eugene, OR 97401

www.wipfandstock.com

PAPERBACK ISBN: 979-8-3852-2241-4
HARDCOVER ISBN: 979-8-3852-2242-1
EBOOK ISBN: 979-8-3852-2243-8

Cataloguing-in-Publication data:

Names: Roochnik, David [author].

Title: Deaths of famous philosophers : an imaginative history of ancient Greek philosophy / David Roochnik.

Description: Eugene, OR: Cascade Books, 2024 | Includes bibliographical references.

Identifiers: ISBN 979-8-3852-2241-4 (paperback) | ISBN 979-8-3852-2242-1 (hardcover) | ISBN 979-8-3852-2243-8 (ebook)

Subjects: LCSH: Philosophy, Ancient. | Death. | Philosophy.

Classification: B171 R66 2024 (paperback) | B171 (ebook)

VERSION NUMBER 12/03/24

"Philosophers? They spend their lives preparing for death."

(PLATO, *PHAEDO* 67E)

Contents

Prelude

"Who am I?" the book asked.

"Hard to say," I replied.

"Where do I fit? What genre?"

"Don't know. Sui generous, maybe."

"Stop it!"

"Sorry. How about I give you the back story?"

"You've got to give me something," the book said, "because right now I can't make sense of myself, and I'm thinking no one else will be able to either. I'm about ancient Greek philosophers, several of whom I'd never heard of, and each of them is either dying or dead. Why in the world? And so much silliness! Like chapter 4. Heraclitus' whole body covered in tattoos! Or 5. Parmenides visits a prostitute. Were you just fooling around when you wrote this? If so, then why do I have so many footnotes?"

"Scholarly conscience. Or at least vestiges thereof. Can't stand to pass stuff off as my own when it's not. Don't worry, though, readers can skip the notes and not miss a beat."

"And the profanity! Socrates saying the f-word! I don't believe it. Why couldn't you write a regular book? I'm a hybrid, some twisted blend of scholarship and frivolity, and I'll probably wind up on a shelf, ignored."

"Ah, that's it. You're worried about sales." I asked.

"I want people to take me home," the book replied. "My pages are meant to be turned, aren't they? So tell me: who will my readers be? You should know, you're the writer."

"I wish I did," I said. "Truth is, I've never understood who my readers are. Or who I hope them to be. Or even if any of them actually exist."

"Oh, poor you." There was a nasty edge in the book's voice.

"On the one hand," I continued, "I'm no more than an above-average academic who's published mostly on Plato and Aristotle. My work has been cited by a thimble full of other academics. And yet, I've always had an urge to . . . to . . . to do what? Write something that matters, whatever that means? Make the world a better place? Reach a wider audience? I wrote a few books aimed at the 'general reader' who, I hoped, might be open to the possibility that, even today—especially today—the ancient Greeks can teach us important lessons and even change the way we think. But by and large my work has fallen on deaf ears. It's academic, but not particularly aggressive on the scholarly front. It's clearly written and accessible, but almost always it's about old books only a few people have ever read.

"So who am I writing for? Subscribers to the *The New Yorker*? Lawyers, doctors, non-academic friends? My father? Students longing for a worldview more humane than our technocratic own? Oprah Winfrey? Environmentalists who know full well the modern world is devouring itself but don't understand why? Or maybe misfits who were tempted by Buddhism but now realize their best hope lies in the European tradition itself."

"Enough already! Just get on with it. Tell me who I am."

"I'm trying. I was nearing retirement . . . ."

"Ah, that's it," the book interrupted. "I've been written by a geezer!"

Barely able to retain my composure, I continued. "I'd lost what interest I had in university life. Rankings, conferences, branding, best practices, journals, meetings, self-absorbed professors, online education, digital humanities, outcomes assessment, students as pampered customers, neuroscience everywhere you look. I couldn't take it any more."

"I suppose having tenure was a terrible burden."

I winced, but again managed to ignore the remark. "I'd dabbled in fiction for a long time and one day a few years ago I got it into my head to write a story about Socrates. I imagined him awaiting death in his jail cell and talking to a childhood friend I called Megacles. Hoping to turn up some juicy tidbits, I consulted the chapter on Socrates in Diogenes Laertius' *Lives of the Eminent Philosophers*."[1]

"I've been wondering about him! You quoted him dozens of times but you never bothered to explain who he was."

"Well, I'm doing it now, so calm down. He lived somewhere in the Roman Empire, and his book, which was likely written in the third century, is a collection of biographies of Greek philosophers, about eighty in all. They range from the most famous, like Plato and Aristotle, to un-knowns like Metrocles and Stilpo."

"Oh," the book said.

"The *Lives* is a strange bird, a hodgepodge of tall tales, second-rate philosophical summaries, and contrived succession narratives.[2] Most professional philosophers—people with my sort of training—don't take it seriously. And even Herbert Long, who wrote the Introduction to the edition I was reading, says Diogenes is superficial at best, unreliable at worst. He mostly just compiled stories written by other authors. Apparently, biographies of Greek philosophers were quite a thing in antiquity. Anyway, as Long puts it, 'Diogenes is a veritable tissue of quotations from all sorts of authors and on most conceivable, and some inconceivable, aspects of philosophers' lives . . . much of this quoted material is trivial, merely amusing, or probably false.'[3] Tad Brennan is nastier. Diogenes 'prefers a juicy piece of gossip to a solid piece of thinking any day. . . . He is not careful in his selection of sources, compiling all kinds of unlikely rubbish.'"[4]

"My god," the book gasped. "I'm based on rubbish!"

"Not based on, but, yes, I did take my bearings from Diogenes. The *Lives* may be, to quote Brennan again, a "third-rate Reader's Digest Guide to Ancient Philosophy,"[5] but it's been a boon to me. Its stories are often wild and typically they are abrupt and undeveloped, but that's exactly why they were such good fuel for my imagination. Diogenes gave me the nudge, and I filled in the details. Let me give you an example. I'll read it to you."

"Oh joy," the book said, its voice laced with contempt.

> *Hippobotus says that Empedocles made his way to Etna, and when he got there he leaped into the fiery craters and disappeared; for he wished to strengthen the rumor that he had become a god. But later the truth came out when one of his boots was disgorged by the volcano. For it was his habit to wear boots made of bronze.*[6]

"Yes, I recognize it. It's from chapter 8. Which is not your worst."

"Now, this story of Empedocles' death is obviously ridiculous, but it also gets to something important about philosophers. They're at risk of becoming totally full of themselves. Empedocles fits the bill. According to Diogenes, he thought he was god's gift to humanity. He wore fancy clothes and gave lectures to big crowds. In my version, he is a rich and famous celebrity, and he and his boyfriend are living the high life together. Until he is overwhelmed by the pressure of his fame and runs away."

"You took liberties."

"To put it mildly. But Diogenes gave me the permission to do this. He invited me to explore, through my imagination, the question of whether fame would be ruinous to a serious philosopher."

"Good thing you won't have to face that question yourself."

I chuckled. "Here's another example. I wrote a story about Zeno, the student of Parmenides who came up with the famous paradoxes. You know, like the one about Achilles and the tortoise."

"Of course I know! I'm the book, remember?"

"Right. But Diogenes adds a layer. In addition to being a great logician, Zeno was a patriot and a very brave man who single-handedly inspired a revolution against the tyrant Nearchus. The story is fantastic. Zeno bit his ear and then, after he was stabbed by the guards, he bit off his own tongue and spat it at the tyrant's feet! The crowd went berserk and Nearchus was toppled."[7]

"Yes, it was surprising, I'll grant you. Gory too."

"And it raises the question, what role, if any, should philosophers play in their community, their *polis* as the Greeks would have put it? Should they, like Zeno, become actively engaged in politics, even if it means losing their lives, or should they stay aloof and spin their logical wheels in private? If it's the latter, then does that make them, does that make me, utterly selfish and irresponsible as citizens? Diogenes' story of Zeno is probably no more than a legend, but it got me wondering."

"Okay."

"I'm not the first to use Diogenes as a spur to the imagination, you know. Hölderlin and Matthew Arnold did it. They both wrote poems about Empedocles jumping into the crater of Mount Etna. And in his *Imaginary Lives*, Marcel Schwob makes up stories not only about Empedocles but Crates as well. And check this out: Raphael probably 'used the personal information about the ancient Greek philosophers in Diogenes Laertius to draw the strongly individualized portraits' in his famous fresco, *The School of Athens*."[8]

"Trying to sound sophisticated, are we?" the book said softly.

"Sorry. They teach you to do that in graduate school, and old habits die hard. Anyway, the point is simple. Diogenes has been mighty influential in shaping the European conception of ancient Greek philosophy."

"Bully for him," the book said. "But why am I so morbid? All your philosophers are near death, and some even die on the page. Why?"

"The easy answer is that Diogenes himself typically includes a death story.[9] This seems to have been a significant feature of the biographic tradition he was drawing upon. Ana Chitwood's *Death by Philosophy: The Biographic Tradition in the Life and Death of the Archaic Philosophers*, and Sergi Grau's, 'How to Kill a Philosopher: The Narrating of Ancient Greek Philosophers' Deaths in Relation to Their Way of Living,' address this topic.[10] You might enjoy what they've written. They're serious scholars."

"Unlike you?"

"Afraid so. The truth is, although I was glad to learn a bit about it, I was not inclined to study the biographic tradition. That's a philologist's job. Or a historian's."

"Too hard for you?"

I didn't take the bait. "No," I replied, "I'm just not interested in detective work. Instead, I used Diogenes' death stories for my own purposes. They prompted me to conjure up stories about philosophers taking stock at the end of their lives."

"Oh, now I get it! You're a battered old professor who's worried his life's work doesn't amount to much. You were taking stock of yourself in this book."

I felt a stab, but it didn't hurt much. "I've been teaching and writing about ancient Greek philosophers for such a long time that it was easy for me to summon their voices. I tried to bring them to life and imagine what they were thinking at the end."

"And you dispensed with the facts," the book said sadly.

"Look, if it's facts you want, check out books like Dudley's *A History of Cynicism*. He debunks Diogenes Laertius' claim that Diogenes the Cynic studied with Antisthenes. As he puts it, 'it is extremely unlikely that there was any personal contact between Antisthenes and Diogenes.'[11] And he supports his assertion with an actual argument. As you know, in my version they had a meaningful relationship. You remember don't you?"

"Of course. Based on nothing more than your beloved *Lives*, a book you acknowledge to be unreliable at best, you turned Antisthenes into Diogenes' teacher and said he was thinking about him on the day he died."[12]

"'Beloved' is too strong a word, but, yes, I am grateful to the *Lives*. And it's not in spite of its obvious demerits; it's because of them. You know what William Styron once said, don't you?"

The book seemed annoyed and did not respond.

"The historical novelist works best when fed on short rations."[13]

"So there you have it," I said. "Diogenes' tall tales and weird concoctions, tantalizing in their brevity, gave me the push to write something I've long wanted to try: a blend of philosophy and storytelling. You know, like Plato's dialogues."

"Trust me, you're no Plato."

"Trust me, I know," I replied.

"Another question, if I may," the book said.

"Shoot."

"Why the profanity?"

"It packs some punch, and it's the way people actually talk when they get excited or angry. Or at least I do. And it's justified, I think, when it comes to Heraclitus and the Cynics, and maybe Socrates too."

"Or perhaps it's no more than an exercise in macho posturing? Good god, man, I'm a book about obscure Greek philosophers known only to a handful of academics. Its author should sound like a scholar, not a longshoreman from New Jersey."

"How'd you know I grew up in New Jersey?"

"You'd be surprised what I know," the book said with a nasty smirk.

"Well, I am a scholar, but in my own way. Respectfully, but never wholeheartedly. One foot in, one foot out. Just like Socrates."

"You're no Socrates! As you admitted, you're an average academic . . ."

"Above average!" I interjected.

"So why didn't you just stick with that? It's an honorable profession."

"It is. And the hours are good. Truth is, I didn't have much choice. It was either a book like this or give up writing, which is something I can't do. I have too much energy, and I can't think without it."

"Self-indulgent," the book said.

"No doubt. Look, I started writing you in the pandemic year of 2020. There were long stretches during the lockdown when I spent hours staring out the window, imagining invisible aerosols, like Democritean atoms, floating through the void, poised to enter my bloodstream and destroy my lungs. In such circumstances, I had no interest in writing yet another book on Aristotle's *Metaphysics*."

"Why not? At least there would be a proper place for it in the library. Now, who knows where I'll be classified. I'm a mongrel. No one will want to read your fanciful, vulgar stories about dead Greek philosophers."

"You never know."

"The academics will ignore me."

"Probably."

"You don't get it, do you? Only academics will recognize the names of your famous philosophers and consider picking me up in the first place, and yet you didn't write me in the language they're accustomed to. Then who did you write me for? Certainly not 'general readers,' whoever they may be. They won't be enticed by a book that features such notables as Crates and Aristippus."

"I know. I'm in the same bind I've always been in. I want to be understood by people who aren't scholars, and so I write as clearly and simply as I can. But my thinking has been decisively shaped by my study of the ancient Greek philosophers, and I need to bring their books into my own writing. Without them I wouldn't have much to say."

"If you wanted ordinary people to be your readers," the book said, "you should have written a historical novel with a good deal of sex and violence."

"Hey, I put some sex, even a little violence, into you."

"Pretty tame stuff. Face it, I'm not going to sell."

"It is what it is," I replied stupidly.

"Enough of your blather!"

Suddenly I felt a wave of exhaustion wash over me. "Look," I said, "we're done here. You're just going to have to do the best you can with what you've got. Most likely you'll be ignored, and if you do get read, you'll probably be misread. You can disown me if you want. I don't care. The world was rotten before you were born and it will only get worse when you're gone. The bottom line is I wrote what I wanted to write. I was cooped up in my house for months and months and because of you I managed to pass the time in an agreeable fashion. So, my friend, off you go. As Aeschines said to Aristippus 2,300 years ago, *vaya con dios, amigo.*"

"You're insufferable!" the book replied.

1

Thales the First

(Thales: 630–552 BCE; Anaximander: 610–546 BCE;
Anaximenes: 586–536 BCE)[14]

As Thales watched the games,
You snatched the sage from the stadium.
I commend you Zeus, Lord of the Sun, for drawing him toward you;
For he could no longer see the stars from earth. (DL I.39)[15]

IT WAS THE FIRST day of the fall term and, despite his misgivings, Anaximander was determined to address the new students. He had resolved to do so only a few hours earlier, at dawn. For the past two weeks, his steadily worsening cough had kept him from sleeping much, his urine was streaked with blood, and he had no appetite. He seriously considered retiring and passing the torch to his most capable student, Anaximenes, but when the sun finally rose, he could not bear to do it.

As he had for the past five years, he began by saying, "Welcome, gentlemen, to the Milesian School of Philosophy." Afraid of triggering his cough, he kept his voice soft and his breathing shallow. "Today we shall discuss the question, how is it that the whole of earth, for all its great weight, forever remains at rest?"[16]

"Before I begin my lecture, however, I would like to say a few words about our founder, Thales of Miletus. He was, as you surely know, the first. Not just the first head of our school, but the first philosopher in all of Greece."

He paused and glanced at the notes written on his wax tablet. He blinked in dismay when he realized they hadn't changed one iota since he delivered his inaugural lecture on the day he succeeded Thales as head. For five years he had told exactly the same story. Thales was a revolutionary. Prior to him the teachers of Greece had been the poets who, however beautiful their songs, relied on the Muses for inspiration and had no way whatsoever of demonstrating the truth of their claims. Thales was the first to dispense with myth, music, and meter, and to study the world with only his mind. He was the first to predict a solar eclipse and prove a circle is bisected by its diameter.[17] It was he, not Homer or Hesiod, who discovered stability standing behind the flux, unity behind multiplicity, Being behind becoming. He was the first to be called a sage, and rightly so, for it was he who elevated reason over imagination, science over poetry, seeing over making, *logos* over *mythos*. He arrived at his famous proposition, that water is the ultimate and abiding source of all things, through rational argument alone. *Observation #1*: water falls from the sky. *Observation #2*: water is under the earth. *Observation #3*: living beings need water. *Observation #4*: land masses are surrounded by water. *Conclusion:* water is the first principle, or what we Milesians call the *archē*.[18]

When Anaximander saw this word on the tablet, he grinned. For it was he who convinced Thales to use it. And what a perfect word it was, for not only did it mean beginning, origin, and first cause, but also power, rule, and authority. The *archē*, Thales had taught him, is what the philosopher must strive to understand and to explain. And while, no doubt, his teacher took the crucial first step, and for this deserves enormous credit, he got it wrong. For years Anaximander had argued that, precisely because the *archē* was the source of all things, it had to be essentially different from them. It could not possibly be a determinate entity, a specific thing, a this rather than a that, as water, which is not fire, surely is. That would be illogical. No, he concluded, the *archē* must be the indefinite, the unlimited, the infinite.

He took a sip of water from the cup sitting on the speaker's platform. Yes, he thought, Thales was surely wrong, but so what? He had been his teacher and his friend, a wonderful man who was smart, warm, loyal, and funny.[19] He remembered when Anaximenes asked Thales why he had no children. Because I love children too much, he replied. And when his mother urged him to get married, he told her it was too soon, and when she repeated herself a month later, he told her it was too late. Once a smart aleck asked him, "if there is no difference between life and death, why don't you kill yourself right now?" He answered without a moment's pause: "because there is no difference." And then there was the golden tripod. A fisherman found it in his net. He was so astonished that he asked the oracle at Delphi what should be done with it. The priestess replied, it should go to the wisest of all men. So he gave it to Thales. And what did he do? He presented it to Apollo at his temple in Didyma.

Anaximander remembered the night when the two of them were observing the stars. Thales was so intensely absorbed he fell into a ditch. Fortunately, he wasn't hurt and so Anaximander said to him, "how do you expect to know all about the heavens, Thales, if you can't even see what's under your feet?"[20] Then he made the mistake of telling a fellow student the story, and within days it was being repeated throughout Miletus, and Thales became a laughingstock. But he had his revenge. Through his astronomical studies, he calculated that there would be a bumper crop of olives in the fall. So in the spring he borrowed money and rented all the olive presses in Miletus. When harvest time arrived, he charged an exorbitant fee for those presses and made a fortune. His objective, though, was not to get rich, but only to show people it would be easy for philosophers to make money if they wanted to. But they don't.[21]

Anaximander shook his head sadly. Even this remarkable turn of events never quite extinguished the story of Thales and the ditch. In fact, after he died the rumor spread that this is what killed him. But it wasn't true. He had died from heatstroke after spending an entire afternoon in the blazing sun, watching athletes compete. Naturally, he was not there to cheer on anybody in particular, but to contemplate human excellence in its physical form. A fitting death, Anaximander thinks, for a philosopher.

He was sure that had he not met Thales when he was teenager he would have become a merchant like his father. It only took one lecture for Thales to turn his soul around and ignite in him a burning desire for knowledge of the world. He studied with him for nearly twenty years, and then for the next twenty served as his assistant. On his deathbed, Thales took his hand, smiled, and whispered, "Your turn now."

At first he was astonished that Thales named him, Anaximander, his successor. After all, they disagreed about the nature of the *archē*. But the more he thought about it, the more he realized that even at the end Thales was teaching him a lesson. A philosopher strives for wisdom but, because he is a man and not a god, he will always fall short. He delights in intellectual competition between friends, but loves truth far more than victory.

It took a while, but Anaximander gradually made this principle his own. This is why he felt not a twitch of anger when he was challenged by his own student. Anaximenes argued that, no, the *archē* was not the indefinite, but air.

He turned to his small audience, which had been waiting patiently for him to continue. "You must understand, gentlemen," he said slowly, his voice weak but audible, "Thales was a revolutionary. Not only was he the first head of the Milesian School, but he was the first philosopher in all of Greece. Many years ago he predicted an eclipse. I watched him do it myself."

2

Solon Reaches the End

(630–560 BCE; Archon of Athens, 594 BCE)[22]

Distant Cyprion fire consumed the body of Solon.
Salamis harbors his bones,
Their dust has nourished grain. (DL I.63)

"HOW ARE YOU FEELING?" the young doctor asked gently. He was a small, delicate man, with bright eyes, a thin nose, and twitchy fingers.

"Better," Solon replied. He sounded unconvinced.

The doctor put his hand on his forehead and nodded. "Yes," he said with as much cheer as he could muster. "The fire has died down. Did you get some sleep last night?"

"I did."

"No sweats?"

"No."

"And did you have an appetite this morning?"

"No, but I forced myself to take a few spoonfuls of broth. And to drink some of your tea."

"It's made from willow leaves," the doctor said, "and it's why you feel better."

"Perhaps," Solon replied. "Thank you for moving my bed closer to the window. The sea breeze is wonderful, and I like looking at the beach. Especially that giant rock just off the shore."

Barely having the energy to raise his hand, he managed to gesture towards the sea.

"I'm glad," the doctor said. "Do you know what it is?"

"No."

"The Rock of Aphrodite. It's where she was born. You know the story, I'm sure. Cronus castrated his father Uranus and threw his genitals into the sea. The water bubbled and foamed, and from the whirlpool emerged Aphrodite. Right there, on that very beach, she came to earth, to delight and torture us all."[23]

Solon tried to smile. "Ah, yes, of course, the goddess. She was born here, in Cyprus."

The doctor was pleased, almost proud. "We are honored to have you with us, Solon."

"Thank you. But I had hoped to die on my own island of Salamis, not on yours."

"You're not going to die here, Solon. You . . ."

"I'm finished, and you know it," he interrupted with surprising vigor.

The doctor drooped his head in shame.

"Oh, come now," Solon said. "You've done a good job. You made me comfortable. My mind is clear for the first time in days, and I have the energy to talk with you, which is a great treat. Don't feel sad. I'm eighty years old and have had a long life.[24] An interesting life."

The doctor studied his wrinkled but still handsome face. His hair and beard were thick, his eyes deeply set and thoughtful. Only the grayish flush on his cheeks suggested he was ill. He wanted to say something, but hesitated. He closed his eyes for a few seconds and summoned his courage. "Count no man happy until he has reached his end," he said quietly.

He was amazed when Solon grinned. "Ah, my famous words," he said. "They've spread far and wide, haven't they. I actually heard a fisherman at the harbor say them to his friend. He was talking about his dead fish, though, and laughing."

The doctor, unsure of himself, nodded. "Yes, it's a well known saying here in Cyprus."

"A cliché, you mean," Solon chided him.

The doctor, embarrassed, shook his head. "I've been told you said it to Croesus, but that's all I know. Maybe you could tell me the story?"

"Don't you have other patients to see?" Solon asked.

"I do, but they can wait. It's not every day a sage comes to Cyprus."

"Nonsense," Solon said. "I'm no sage. Some say I'm a philosopher, but that's not true either. If anything, call me a lawgiver. I did my best for the city of Athens."

"Still," the doctor pressed on, "I'd love to hear the story. Why don't I get you another cup of tea, and you can tell it to me."

"I'll try," he replied.

The doctor brought the old man his drink and helped him take a few sips.

Solon began.

"When I got Croesus' letter inviting me to visit him in Lydia, I declined. I was polite, though. I didn't tell him that the prospect of being entertained by a tyrant repulsed me. After all, at the time I was doing everything I could to stop Pisistratus. He was consolidating power in Athens, and he had his eye on becoming a tyrant himself. Once I even came into the Assembly wearing my shield and carrying my spear. I looked like a fool, and the people thought I was insane, but I knew what I was doing. Trying to wake them up to the threat Pisistratus posed to our freedom."

Solon closed his eyes. The doctor was afraid he was on his way out, but the old man surprised him again. "We were friends once, you know," he said, his voice gaining strength. "Back when we were young. But he became an unbearable man and was always spoiling for a fight.[25] He got fat and had yellow hair that looked like a gust of wind had blown it upwards, a jaw that was perpetually thrust forward, and the narrowed eyes of a predator. It took me a long time, but I finally realized that Pisistratus cared about absolutely nothing except himself. His famous motto, *Make Athens Great Again*? Total nonsense."

Solon bit his lower lip and sighed. "I could have been tyrant myself, you know. The people wanted me to. That's because my first act as *archon* was to cancel their debts. They used to offer themselves as collateral for loans, and many of them had become indentured servants, little better than slaves. They trusted me because I lifted them out of poverty and restored their citizenship. But I refused to become their leader. Power belongs to the people, I told them, not to a single man."

He was speaking rapidly, but his breathing was labored and the grayish flush had spread to his nose and forehead. The doctor recognized what was happening. Before the old man succumbed to the fire burning inside him, a burst of energy would flow through him. Bombarded by memories, he'd feel an urgent need to talk. And then he would die. The doctor's only hope was that Solon would have enough time to finish his story and his end would come without too much pain.

"When the tide began to turn Pisistratus' way," he continued, "I realized my days in politics were over, and it was time for me to leave Athens. I began my ten long years of travel and let the Athenians fend for themselves.

"The first thing I did was to reconsider Croesus' invitation. I sent him a letter asking if I might still be able to visit. He wrote right back and said he would be delighted to have me come.

"When I arrived in Sardis, he greeted me enthusiastically, housed me in opulent guest quarters, assigned three servants to attend me. Before I had even unpacked my bags, he gave me a tour of the royal treasury. It lived up to its reputation. Croesus kept a vast collection of coins, statues, jewelry, all of it made from gold. He was a Midas indeed, and proud of it.

"My first dinner in the palace was pleasant enough. We had a luxurious meal—too rich for my taste—and then we talked late into the night. Croesus was intelligent, respectful, and genuinely interested in my poems. The second night, though, was different. We were beginning our dessert when, out of nowhere, he asked me who was the happiest man I had ever known.

"It took me a moment to recover from the shock of his question, and of course I knew what answer he anticipated. But even though I was a guest, I refused to gratify him. Instead, I told him the truth. The happiest man was an Athenian named Tellus. He was a farmer who had a faithful wife and four sturdy sons. Most important, he served his city and the end of his life was superb.[26] He was in the army that routed the Eleusians and he died honorably on the battlefield. The Athenians rewarded him with a public funeral.

"Croesus didn't like my answer. He couldn't understand how a mere soldier, an ordinary man, and someone who was already dead, could possibly be happiest. But he managed to control his frustration, and he asked me who came in second. It was a tie, I told him, between two brothers from Argos, Cleobis and Biton. They lived in a village six miles from town. One day their mother wanted to attend a festival in honor of Hera. The boys were preparing the ox cart that would take her to the temple when they learned the oxen were still working in the fields and could not be spared. So they put their mother in the cart, strapped it to themselves and dragged it for the entire six miles. When the trio finally reached the temple, people were amazed and they congratulated the mother on having such splendid sons. Glowing with pride, she prayed to Hera to reward them with the best of all possible gifts. That night the two boys lay down to sleep in the temple and never awoke again. Like Tellus, the end of their lives was most excellent.

"When he heard that, Croesus started to get mad. He asked me if I thought it was better to be dead than alive, but he didn't let me answer. Instead, he blurted out another question, the only one really on his mind. What about me? Surely I rank higher than two boys who treated their mother well and then died young!"

Solon paused. His lips were quivering, and the flush had changed from gray to an angry red. The doctor helped him take a few more sips of tea and then wiped his chin where it had dribbled.

"I tried to talk sense to him," he continued, his voice firm. "In the blink of an eye good fortune can turn to bad, which means it's a terrible mistake to call someone happy while they are still alive, for they remain vulnerable to chance. Not even you, Croesus, I told him, are immune from upheaval, at least not before you have ended your life well. And then I uttered the words you Cypriots like so well. 'Count no man happy until he has reached the end.'

"That was the final straw. He stood up from the couch and screamed, 'Is that it? You want me to die?'

"For a moment, I thought he would have me killed on the spot. Fortunately, though, he just sent me away in disgust. But why? I was only telling him the truth. We hang by a thread."

Solon, his cloudy eyes open wide, looked amazed. The doctor put his hand on the old man's forehead. Despite the willow leaves, it was hot.

"And what happened to Croesus?" the doctor asked, desperate to hear more.

"A catastrophe," Solon said. "One night he dreamt his son, a boy named Atys, was killed by an iron weapon. From then on he would not allow Atys to get near a knife or leave the palace grounds, and he gave him a personal bodyguard named Adrastus. Croesus had great confidence in this man, and so he granted Atys his most fervent wish. To join the men on a hunt for wild boar. The boy was excited. Too excited, I'm afraid. When Adrastus told him to stand next to a tree while he and the servants flushed out the boar, Atys could not stay still. He followed the men and snuck into the bush without them seeing him. When Adrastus threw the first spear, it hit Atys square in the chest. He died instantly."

"Friendly fire," the doctor said sadly.

"Yes, but there's more. Croesus mourned for two full years. When he returned to the throne the first item on his agenda—the very first!—was to go to war against the Persians and their king Cyrus. But before doing so he consulted the oracle at Delphi. The priestess told him if he attacked the Persians a great empire would be destroyed."

"Oh my god," the doctor said, realizing instantly what would happen next.

"Yes," Solon said. "Even after his son's death, Croesus was sure of himself and he proceeded to attack the Persians. The result? Lydia was destroyed, and he was taken prisoner by Cyrus. When he was on the pyre ready to be burned, Croesus remembered my words. Count no man happy until he is dead. Then he said my name out loud. Cyrus was intrigued, had the fire doused and asked him who this Solon was. A sage, Croesus said. He told Cyrus the story. All of us, no matter how rich or poor, are subject to chance. As Homer said, 'Zeus, being all powerful, gives all of us, in turn, good luck and bad.'[27]

"Cyrus spared poor Croesus' life, and thus began my career as a sage. But it's silly. My saying is no more than a bit of folk wisdom."

Solon had difficulty clearing his throat. After the doctor helped him take sips of tea, his head sank deeper into the pillow. Afraid he was losing him, the doctor asked one more question. "And you, Solon, what about your end? Are you happy?"

"Me?" he said, reluctantly. He stared at the ceiling for a long moment, and then chuckled. "Before I came here I was in Egypt, and my hosts told me no ships would be sailing to Cyprus for at least two weeks. But I went to the harbor anyway just to check, and sure enough, one was getting ready to depart that very day, and a single berth was still available. When I told the other passengers what happened, they congratulated me for being so lucky, and indeed this is precisely what I myself thought. Of course, the first thing that happened when I arrived in Cyprus was to catch the fire, which will kill me soon. What seemed to be good luck turned out to be bad, but, as always, this could only be known after the fact."

The doctor grimaced.

"On the other hand," Solon replied, his voice suddenly becoming weaker, "right now I'm not in pain. And you, dear doctor, are good company. I'm comfortable, and I'm looking at the Rock of Aphrodite. Mine is not a glorious death like that of Tellus. But it's not too bad, at least if I die soon. Who knows, had I stayed in Egypt, it may have been much worse."

"Only when it's over . . . ." The doctor did not finish his sentence.

Solon, now exhausted, whispered, "Do something for me."

"Of course, Solon. Anything."

"After I die, send my bones to Salamis."[28]

Solon's words hit the doctor's chest like a spear. He tried to muffle his cry, but could not.

"Come, come, dear boy," he said, barely audible.

The doctor took a breath, regained his composure. His eyes met Solon's but the old man no longer registered his presence. Still, the doctor spoke.

"I don't understand, Solon, really I don't. You say we cannot know whether our luck is good or bad until it has run its course and we have reached the end. But what does that mean? That at every moment of every day we must remind ourselves that if any little bit of good fortune happens to come our way it can be obliterated in the blink of an eye? Are you telling me the most we can hope for is that it all ends before catastrophe strikes?"

Trying to think harder, he put the palms of hands over his eyes and pushed, as if to drive Solon's maxim deeper into himself. He sighed when he realized he couldn't.

"I wish you could meet my son, Solon. He's only three, and there's nothing in the world I like more than being with him. He talks well already, and he's interested in everything, especially chariots and carts, anything with wheels. And he loves ants. He never steps on them, he only points and smiles. He's a sweet boy, a gentle boy. And what would you have me do when I'm with him and feeling blessed? Should I stifle my happiness? Should I tell myself that, like Croesus, my boy may be taken away at any moment, and if he were, I would suffer beyond words? I believe my son's birth was great good fortune, but, who knows, maybe I'm wrong. What's worse is I cannot know until all my chapters have reached their end. But then I will know nothing at all.

"I don't understand! How are we supposed to live? On edge, facing an unknowable future, always ready for the worst? When I'm with my son, I can't possibly think like that. Happiness has become a habit, and I'm not sure I can break it. I'm not sure I want to."

Solon's eyes were closed, his breathing shallow. The doctor looked at him for several minutes and then he spoke again.

"Or is it the other way around? Maybe your pessimism makes us more appreciative of the little we have. For it is true, my son is a delicate flower who can be trampled by a careless step. Is he all the more precious for that?"

The doctor rested his hand on the old man's forehead. The fire was burning fiercely and, he was now sure, there was nothing more he could do. He lifted his hand and brought it to his lips. Then he closed his eyes and silently prayed to Aphrodite. He vowed he would deliver Solon's bones to Salamis himself, although this meant he would not see his son for weeks. And when he told the story, he would make sure it ended well.

3

Pythagoras Flying

(580–500 BCE)

To avoid trampling the beans
He was slain at a crossroads
by the Agrigentines. (DL XIII.45)

Eyes closed, tranquil smile, hands clasped at the belly. As always, wearing an immaculate white robe, trousers, and a golden wreath on his head.[29]

A musician at his bedside, gently strumming a lyre.

Not long for this earth. But do not fear, he will come back as a swallow, harbinger of spring. Or maybe a hawk. Or even a crow. It does not matter, as long as he can fly.

Some say he is Apollo, come down from the Hyperboreans in the far north.

Once, when he crossed the river Nessus, it greeted him with a song.

A disciple saw him naked and reported that he had a thigh of gold.[30]

Music turned him on. One day, only a child, he walked by a forge. Blacksmiths beating their hammers on anvils, each striking a different note. And then, a miracle: cacophony became euphony. Different notes harmonizing. The smiths let him enter. He measured. The size and weight of the hammers determined the sound. Went home. Reproduced the same intervals in strings.[31]

Behind the harmony we hear: ratio!

The lyre, no more than a wooden box laced with sheep gut strings. But tuned properly, its music is glorious. From the longest string (lowest in pitch) to the middle . . . a fourth. From the middle to the shortest (highest in pitch) . . . a fifth. From the shortest to the third . . . a fourth. From the third to the longest . . . a fifth. The fourth 3:4, the fifth 3:2, the octave 2:1.[32]

Ratio! Portal to the cosmos.

He started seeing it everywhere. In Eurymenes' body. Bottom of chin to top of forehead is to the length of whole as 1 is to 10. Bottom of chin to bottom of nostrils is to the whole face as 1 is to 3. In his teachers. Amasis: insistent, but never demeaning. Attentive to students, but kept his distance. Equal parts water and fire. Pherecydes: prone to outbursts of anger. Unbalanced. Hermodamas: prone to melancholy.[33] Unbalanced. In the 4 seasons of a man's life:

20 (boy)	*20 (youth)*	*20 (man)*	*20 (old man)*
spring	summer	autumn	winter[34]

In rams's horns, vine tendrils, nautilus shells, fern fronds.

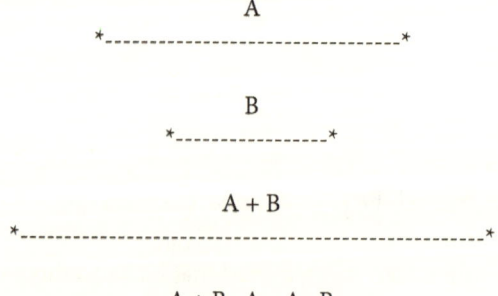

$$A + B : A :: A : B$$

The cosmos, intelligible at heart. Divine.

The heavenly bodies, rotating in circular orbit around the earth, velocities synchronized. On each, a Siren, singing a single note as she is borne around in its revolution. From all 8, a harmony.[35] Of the spheres.

3, the prince of numbers. Left, right, center. Length, width, depth. Above, below, level. Future, present, past. Sky, light, earth. God, human, beast. Beginning, middle, end. And, of course, the triangle.

10 pebbles, arranged thus: an image of perfection.[36]

.

. .

. . .

. . . .

The One: *Archē* of all things. From The ONE, The Indeterminate Dyad; from The ONE and The Indeterminate Dyad, numbers; from numbers, points; from points, lines; from lines, plane figures; from plane figures, solid figures; from solid figures, perceptible bodies, of which there are four: fire, water, earth, and air; from them, the cosmos, alive.[37]

The book of nature written in mathematical characters.

Without number, it is not possible to think or know.[38]

Arithmos: a number (or count) of units (of 1s). Therefore, the first number is 2.

The One: *archē* of number but not itself a number. The One: fount of the cosmos, origin of knowledge. But it cannot, itself, be counted. It cannot, therefore, be known. Only revered.

Bodies change, deteriorate, fall apart. Not numbers. 3 sticks, 3 stones, 3 applies, they all come and go. But not 3. It always is.

So too is the soul that does the counting. Like numbers, it is divine and moves on when body is gone.[39] To other animals.

Transmigration of souls. Therefore, do not eat meat!

> *Abstain! Preserve your bodies unabused,*
> *mortals, with food of sin!*
> *How vile a crime that flesh should swallow flesh,*
> *body should fatten greedy body; life*
> *should live upon the death of other lives!*
> *With all the bounteous riches that the earth,*
> *best of mothers, yields, can nothing please*
> *but savage relish munching piteous wounds?*[40]

By virtue of their windy nature, beans partake most of the breath of life.[41]

He was trying to escape from a band of thieves when he reached a bean field. He refused to cross it. They caught him. Now he lies here.

He will be back among us in 207 years.[42] Just wait.

4

Heraclitus Rants

(540–480 BCE)

Heraclitus lived a troubled and ill-fated life
And then died.
An awful disease, flooding his body,
Extinguished the light in his eyes and brought on darkness. (DL IX.4)

HE'S TERRIBLY ILL, NEAR death really, but still he visits me once a week. Without fail. This afternoon, after he slowly shuffled into my office, in obvious pain, feet so swollen he could no longer wear sandals, I let him release some of his pent-up rage.

"Why do people keep gushing over Hecataeus?" he asked me. Of course he answered his own question. "He's no more than a two-bit sight-seer!" he screamed. "Scythians, Persians, Egyptians . . . who gives a shit!"[43]

His language is becoming increasingly vile. Filthy, really. Look, he's always been abrasive, and even as a kid he would lay into people, but ever since Hermodorus died he's been getting steadily worse. His one friend, the only person with whom he softened. They grew up together and as kids they were inseparable. When Hermodorus was banished from Ephesus, Heraclitus went berserk. "He was worth ten thousand of you shitheads!" he howled, tears rolling down his cheeks. "Why don't you do us all a favor and hang yourselves!"[44] He said these things in public! Can

17

you imagine? And then for weeks afterwards he would spend hours sitting alone on the banks of the river Kaustros. Just watching it flow by, mumbling to himself.

He's my older brother, but I've never liked him. Yes, yes, I know, I owe everything to him. When he renounced his claim to the kingship twenty-five years ago, I was next in line.[45] I've always tried to treat him respectfully, which, trust me, hasn't been easy. But now he's gone over the edge. I know he's going to die soon, but even that doesn't excuse his appalling language.

As a child he was a prodigy. He memorized Homer and the poems of Archilochus before he was ten. He liked to torture me by reciting passages from the *Odyssey*. Sometimes, when he was in the mood to really show off, he'd recite them backwards. But by the time he was twelve and—how shall I put it?—coming into his own, he started to rail at both of them. Said they should be whipped! And by his early teens he was mocking his teachers. To their faces he'd call them sleepwalkers and tell them they didn't understand a word of what he was saying. Look, it's true, the teachers here in Ephesus aren't always the best, but most of them try hard. Still, Heraclitus held them all in contempt. He used to brag that he was self-taught. At least he was honest about that.

With Hermodorus, though, he was a totally different person. Quiet and completely at ease with one another, they would spend hours playing knucklebones. They'd throw a few into the air and try to catch them on the back of their hands or on the top of their heads. Or they would toss them into a pot. It didn't matter what they did, they were always together, having fun. They'd wrestle and laugh and talk in what sounded like their own private language. Of course, they never let me, the little brother, in on any of it.

They stayed close for years and years, up to the day when Hermodorus was exiled. And that's when Heraclitus started to get strange. By then he had finished his first book, which he modestly titled *On Nature*. Truth is, though, he never actually finished it. To this day parts of it are still fragmentary. But at least he stopped tinkering with it and allowed it to circulate. His main objective, as far as I could tell, was to make it as confusing as possible so that no one—except Hermodorus, I suppose—could understand it. I mean, half the time he didn't even use verbs. "Bound together, whole not whole, in tune out of tune." Good lord, what's that supposed to mean? Or "the most beautiful harmony from things torn asunder." Or "road up down one and same." Totally incomprehensible! I'm surprised I remember them.

Once I asked him why he wrote this way. He looked amused and said in his most condescending voice, "nature loves to hide."

Oh, my brother. What an insufferable man.

But Hermodorus could suffer him. Indeed, he seemed to love him.

For reasons I cannot fathom, his book made quite a splash. In fact, the great king, Darius himself, somehow got hold of it and wanted to meet him. He sent Heraclitus a letter in which he said that he found *On Nature* to be fascinating but hard to understand and that he would like him to come to Persia and explain it. So how did my brother respond? With his typical arrogance. "Earth-bound ninnies like you care only for fame and fortune. I detest your splendor. Thanks, but no thanks." To the king of Persia, that's what he wrote!

He liked animals better than people and often talked about them. He would point out obvious things as if they were amazing discoveries. Pigs, he once excitedly told me, prefer mud to clean water. Oxen eat vetch even though it tastes terrible to us. Birds clean themselves in dust. Give a donkey a choice, and he'll take trash over gold every time.[46] I tried to understand why he thought these trivial remarks were profound but, to be honest, I never got close.

I will say this. He was always exceptionally good with children. He would get down on his hands and knees and play knucklebones with them for hours. He was never condescending, and he didn't talk to them in the sing-song voice adults typically use. Instead, he genuinely enjoyed their company. Preferred them to adults. When he was twenty, he got his first tattoo, on his right forearm. *Child at play.*[47] Ugh.

Now he's covered in tattoos. Too many to count. There's a thunder-bolt on his left bicep, *war, father of all* is on the side of his neck, and *anarchy rules* is across his back. He's old and sick, and his painted skin hangs on his fragile bones like wet papyrus sheets. Disgusting, really.

You wouldn't believe what he said about the Pythagoreans this afternoon. "Numbers, numbers, numbers. Yap, yap, yap. The morons actually believe their own bullshit. Cosmos, order, harmony! A crock of random shit, I say. I should shove their sacred beans up their asses. Make them fart until they explode. Their souls already stink."

Look, I'm not crazy about Pythagoreans either, but that's no reason to be nasty.

I hate the sound of his voice but, in accord with the oath I swore on my mother's grave, I don't say a word when he goes on a rant. Thank god he only comes once a week and doesn't stay long.

If he weren't going to die soon, I'd have him killed on the spot!

No, I'm sorry, I didn't mean it.

As usual, this afternoon he launched into his favorite tirade. "God-damned Ephesians! Not one of them could hold a candle to Hermodorus. He was the best of the best, and so what did the stupid bastards do? Exile him! Mediocre pricks couldn't abide excellence in their midst!"

He simply can't let it go.

After Hermodorus was exiled and living in Colophon, Heraclitus visited him often, and he always seemed depressed when he returned. He was shattered when he got the news of his friend's death a couple of years ago. He didn't cry, didn't say a word, he just started walking towards the mountains. He stayed there in complete isolation for two weeks. He brought no food or blankets with him. God knows how he survived. And when he finally did come back to town, he was emaciated, and his feet were so swollen he could barely stand on them. It was dropsy, which, I have to say, is rather ironic. One of this tattoos, on his right buttock I think, reads *water is death*.[48] He tried to cure himself by burying himself in our cowshed. He thought that the warmth of the manure would draw out all the liquid that was filling him up. Needless to say, it did not go well. Because he was too weak to protest, I had the court physicians treat him and a nurse force-feed him. Eventually he recovered, somewhat, but when he did, he was even more of a misanthrope than before. That's when he started visiting me for his weekly ranting sessions.

The ambassador from Colophon informed us that Hermodorus had been killed in a house fire. I hate to say it, but that was fitting. When they were kids there was nothing those two liked more than playing with fire. Heraclitus would steal the iron and flint from the kitchen, and they'd start blazes behind the storage shed near the pigsty. Once, things got out of control, and they burned the building down. My father whipped Hera-clitus good and hard, but he never cried. That night, when we were in our beds, he told me that watching the shed go up in flames and hearing those pigs squeal in terror was the most fun he'd ever had. That was a little scary.

When he was a teenager he was hyper-active, but at least he stopped playing with fire. But to this day, he has always loved sitting in front of a hearth and staring into the flames. One of his tattoos, on his left shoulder I think, is *fire judges all*.[49]

He did surprise me today, though. "Fools!" he screamed, and I didn't know whom he was talking to. "Be not deceived. It is the fault of your myopia, not of the nature of things, if you believe you see land somewhere in the ocean of coming-to-be and passing away. You use names for things as though they rigidly, persistently endured; yet even the stream into which you step a second time is not the one you stepped into before."[50]

For once, no curse words. But I wonder what "myopia" means. Anyway, after that he turned to leave the room, of course without saying good-bye. As he was shuffling toward the door he hardly looked like a fire-breathing philosopher. Just a feeble old man, his body gorged with fluid and soon to die. Before he left, he turned around and looked at me. The mad fury was gone, his eyes were clear, and for the first time in years I saw . . . I saw my brother. My big brother, who never liked me or played with me, who always made me feel stupid and small. But who never hit me either. And on his face I saw the gentle visage of my beautiful mother. We both adored her. Naturally, she favored Heraclitus. He was nothing but trouble, but he was so bright and energetic, so playful and quick to laugh. Me? I was the good boy. Reliable, attentive, obedient. Boring.

She died when we were young. A lump appeared in her breast. She was remarkably open about it and tried to explain to us what was happening. In fact, she even let us touch it. I was appalled. But Heraclitus was fascinated.

As she got weaker, she spent most of the day in bed. One evening she told us that the lump had gotten bigger and was spreading its poison throughout the rest of her body. Totally calm, she said she would die soon, but that we shouldn't be sad. That night, when we were in our room, I couldn't stop crying. And Heraclitus, well, he told me to dry my eyes and to look into his. He put his hand on my shoulder. He didn't say anything, but after a few minutes I did stop crying.

To this day I can still feel his touch. Even though he certainly never said so, and never even appeared to be particularly upset, I think he was wounded terribly by our mother's death. Anyway, the look he gave me before he left today reminded me of that evening long ago when she told us she would die. And you know what he said? "Immortals mortals, mortals immortals; living their deaths, dying their lives."[51]

5

Parmenides and His Goddess

(515–435 BCE)

Parmenides,
Motionless at last.[52]

HE'S IN BED, A shriveled old man, tiny, barely a hair on his head or a tooth in his mouth, and he's dying. I'm sitting on a stool next to him. To my surprise, he speaks.

"I never told you this, Zeno."

"Never told me what, Parmenides?" I ask quietly.

"The truth. I never told anybody. And that's the truth."

He closes his eyes. For the past two weeks, he's only been conscious for short stretches, and when he is, he doesn't make much sense. Whatever the disease, it's ravaging him, body and mind.

You can't imagine how hard this is for me to witness. Parmenides was always the sharpest, most energetic of philosophers. His thinking was meticulous, his words lucid. It was an honor to be his student, indeed, just to be in his presence. And now, to see him like this . . . .

He opens his eyes and turns to look at me. And then he smiles, a joyous, if toothless, smile, the kind you see on the face of a child at play.

"You're not going to believe it," he says. And then, of all things, he giggles, a high pitched cackle! I'm absolutely bewildered, but I don't say a word.

"My journey; my journey to the Goddess. You remember her, don't you?"

Of course I do. He is referring to his famous Proem. Every kid here in Elea has to memorize it. It's a story of a young man who is being taken to visit a Goddess.

> *The steeds that drew my chariot brought me to the*
> *farthermost reach of my desire, and carried me on the*
> *resounding road of the Goddess, along which one who*
> *knows is borne through all cities. On her path I was*
> *driven—yes, the wise horses drew me in my chariot, while*
> *maidens led the way.*

These maidens turn out to be daughters of the sun. The chariot, its whirling axles whistling like flutes, flies high to the gate of night and day where it is halted by a guard, Justice herself. The maidens persuade her to allow the young man to enter. The Goddess takes him by the hand and says,

> *Young man, accompanied by immortal charioteers . . .*
> *welcome! No evil destiny sent you forth to travel this road,*
> *which is far from the path beaten by human beings.*
> *No, it was Right and Justice that did so.*
> *For you must learn all things,*
> *both the heart of well-rounded Truth, which does not tremble,*
> *and appearances, in which there is no true trust at all.*[53]

So, yes, I tell Parmenides, of course I remember his journey to the Goddess.

He giggles again, the same high pitched cackle. His eyes are wide open and burning bright. Somehow the cloudy layer that had occluded them just minutes ago has vaporized. I wonder if he has lost his mind.

"She was Thalia," he says, "and never was a woman more aptly named. For she was of abundant good cheer."

I have no idea what he's talking about.

"I met her during the summer of my sixteenth year. During those long hot days, I used to spend afternoons with the boys from the local Pythagorean school. We would sit together under the shade of an ancient tree. By and large they were an uninspiring bunch. Still, they were better than nothing. They helped me idle away those stifling hours.

"There was one boy, though, who did catch my eye. A rich kid, like me, but older.[54] He wasn't from the school, and he seemed to do nothing but wander around town. Nonetheless, he had a confident air about him, as if he knew exactly where he was going, and why. He was tall, his long limbs moved with ease, his black curly hair was short, and he had a faint trace of a beard. When he passed by our tree, which was often, he didn't seem to notice us sitting there. But I would watch him intently. One day, he returned my gaze. And then he did something astonishing. He winked! He winked, and I was dazzled."

Parmenides is speaking intelligibly for the first time in weeks, and even if I have no idea why he is telling me this baffling story, I'm delighted by his resurgence.

"A few days later," he continues, "in the late afternoon when the heat had died down and the other boys had gone back into the school, I was walking home, and I bumped into him in front of the temple of Poseidon. He smiled at me and asked my name. I told him, but, too nervous to think straight, I forgot to ask him his. Later I learned it was Terpsion. He invited me to sit down on the steps of the temple with him, and we talked there for a while. Although our conversation was about inconsequential matters, I found him engaging. His intelligence was palpable.

"Soon we were meeting every late afternoon in front of the temple, where we would sit and talk into the evening. Actually, most of the time he would talk, and I would listen. It quickly became clear that even though he was extremely smart, he was no philosopher. Every time I tried to broach a serious topic, he'd change it. I'd be telling about my latest thoughts on indivisibility, and he'd interrupt with a story about the blacksmith whose wife who was dividing her time between him and the potter next door. I wasn't interested in this sort of thing and I couldn't understand why he was. Perhaps that's the reason I found him so interesting. He was thoroughly unlike me. Remember, I was young and had led a very sheltered life.

"One day we were talking as usual when out of nowhere he asked me, 'Are you a virgin?'

"At first, I was too stunned to reply, but then I managed to mumble, 'Well, yes, I guess so.'

"'You guess so!' he roared. 'Surely you must know whether you are a virgin or not!'

"Strange, but that morning I had been wondering about this very question: How do we know anything at all? Still, I was too flustered to reply.

"'Come on kid, get your act together,' he said. 'And I know just the place where you can do that. Meet me back here at sunset.' And without waiting for a reply, he walked away.

"I was confused, going back and forth, back and forth, about whether I should heed his call. I had never given my virginity a moment's thought, and was not particularly eager to begin doing so. But there was something magnetic about Terpsion. Even though I was unable to explain why, I decided to return to the temple that evening."

Listening to Parmenides, I too am going back and forth. On the one hand, it's wonderful to hear his voice again. On the other, in all the years I've known him, I have never once heard him say a word about his private life. He was always at ease in social situations, but his métier, by the widest of margins, was logical analysis, not autobiographical outpour. When he put on his philosopher's hat, as he always did with us in class, his demeanor was severe, his focus sharp and unyielding. On balance, though, I'm glad he's talking in full sentences again, no matter what he's saying, and I hope he's able to continue.

Fortunately, after resting for a moment to regain his breath, he resumes.

"As soon as the sun dipped below the horizon, I left my house and walked back to the temple. But when I arrived, Terpsion wasn't there. For a moment I was afraid I'd been duped. Thankfully, however, that wasn't the case, for I soon saw him sauntering toward me in his familiar, slack-limbed manner.

"He patted me on the back and said, 'Glad to see you, my dear boy. Are you ready to roll?'

"'Roll?' I asked myself. I had no idea what he had in mind. As usual, though, I followed his lead and soon we were darting down the street.

"We made a few turns and then suddenly we stopped in front of a good-sized house, nondescript but well kept. 'Welcome,' he said, 'to the Eleatic School of Symposiastic Arts.' He grinned. I stared at him and wondered if he was drunk. Before I could decide, he grabbed my arm and dragged me through the door, which he didn't bother to knock. We entered a large sitting room. There were couches and cushions strewn on the floor, and four or five flutes leaning against the wall. 'Hello hello hello,' he yelled at the top of his voice. 'Thalia! You home?'

"At first there was no response and I thought we were going to leave. But then a woman entered from the rear of the house. She was middle-aged, with jet black hair down to her shoulders and lips painted ruby red. Large and well proportioned, she moved as if she didn't have a care in the world. She was wearing a purple gown, and when she entered, the room felt warmer. She smiled and said, 'Ah, dear Terpsion, who else could it be?' She approached him and kissed him twice, first on the right cheek, then the left. She put her hands on his shoulders and looked him in the eye. 'Bienvenuto amore. So very nice to see you.' Her accent told me that she was not from our part of Italy but probably from the north.[55]

"'Thank you, Signora,' Terpsion replied. 'May I present to you my friend, the honorable Signor Parmenides.' He turned to me. 'Signor Parmenides, this is Signora Thalia. She is the proprietress of this fine establishment, the Eleatic School of the Symposiastic Arts. Here young ladies from all over southern Italy come for training in song and dance. They learn how to entertain the very best of men—such as ourselves—in the most elegant of settings.'

"With that, he winked at Thalia, who smiled in return. Then she turned to me. 'Piacere, Signor Parmenides,' she said.

"I was unable to reply or even to look her in the face. She detected my discomfort immediately. As I came to learn that night, she was a highly sensitive woman. She stood before me and took my hand. Her touch was reassuring, but it also sent an unfamiliar, although not unpleasant, charge through my arms and torso and into my loins. 'Young sir,' she said, 'no evil destiny has sent you here. For mine is a house of ease. Please, join me if you will, and I will teach you what you need.'

"She led me to a bedroom in the rear of the house. I was so taken by her fragrance that I forgot to say goodbye to Terpsion."

I'm flabbergasted! He's like an actor playing different roles, speaking in different voices, and what he's saying is absolutely incredible. Like everyone else, I've always assumed Parmenides' Goddess was no more than a symbolic representation of Wisdom, and a bit of a heavy-handed one at that. And now, here on his deathbed, he's telling me she was inspired by an actual flesh-and-blood woman! How bloody weird! I mean, this is Parmenides after all, the analytic philosopher *par excellence*.

I remember, years ago, being captivated when he gave his famous lecture. Change, he told us, cannot be, for it is composed of two constituents: what is and what is not; being and non-being. But non-being cannot be. Nor can it be thought, for when we think, we think of this or that, of something that is.[56] So too must it be unspeakable, for when we speak, we say this or that. To say is to say something, not nothing. It follows, therefore, that change, a concept in which non-being is embedded, cannot be. Only Being—changeless, motionless, and eternal—is.

That was Parmenides at his rigorous best, pursuing a thought to its logical conclusion, however offensive to commonsense it might be. Of course, I assumed the Goddess of his Proem represented the wisdom of pure reason! How could I not? But now here he is telling me she was a full-bodied woman with jet black hair and ruby red lips. Not only that, he's speaking in her voice! On his deathbed! Thalia, not logic, has brought him back to life.

I'm feeling a little wobbly.

Parmenides looks exhausted. He closes his eyes, and I'm afraid he'll either fall asleep or lapse back into senile muttering. Or die. Fortunately, he's only gathering the little energy he has left. He resumes his story.

"She was the most marvelous of teachers, my dear Zeno," he says with a curious grin on his face. "Cheerful, patient, and entirely accepting of my inexperience. When she was undressing me, my skin being touched by a woman for the first time since I was a small child, I experienced a sudden stiffening between my legs. On the one hand, this was familiar, for most mornings I woke up in a similar condition. On the other, it was mysterious, and I had no idea why it was happening. I looked at it as if it would give me the answer, and Signora Thalia laughed. 'Yes, it's wonderful, isn't it? Eros, first of all the gods,'[57] she said with gusto. Then she gently stroked it. After no more than a minute, it exploded like a volcano and emitted a stream. I groaned, the pleasure was so intense, but when the spasm ended, I was aghast, and I covered my face in shame. After she washed my member, and her hands, with a soft towel, she lifted my chin and forced me to look her in the eye. 'Trust me, young sir, it is good.' I didn't understand what she meant, but the tone of her voice, the feel of her hands, the proximity of her ample bosom, calmed me, and trust her I did."

Parmenides falls silent. He turns his head away from me and stares at the ceiling. And then, lo and behold, he giggles for the third time. "I never would have guessed," he says, "that the organ of urination is also the organ of highest fulfillment!"[58]

He begins to laugh, but almost immediately it turns into a nasty cough. I give him a cup of water, from which he takes two or three sips, and he relaxes. Then he whispers, "That old fool Heraclitus, he would have loved it."

He falls silent for a minute, and then turns to me and says, "It was long ago, and yet when I summon the past it becomes present. As if there were no time at all. Which is the whole point, isn't it, Zeno my dear?"

I have no idea what he's talking about, so I just say, "Yes, Parmenides, it is."

6

Zeno (of Elea) Bites His Tongue

(495–430 BCE)

You desired, Zeno, and your desire was noble,
To slay the tyrant and deliver Elea from slavery.
But you were defeated: for the tyrant caught you and beat you to death.
But what am I saying? It was your body he beat, and not you. (DL IX.28)

HE DOES NOT ALLOW himself to cry, for if he did the pain would be unbearable. His ribs are shattered, and so he breathes as little as possible. He tries not to move what's left of his tongue, but he's choking on his own blood. The guards dislocated both his shoulders and stabbed him in the back. He's lying on his stomach, waiting, hoping it won't be long.

But he has no regrets. None whatsoever. For the tyrant is dead.

Nearchus was a monster who crushed anyone who stood, or might some day stand, in his way. Even his brother and an uncle. A platoon of thugs guarded him day and night, and he trusted no one else. He raped every new bride in town before allowing them, bruised and humiliated, to return to their husbands. He taxed his subjects without mercy, reduced them to poverty, and used the money for grandiose building projects, all of them monuments to himself. He outlawed symposia and pederasty, and imprisoned the booksellers. He closed the Pythagorean school and when its director protested, he cut his throat in the *agora*. And seemed to enjoy doing it.

Not to fight back: it was a shame Zeno could not endure.

His only relief, and it is no more than a sprinkle, comes when he reminds himself that Parmenides is already dead. When it came to politics, he was a total innocent. Nearchus would have crushed him without batting an eye.

Zeno loved Parmenides and studied with him for years. In truth, however, he was never entirely serious about philosophy. For he enjoyed cooking up puzzles and poking fun at commonsense more than practicing dialectic. His favorite was called the Achilles. In it, he showed why the fastest of all men could never catch a tortoise who had a head start on him. For during the time it would take Achilles to reach the place where the tortoise started, the tortoise would crawl forward a tiny bit. Achilles would then have to traverse that distance and, however short it might be, this would also take time. Which meant that once again the tortoise would inch forward, and Achilles would have to catch up again. Since this would happen every time he reached the place where the tortoise had been, Achilles would have to make an infinite number of finite runs in order to catch the tortoise. But this is impossible. It follows, therefore, that the fastest man can never catch the slowest animal on earth.[59]

Far more than his puzzles, though, what Zeno loved best was his city, which is why he dared to criticize the tyrant during his lectures. One of his students, we'll never know who, denounced him to the authorities, and Nearchus had him thrown into prison. The guards strapped him to a board and poured water into his nose and mouth. Every time his lungs were about to burst, they'd stop and let him vomit. Then they did it again. When they were finished with that, they beat him. They wanted names. Realizing he would be unable to think straight for long, he decided to give them names. Of men he knew to be loyal to the tyrant.[60]

His ploy worked. Nearchus executed the men whose names Zeno gave him and then not only released him from prison, but praised him as a model citizen. To celebrate, Nearchus presided over a town meeting in the *agora*, which every citizen of Elea was required to attend. He told the crowd that Zeno had given him the information he needed to keep the city safe from its enemies, and every loyal subject must do the same. During this excruciating speech, Zeno strained every muscle on his battered face to make himself look pleased, even though his fingers were itching for the tyrant's throat. When Nearchus finally finished and was about to place a wreath on his head, Zeno told him he had one more name to give, but it had to be whispered into his ear. The tyrant, a stupid man blinded by his lust for power, smiled widely and made a big show of moving his head close to Zeno's mouth. To the shock of every person standing in the *agora*, he bit the tyrant's ear with the ferocity of a mad dog. He ripped it off and spat it on the ground. Nearchus, blood spouting, screamed in agony. Zeno, his mouth and chin drenched red, turned to the crowd and raised his arms in triumph. Two guards grabbed him from behind, and broke his shoulders in the process. But ecstasy overwhelmed pain and he glared at Nearchus, thrilled to see him suffer. A servant gave the tyrant a towel to stanch the bleeding. Holding it to the side of his head, he pointed at Zeno and squealed, "Kill him, kill him, kill him now!" Zeno was ready to explode, but he couldn't move. And so he bit off the top of his own tongue and spat it into the tyrant's face. Like a little girl, Nearchus screamed in terror. A guard stabbed Zeno three times in the back, but before he could land the killing blow, the crowd rushed onto the stage. They stomped the tyrant and his thugs to death, and the revolution was over the very moment it began.

7

Anaxagoras and the Failure of Wisdom

(Anaxagoras: 500–428 BCE; Archelaus: 480–397 BCE)

He once declared the sun to be a mass of red-hot iron,
And for this Anaxagoras was bound to die.
His friend Pericles saved him, though he himself,
His wisdom failing, ended his own life. (DL II.15)

"YOU WANT ME TO talk about him before I pass away, don't you?" Archelaus said.

A little embarrassed, Sotion glanced at his feet.[61]

Archelaus chuckled. "Don't worry, son, I'm not going anywhere soon. I'm old, over eighty I think, but still kicking. My energy is good today. Probably because I only had to pee a few times last night. So I'm glad to talk, especially about him. He was my teacher, you know."

"I do," Sotion said politely.

"I'll begin at the end, if you don't mind."

"Of course."

Archelaus took a breath, exhaled slowly. Then he spoke, his voice shaky. "He cut his own throat."

"My god," Sotion gasped.

"I found his body. He was at his table, slumped over, forehead on top of the papyrus, which was drenched in blood. The knife was on the floor. I remember wondering how in the world he had the strength to do it." He shook his head in disbelief.

"I arrived the day before," he continued, "and as soon as I got off the ship in Lampsacus, I went to his house. A servant led me to his room and opened the door. I was shocked by what I saw. It was before noon, but instead of reading or writing, which is what he had done every single morning for all the years I had known him, he was asleep on the couch. He looked horrible, and he didn't smell good. He'd always been portly and shaped like a pear, but now he was emaciated, his hair was long and stringy, his cheeks unshaven. And it had been less than a year since I'd seen him last! He'd never been jovial, but now his face, even in sleep, was locked into a terrible grimace. I couldn't take my eyes off him. He'd been my friend for a long time."

Archelaus sighed and stared blankly out the window. But he caught himself and grunted slightly. "I remember the day I first heard him. I was only fifteen, and as usual back then, I was wandering around Athens, lost in thought. But had you asked me what I was thinking about, I wouldn't have been able to say. I only knew I was lost. Regardless of where I was—at the table with my family, in class reading Homer with tutors, or on the streets—I was uncomfortable, restless, longing for something but no idea what.

"Sorry, I'm drifting, aren't I?"

"No, no, it's fine, Archelaus," Sotion assured him. "Just say whatever comes to mind. It doesn't matter in what order. I'm taking notes, and I'll sort them out later. Please, don't worry."

"Okay then," Archelaus said appreciatively. "But where was I? Ah yes, at the beginning. I was a kid, wandering around Athens, aimlessly I suppose, when I turned a corner and stumbled on a lecture being given by a large, pear-shaped man. His voice was deep and dignified, but his accent made it clear he wasn't from Athens. He spoke with great animation, but the strange thing was, he seemed to be oblivious to the audience. He paused frequently and gazed up at the sky. His name was Anaxagoras. And he's the one you're interested in, not me. Right?"

Sotion's face crumpled.

"It's okay, son," Archelaus said. "He was a great man. He deserves a biography, and good for you to be the one writing it."

"Thank you, Archelaus," Sotion replied. "But I'm planning to write a chapter about you too. After all, you were Socrates' first teacher."

"Socrates," he said, savoring each syllable. "The Athenians are going after him, just like they did with Anaxagoras. They accused him of being an atheist, you know, because he claimed the sun was made of iron.[62] But had they ever read his books or studied his cosmology? Of course not! Athenians like to brag about how cultured they are, but anti-intellectualism runs deep in this town. Whenever the politicians need to bolster their support from the people, they accuse a philosopher of atheism. It makes them look like they care about something other than themselves, which they don't. So, yes, I'm worried about Socrates. Anaxagoras barely escaped with his life."

Archelaus shook his head. "All right already, let's get back on track, shall we? I was a kid wandering around Athens when I stumbled on his lecture. Truth is, up to that point in my life, I hadn't been much of a student. I wasn't a troublemaker, but my elders, well, they bored me, and I didn't pay attention to a word they said. To my surprise, though, I was intrigued by this chubby, fidgety man lecturing in the *agora*, and I moved closer to the speaker's platform so I could hear what he was saying."

He closed his eyes and began to recite.

> *In the beginning, all things were together. Earth, air, fire, water, the seeds of all things, all mixed together. No thing stood apart on its own, clear and distinct.*

> *And then Mind, itself by itself, mixed with nothing other than itself, caused the great undifferentiated mass to rotate, and there was separation. Earth below, with its forests and fields, animals and cities; clouds filled with water above; moon and fiery stars above the clouds.*

> *But never forget, in all things there is a portion of every thing.*[63]

"At first I thought he was reciting verses from Hesiod. But as he continued to speak, I realized he was no poet. No, he was trying to explain things. All things. But how, I wondered, could anyone possibly do that?"

Grinning, Archelaus scratched his hairy ears.

"The next day I returned to the *agora* to listen to him again. I barely understood a word, but I knew this strange man had something to say, so I came back every day for three weeks. Finally, I summoned the courage to approach him after his lecture. If everything is in everything, I asked him, how can Mind be mixed with nothing? He glared at me for a few seconds. Then he said I could join a group of students who came to his home in the evenings. Somehow he knew my name."

"You must have felt honored," Sotion said.

"I did, but at first I was sure he'd made a mistake. After all, I was the youngest person there, and I was in way over my head. They kept using names I didn't know. Thales, Anaximander, Anaximenes, Pythagoras, Heraclitus, and, most of all, Parmenides. I realized how hard I would have to work to catch up with the other students. That's when I began my habit of reading late into the night. Which I still do."

Archelaus scoffed at himself. "Well, truth is, I can't read much any more. My eyes aren't what they used to be, and even when I make out the words, I have trouble holding on to them. As my grandfather used to say, getting old isn't for sissies. Anyway, where was I?"

"You began your life-long habit of reading late at night," Sotion answered.

"Right! Of course I started with Parmenides. Anaxagoras never mentioned him by name, you know. Always called him the Eleatic monist. Anyway, at first I didn't like his book much. It begins with a story of a young fellow going on some sort of mystical journey to visit a goddess. Obviously a representation of the quest for wisdom, and not particularly imaginative. But as I read further, I came to see the power of his argument. There's a reason that, even today, we call him Father Parmenides. And do you know what it is?"

Sotion didn't stop writing, but shook his head to say no.

"Because he was the first to think about Being itself. Not *a* being, like a dog or a tree, but Being simply *as Being*."

Sotion looked up from his wax tablet.

Archelaus shifted into his teaching mode. "Okay, I'll try to explain. Parmenides' first move was to show that non-being—call it 'nothing' if that's easier for you—is unthinkable. Of course, he was right. Just try to disprove it, and you'll see why. Go ahead, son, try to think about nothing."

Sotion was confused.

"Come now," Archelaus said, as if talking to a child. "It's simple. Close your eyes and try to think about nothing."

He dutifully closed his eyes for a long moment. When he opened them, Archelaus pounced. "Can't do it, can you? You were thinking of something, weren't you?"

"Yes," he acknowledged.

"Which means that Parmenides was right. Non-being is unthinkable because when you think you think of this or that. Of something that is. Or as he put it, 'the same it is to think and to be.'"[64]

Sotion resumed writing.

"Now, by itself this may be no great insight. But when you get to his second move, you'll see how much he built on it. Ready?"

"Yes."

"The world seems to be filled with a great many things which seem to be moving, changing, coming-into-being and then passing-away. Right?"

"Of course."

"In fact, however, none of them is really real, at least not according to Parmenides. He placed all of them in the category of what he called *Becoming*, which he argued was a concept as impossible as non-being. For Becoming is essentially the transition from Being to non-being. For example, you might say I'm becoming old, which means that once I was young but now I am not. Or you might say the air has become cool, which means that earlier it was hot but now it is not. But these very words, 'it is not,' state a contradiction. For what is not cannot be. Nor can it be thought or said. In short, non-being is a conceptual impossibility. Parmenides' shocking insight was that the same must be true of Becoming. For it, after all, depends on non-being. From this it follows that only Being is, and it is changeless and eternal."

"I don't understand," Sotion interjected. "It's obvious things are changing all the time! I mean, look at me." He began waving his hand at an imaginary friend. "My hand is moving right now. Its location is changing. How can you say this isn't real?"

"I didn't say it. Parmenides did."

"But that doesn't make sense. Of course there's change. I mean, that's just the way the world is."

Enjoying himself, Archelaus grinned. "The way the world is, or the way the world *seems* to be?"

Sotion looked puzzled.

"This is the key distinction for Parmenides. Of course, things *seem* to move and change. But if we analyze the concept of Becoming, we encounter non-being, which means that while the concept of Becoming may seem to make sense, upon analysis it doesn't hold up."

Sotion was scribbling furiously.

"And there's more," Archelaus said. His raspy voice was getting louder. "Parmenides argued that Being must be a single, indivisible whole. For if it had parts, they would have to be different from one another. And then each part would have to be both what it is and not be what it is not. Divisiblity implies multiplicity, which in turn implies non-being. But no being can both be and not be, for that would be a contradiction. It follows, therefore, that Being has no parts, which means it is one."

"Eleatic monism," Sotion whispered.

"Precisely!" Archelaus replied. "Motion, change, multiplicity, the world as we ordinarily experience it, well, it's just not the whole Truth."

He paused to catch his breath.

"Are you okay?" Sotion asked.

Archelaus ignored the question. "Way back then," he said, "when I was a kid studying with Anaxagoras, I was like you. I thought Parmenides was crazy, and I couldn't understand why everybody held him in such high regard. So one day I spoke with an older student. He was charismatic and always ready to talk. I asked him whether Parmenides actually believed that motion and change, everything we see and touch, ordinary life itself, is an illusion. He said, no, not quite. Yes, he explained, Parmenides does believe Becoming is not really real, but he doesn't think it's an illusion. Instead, it is intrinsic to what he calls *doxa*: appearance, opinion, belief, the way things seem to be. And while *doxa* is radically distinct from Truth, it still has its own kind of reality, however blurry it may be, for it is where we live and breath, at least when we leave the lecture and return to our ordinary lives. Admire Parmenides' logic all you want but don't worry, he assured me, you can still make speeches in the Assembly during the day and tickle your girlfriend at night."

Delighted by the memory, Archelaus nodded his head. "By the way," he said. "You'll recognize the name of this student."

"I will?"

"Yes. It was Pericles."

"Really? You were a classmate of Pericles?"

"For a short while, yes. But soon after our conversation he stopped coming to lectures. He turned to politics and never looked back. But let's return to your question. If you want to understand Anaxagoras you have to begin with Parmenides' rejection of Becoming. On the logical side, it may make perfectly good sense, but on the empirical side, it doesn't. This is why ever since Parmenides published his book philosophers have been trying to find a middle-way, a path between pure reason and the testimony of our senses, between Truth and *doxa*."

"Between Parmenides and Heraclitus," Sotion interrupted in a burst of enthusiasm.

Archelaus looked at him skeptically. "Yes, I suppose you could put it that way. Anyway, Anaxagoras came up with a powerful theory. He argued that, on the one hand, Parmenides was wrong. Multiplicity is real. Remember, in the beginning all things—plural, not singular!—were mixed together. Then Mind caused the primordial mass to rotate, and the multiplicity of distinct beings emerged into the light of day. The world, filled to the brim with diversity and change, came into being, and this is what our senses now detect. We open our eyes, and it certainly looks like there are many different trees, and they're blowing in the wind. And you know what? There really are. So, yes, the senses can be trusted. They do disclose reality. But only up to a point. For Parmenides was also right. Not about the sensible things we see and touch in our daily lives, which do indeed come to be and pass away, but about their component parts, or what he called their seeds. These never change. So, for example, when a dog dies it only *seems* to have perished. For in reality it has been transformed. As its corpse decomposes its seeds, all of which existed before they coagulated to form the dog, scatter. They continue to exist after the dog is gone, and then they will repeatedly be recycled into other things. They are, one might say, little bits of Parmenidean Being. They scatter when things fall apart but then recombine and emerge in other things.

"Is this making any sense?"

"I think so," Sotion said.

"Good," Archelaus said. "And don't forget this. Because Mind is the first cause of all things, the multiplicity and change intrinsic to the world is intelligible. We live in a cosmos, an orderly whole composed of parts whose movements occur in predictable ways."

Archelaus' eyes narrowed. "Make sure to make one thing clear to your readers."

"What's that?" Sotion asked.

"Anaxagoras invented natural science.[65] He had a theory that explained the pattern behind change, the stable order behind the flux, no matter how random it may seem. And that's because everything is in everything. Trees, dogs, rocks, you, me, it doesn't matter; they're all made of the same ingredients, and they all go through the same process of scatter and merge, scatter and merge. And this is why the world is intelligible.

"I remember Anaxagoras once told us that nature is like a book meant to be studied. Strive to understand, he commanded us. Ask questions. Why is the moon bright at night? Why does a chicken's egg have a yolk and a white? Why does sound travel? What is the cause of an eclipse? Why do living things come from slime? Why is the earth flat?[66] Get to work, gentlemen, get to work, he used to implore us."

Archelaus slumped into the couch. "Sorry," he said, "but the fatigue just hit me. I'm tired of explaining. It's all I've done for as long as I can remember." He fell silent.

Sotion waited for a couple of minutes and then became alarmed. He jumped up from his chair and rushed to the kitchen. When he returned with a cup of water, Archelaus was staring at the ceiling. He offered him the drink, but the old man looked at him uncomprehendingly. After a moment, though, he accepted the cup, drank appreciatively, and returned to himself.

"I studied with him for nearly a decade, you know, and when I asked him whether I was ready to open my own school, he said yes. And you know who one of my first students was?"

"Who?" Sotion asked, although he knew the answer.

"Socrates."

Archelaus paused, savored a memory.

"An unattractive boy, working class, with a thick neck and a snub nose. His language was crude, and he had a rather aggressive demeanor. But he was serious and extraordinarily bright, so I allowed him to stay on. I tried to teach him, I really did. I explained how thinking is caused by blood moving through the brain and hearing by sound entering the ear after having been produced by a blow. But Socrates quickly lost interest in my lessons. When I asked him why, he said, with his typical bluntness, he did not have the nature to study nature. I was perplexed. I couldn't understand how an intelligent young man could find animals and plants, stars and clouds, earth, air, water, fire uninteresting. But he did, and I was tempted to give up on him. I decided, though, to give him one more shot. I thought, if anything could grab his attention it would be Mind. I opened my copy of Anaxagoras' book and read. *Mind brings order and is the cause of all things.* 'That's fantastic!' Socrates roared. And then he began to bombard me with questions. 'Doesn't this mean everything in the world is as it is because it is for the best? For that's the way Mind works, doesn't it? I'm talking to you right now because I decided, in my mind, it would be good for me to do so. Isn't that right?' he asked, but then he answered his own question. 'Of course it is!' Then he said, 'And if Mind rules, then The Good must rule too. If the earth is flat, it must be good for it to be flat. Isn't that right?'

"Rather than try to respond to his barrage of questions, I handed him Anaxagorgas' book and told him to go home and read it for himself.

"The next day, he returned to my room. He slammed the book on my table and without even saying hello told me that Anaxagoras didn't understand Mind! Air, fire, and water do all the work! His book is just mechanics, no Mind at all, which is why he doesn't say a single word about The Good!

"I tried to explain to him that Anaxagoras' Mind is nothing like our own. We are purposive beings who aim for goals we believe are good. But Anaxagoras' Mind is a cosmic principle, not a psychological one. It causes the rotation of the original undifferentiated mass, and it is responsible for the order we observe in the world. It is why the world is intelligible, but no, it does not aim for The Good.

"'Then why am I standing here?' he nearly shouted at me.

"What do you mean? I asked him.

"'You know perfectly well what I mean,' he replied. 'Did I walk into your room because my muscles contracted and relaxed and because my bones are hard and have joints? That's what Anaxagoras would say, isn't it?'

"In all honesty, I was befuddled, and I'm afraid I just said yes.

"Socrates looked triumphant, and he told me that he walked into my room because he decided, all things considered, it would be best for him to do so. If he had thought it would be better, he could have walked to Megara.

"I have to admit, he floored me. I managed to regain my composure, but my counter didn't amount to much. Surely, I said to him, you couldn't have walked here without your muscles and bones.

"'Of course not,' he snapped. 'But they are merely necessary conditions, not real explanations of why I'm standing here now.'[67]

"Without giving me a chance to respond, and at that point I'm not sure I could have, he stormed out of the room.

"He was only a youngster but I was shaken to my core."

Breathing rapidly, lost in thought, Archelaus fell silent. After a long moment, though, he resumed, but he spoke quietly. "People say I had sex with him.[68] But it's not true, and if you know the man you'll know why."

Sotion nodded. "Did Socrates ever meet Anaxagoras?" he asked.

"Oh, good lord," Archelaus replied, "I've been drifting, haven't I?" He laughed heartily, and then took a long swig of water. "Let me put it this way. What Anaxagoras really cared about was the study of nature. He had no interest in The Good, which is why he had no interest in politics. I once asked him if he ever thought about his home city. He looked at me, cold as ice. 'Of course I do,' he said. And he pointed to the sky."

"Perhaps we might go back to the beginning?" Sotion said cautiously.

"Course we can, son," Archelaus said, a mischievous grin on his face. "But you'll have to remind me what it was."

"You arrived in Lampsacus, where Anaxagoras settled after leaving Athens. When you entered his room, he was asleep on the couch, and the next day you found him dead at his table, with his throat cut."

Archelaus looked at Sotion as if he were disappointed in him. "Yes, I'm afraid so."

"But why did you go to Lampsacus in the first place?"

"Ah, that," he sighed. "The jury found Anaxagoras guilty of atheism, and when the sentencing phase of the trial began, the prosecutor asked for the death penalty. I was sitting next to him at the time, and I put my hand on his shoulder. You know, to comfort him. But he was annoyed. And you know what he said?"

"What?" Sotion asked, eyes glued to his wax tablet.

"'Nature condemned me to death long ago.'"

Sotion continued to write even faster.

"And that was when Pericles intervened. He pleaded with the jury to spare Anaxagoras' life. He wielded enormous power in those days, and the people trusted him. As usual, he won them over. The sentence was reduced to a fine and exile.

"We walked out of the court together and Anaxagoras didn't seem the least bit upset. When we got to his house, he began to pack his belongings. I was helping him when a messenger came by. Horrible news! Unthinkable! Anaxagoras' wife and children had died. I didn't even know he had a family. But he did, and they all succumbed to the plague. The same plague that would claim Pericles a few months later. And you know what he said after the messenger left?"[69]

"What?"

"'I knew they were mortal.' That's it! The expression on his face didn't change. Same old grimace." Archelaus sighed deeply and then rubbed his eyes. "So why did I go to Lampsacus? Because I wanted to tell him myself that Pericles, his most famous student and the man who had saved his life, had died. I thought he should hear it from me. Plus, it was an excuse to check up on him. When I got there, he was asleep, which was strange since it was morning and he always spent his mornings reading or writing at his table.

"I sat down and watched him for a while. He was as thin as a rail. He used to be plump, you know. When he finally woke up, he looked at me strangely."

Archelaus blinked back his tears. "He called me Anaximenes.[70] Anaximenes! He was his teacher, and he'd been dead for years. I tried to correct him as gently as I could. I said I was Archelaus, his student, not his teacher, but I couldn't get through. He apologized for not handing in his homework on time. And then, the most pitiful thing I've ever seen."

"What?"

"He began to cry! The man who was indifferent to the death of his own family called me Anaximenes, begged me to forgive him, and kept repeating, 'I promise I'll do better next time!' I tried to behave normally. I told him a plague was ravaging Athens, and it had claimed Pericles.

"When he heard Pericles' name, he snapped out of it and glared at me. 'I offered him the best education in Athens,' he said, 'but he went into politics! I don't care if he's dead or alive.'"[71]

Sotion was writing as fast as he could.

"And then, finally, he recognized me. 'Oh my, it's you Archelaus, isn't it?' he said. I was relieved and said yes, but he didn't look glad to see me. 'What are you doing here?,' he asked me. I told him I had bad news. Pericles had died. He looked totally confused. Before I could explain, he said, as matter-of-factly as if he were reporting the weather, he could no longer write. Why not? I asked. He said he forgot the beginning of a sentence before he'd reached its end. He said he couldn't hold on to a thought."

Archelaus took a sip of water.

"I told him he still had a lot to offer. I reminded him I was his friend and I would be delighted to help him collect his writings and publish them as a book.

"He looked at me, his eyes burning with contempt. 'Leave me alone,' he yelled. And he covered his head with a blanket.

"Trust me, it was rough. I promised him, with as much enthusiasm as I could muster, I would come see him again tomorrow. I told him I had some questions about the original mixture. What exactly was in there? Just the seeds or opposites too? We'd talk, just like the old days.

"'No,' is all he said.

"I left the room.

"The next day . . . well, I already told you about the next day, didn't I?"

Sotion looked up from his notebook and nodded.

8

Empedocles: Gone, Baby, Gone

(484–424 BCE)

He made his way to Etna,
and when he got there
he leaped into the fiery craters and disappeared;
for he wished to strengthen the legend
that he had become a god. (DL VIII.69)

CAN I GET YOU anything? A cup of wine? A bite to eat?

You're sure?

Well, okay then. Why don't we sit down and you can ask me your questions.

Yes, you're right. The light is lovely.

When did I hear? Let me think. The day before yesterday. One of our maids woke me early in the morning. "Signor Pausanias, Signor Pausanias!" she shouted. "They found his shoe!" Her voice was screechy and she grabbed me by the shoulder. "They found his shoe!" she repeated. "Etna coughed it up, and a shepherd boy found it on the slope of the mountain, and he brought it into town, and it has to be his because it's bronze, and he was the only man in all of Sicily to wear bronze shoes!"

I was still half asleep and could barely register what she was saying, but I did catch the last bit, about him wearing bronze shoes. He did, and they looked good on him. Adorable, really.

You've seen them, haven't you?

Good. Well, at any rate, the maid kept blabbering. "Crazy old coot, thought he could survive the flames," she said. "But the mountain spit out his shoe to prove he burned to a crisp. I knew it! Just like the rest of us, he ain't no god!"

She looked triumphant, and slightly deranged. I told her to leave the room, and I wasn't polite about it. Then I got out of bed, splashed water on my face, put on my clothes and some makeup. With my head cleared, I pondered what the poor woman had just told me. I realized right away it was nonsense. First of all, Mount Etna is at least seventy miles away, and he was here at home two nights ago. There's no way he could have travelled that far. Second, even if he had somehow gotten to the volcano, nobody, certainly not him, could have climbed to the top.[72] He wasn't, like, nimble, you know. Third, even if he did jump into the crater, which he didn't, everything, including his bronze shoes, would have been incinerated. Her story just doesn't add up, don't you agree?

Thank you.

But I'm afraid she was right about one thing. Empedocles did think he was a god. Sort of. But he never would have jumped into Etna just to prove his point. He may have been crazy, but he wasn't stupid. No, he was just my baby, my sweet old Empedocles, and he never would have left me without saying goodbye.[73]

I must admit, though, I am getting worried. That night I made a lovely dinner—partridge just the way he likes it, crispy on the outside, tender and juicy on the inside—and we stayed up late drinking wine. A very nice one from Sybaris, I think. He was a little quiet, but he didn't seem weird. Or at least no more than usual. At any rate, when I woke up he wasn't in bed. But that didn't surprise me. He usually gets up early and goes to his study to write. Quality time with himself, I call it. But he wasn't there. So I figured he was out walking, which he likes to do. But when he didn't show up for lunch—cheese, olives, bread, and a bowl of nice dipping oil, which I served on the new silver platter one of his fans gave him—I started to get upset. You see, he's been under a lot of pressure lately. He's booked to give a boatload of lectures—like, seven or eight, I think—and more invitations come in every day, and he hates to say no. And then there are all the sick people who beg him to visit. Even if the doctors say their case is hopeless, they're convinced he can find a cure. He can't even go into town without someone asking him for advice, or an autograph. The other night we were sitting in our favorite tavern and a guy came up to us and without even saying excuse me asked him about the cool weather we've been having. The nerve! I told him to get lost.

Yes, everybody in Sicily wants a piece of him, and, god bless his big heart, he tries to oblige them all. Plus, on top of everything else, he has to keep track of all the money coming in. I'd help but I'm useless with numbers.

How did all this craziness start? It's a long story, but I'll make it short. It was soon after our second anniversary, maybe twenty years ago. It was the summer, plenty hot, and the sirocco was blowing in from Libya. One day, we were having lunch at the tavern when an old farmer sat down at a table near us. He looked exhausted, and his face was beet red. And then he began to cry! Naturally, Empedocles went over and asked him what was wrong. The farmer explained he was on the verge of ruin. His field was being scorched by the hot wind, and he didn't know what to do. Of course, Empedocles offered to help. He went to the old man's farm and surveyed his land. Then he told him to kill his herd of donkeys. The old man was flabbergasted—I mean, who wouldn't be?—and at first he said he couldn't do it. But Empedocles could persuade a Spartan to cut his hair. He convinced the farmer that the survival of his farm depended on his killing the donkeys, which the wretched man finally agreed to do, even if he didn't have a clue why. Then Empedocles told him to have the poor animals flayed and the women of the household sew the hides together. He drew a diagram showing what he wanted them to make. Large bags. The old man was baffled—so was I—but by then he was completely won over by him, and he did precisely as told. While the women were hard at work, Empedocles went back to the fields and took measurements and scribbled notes on a little piece of wax. When the bags were finished, he took them into the field and positioned them carefully on the western border of the farmer's field. "What in god's name are you doing?" I asked him. "Windbags," he replied. Which was funny because that's what I sometimes call him. Anyway, his crazy plan worked. The bags caught enough of the wind to slow it down. The crops were saved.

The farmer was hugely grateful. He came into town during harvest and gave Empedocles a sack of his best grain. And he kissed his hand. He thought he was a magician and called him the "Wind-Stayer."[74] But as Empedocles explained to me—or tried to explain since I never understand him right when he's being serious—there was no magic, just careful measurement. He had figured out the path the wind was taking and how to build a barrier with the windbags. Well, the old man started telling everybody about it, and soon people from all over Sicily were asking him for help. A family here in Agrigentum had a son who broke his leg, and they were sure he would never walk again. But Empedocles bound it tight to a stick, and in two months, the boy was walking fine. When mice invaded Gela, he had the people build hundreds of tiny houses. They put resin on the floors and on top of that a piece of cheese. When a mouse entered a tiny house, its feet got stuck, and it would die. Empedocles made sure every barn and kitchen in town had one and soon the infestation was over. He saved Selinus when its river was stinking something terrible. He had the men dig a canal to divert a nearby stream and run it into the river. Sure enough, the water became sweet. The people held a feast to celebrate, and when Empedocles arrived, they actually bowed before him. I saw it myself!

He always said this stuff wasn't really that hard, at least not for someone who understands how things work. Everything is made of fire, water, air, and earth. Parmenidean bits, he called them, because they don't get born and do not die, just scatter and merge. And there are two forces. Love, which draws things together, and Strife, which pushes them apart. And there you have it! The whole world!

For some reason he always used bone as his example when he was trying to explain his theory to me. Maybe because he'd always have a boner when we woke up in the morning.

Sorry. Please don't write that down.

Thank you.

Anyway, bone is, like, two parts earth and three parts water and four parts fire, or whatever, and it's all held together by Love. But bone doesn't have any air because Strife keeps it away.[75] There you have it, dear Pausanias, he used to say. The keys to the kingdom.

Yes indeed, it's what he used to say. My baby.

Sorry. I don't usually cry.

Did you know he dedicated his first book to me? Give ear, Pausanias, son of wise Anchitus. That's what he wrote! Wasn't it sweet of him to say something nice about my father? Although, truth is, I never liked him much.

At any rate, his book was a smash, a bestseller from here to Miletus, and since then, the whole Greek world knows his name. And that's when he started to get full of himself. I used to watch him looking in the mirror.

I mean it sounds crazy but he'd actually wink or practice waving. It wasn't his fault, though, not really. How could anyone as smart and famous as him not feel special?

What finally pushed him over the edge, though, was Panthea. Do you know the story?

No?

Well, she was about the same age as Empedocles. Their families had been neighbors when they were kids, and they used to play together. About ten years ago she got sick and lapsed into a coma. She was barely breathing and hadn't eaten a bite of food or sipped a drop of water for thirty days. Her husband begged Empedocles to visit her, and of course he said yes. I tagged along. My job was to carry his leather satchel. In it there were leaves, roots, and a dead bird. Very yucky.

When we arrived at Panthea's house—a modest little thing on the outskirts of town—her whole family was waiting for us, and it was, like, gloomy. The women were crying, the children looked dazed, the men reeked of sweat. But when Empedocles entered, he was bubbling with good cheer. He patted each child on the head, gently pinched each woman's cheek, and shook the hands of every man. They thought he was crazy, and I did too. He asked Panthea's oldest daughter to boil some water. She did and brought it to him. He told me to pour everything in the satchel into the pot, which he stirred for several minutes. The whole time he was humming to himself. Then he strained out the solids so only a green-brown liquid remained. He announced he would visit Panthea alone. He went into her bedroom, carrying the steaming pot.

We didn't wait long. Within an hour he walked back into the front room and with him, emaciated for sure but alive, was Panthea. "Ladies and gentlemen, beloved friends, citizens of Agrigentum, may I present to you my dear old friend, Panthea."

At first, her family fell silent. Then one of Panthea's sons jumped up from his chair and ran into the street, and we could hear him shouting, "She's alive! She's alive!" That woke everybody up, and they started hooting for joy. Empedocles kissed Panthea on the cheek, and somehow the woman had enough blood left in her body to blush.

As we left the house, a throng of people were waiting for us on the street. They threw flowers in the air and shouted his name and followed us as we walked home. Just before he opened our door, Empedocles turned to the crowd, clasped his two hands together, placed them to his forehead and bowed. The crowd looked at him in, like, awe.

The next day, at the market, I overheard two ugly old cows talking about him. They were saying it wasn't a miracle since Panthea had fallen into trances ever since she was a little girl. They were very nasty. When I told him about this over dinner, he looked at me sadly but didn't say a word.[76]

Well that sure as heck was the end of normal. Boy, did he think he was a big-shot. Which he was. I mean, he brought a woman back from the dead! He started wearing fancy clothes. His favorite outfit was a purple robe with a golden girdle, a laurel wreath and, of course, his famous bronze shoes. Now, I like nice clothes too, but this was, like, way off the charts. Except the shoes of course. They were so cute on him!

Did you ever see him decked out like that?

Oh good, I'm glad.

Anyway, he started to change. For one thing, he lost interest in his students. One day, when I was polishing the silver, I overheard one of them say to him, "Sir, you told us we would have an oral examination at the end of the semester. When will it be, sir, and what will it be like?" It was obvious Empedocles hadn't given this a moment's thought, and I listened carefully, eager to hear what he would say to the boy. "Don't worry, son," he said. "You'll come to my study, and I'll ask you a question. Then I'll answer it because I can't stand to listen to other people talk." I chuckled, but later, when I was in the kitchen cutting vegetables, his remark made me sad.

And I also got upset when he started saying mean things about his old teacher, Anaxagoras. He used to, like, revere him, but after he got famous, he made fun of him. Said his mixture thing was just a pile of hooey.

What bothered me most, though, was his boy band.[77] These were five cute little guys Empedocles had selected from the neighborhood. He taught them to sing and one of them how to play the bongo drums. He dressed them in white linen. Before he gave a lecture, they would come on stage and perform one of the songs he had written to warm up the crowd. Then he would arrive, usually to thunderous applause, and step up to the speaker's platform. He'd be lecturing—he has a beautiful voice, you know—and every once in a while he'd stop, snap his fingers, and the boys would belt out a tune. Then he'd start lecturing again. At first, like everybody else, I thought it was fabulous, but after a few months, especially after his big show in Syracuse, it was starting to get sort of like, I don't know, sad. It was painful to watch my baby going off the rails.

I have to tell you something, and make sure you write this down. Empedocles always treated those boys well. He hired tutors and trainers for them, and he paid their families to boot. Plus, he never, ever touched them. He wouldn't do that in a million years. He's always been faithful to me, you know. I mean, he may tell people I'm his servant, but our friends know we're a couple.

Yes, yes, I know, this is on the record and you're going to write about it. That's okay. I don't care if everyone in town finds out about us now.

At any rate, a few years later he published a book called *Purifications*. I could tell it was good because when he read it out loud it sounded nice, even though I couldn't understand a word. I mean, I never understood his first book either. That one was called *On Nature*, and it had a bunch of formulas that made no sense to me at all. But *Purifications*, oh my god, it was, like, total mumbo-jumbo. But, oh my god, was it a hit! He recited it at the Olympics, with his boys singing backup, and the crowd went crazy.

Were you there?

Too bad. Well, let me tell you, it was something else.

Anyway, the next time he went to Olympia he demanded all kinds of things. The fanciest room, freshly picked flowers, grilled partridge for himself and lamb kebabs for the boys. He closed his show by reading a passage that was . . . was . . . you know what? Why don't I read it to you. Sit tight for a sec, and I'll get the book.

Okay now. Listen up!

> *You will learn all the drugs that protect against evils and old age,*
> *since for you alone shall I bring to pass all these things.*
> *You will stop the force of the tireless winds that rush*
> *over the earth and devastate the plowed fields with their blasts.*
> *And, if you wish, you arouse their breath again.*
> *You will change black rain into seasonable dryness*
> *for people, and summer drought you will change*
> *into tree-nourishing waters that dwell in the sky.*
> *And you will bring back from Hades the strength of a dead man.*

And if that's not enough, wait till you hear this one:

> *I go about among you, an immortal god, no longer mortal,*
> *Honored among all, as its seems,*
> *Wreathed with headbands and blooming garlands.*
> *Wherever I go to their flourishing cities*
> *I am revered by all—men and women.*[78]

Oh my poor baby! He was too smart for his own good.

It was completely different when we started out. We met at a symposium at Cleomenes' house. You must have heard about that night?

Really? I thought everybody knew. Oh well, I guess it was before your time. How old are you anyway?

No wonder. What say I get us a drink, and when I come back, I'll tell you the story?

Okay then, ready?

I used to get invited to a lot of those fancy parties. I was the pretty young thing at the time, plus I was quiet and polite, and the big shots liked to have me around. Anyway, it was one heck of a shindig. I was sitting near Empedocles, and he smiled at me when we were introduced, but he didn't say anything. As usual, Cleomenes made himself the master of ceremonies. The rumor in town was he was about to, like, take over the government or something. I don't know if it was true, but he sure took over the symposium that night. And he looked the part. He was a huge, heavy man with yellow hair, and he always looked like he was spoiling for a fight. He wouldn't let anyone touch their wine until they made a speech in honor of him. And if he didn't like the speech, he'd have a servant pour wine over the guy's head. The men at the symposium were scared stiff of him, and they did everything he told them to. But not Empedocles, no sir. When it was his turn, he refused to speak. Instead, he stood up, glared at Cleomenes for what seemed like a whole minute. And then he raised his right arm, his fist clenched tight. "Power to the people!" he bellowed. He lowered his arm, real slow, without taking his eyes off Cleomenes. Then he came over to me and yanked me up from the couch and lugged me out of the room. Cleomenes was too flustered to respond.

When we got to the street, he pulled me toward him and kissed me hard. We've been together ever since.

The next day, he went to the court and filed a lawsuit against Cleomenes. I didn't miss a minute of the trial. Empedocles was marvelous. He begged the Agrigentines to show some spine. No tyrant, he told them, should ever see the light of day in a self-respecting Greek city. Well, not only did he get a conviction, but a death sentence too. That was end of Cleomenes.

Oh where oh where can my baby be? A god took him away from me, I know it. Or maybe the pressure got to him. He's been feeling a lot of stress lately. I know he didn't jump into the crater of a volcano, but, and I hate to say it, he might have cracked up.

I know one thing for sure. No matter what people tell you, Empedocles did not think he was a god. How could he? His health was terrible. He hasn't been able to put on his bronze shoes by himself for months. He has to pee all the time, and if he eats the wrong foods, his stomach hurts. I have to force him to do his exercises every day. He knows he's going downhill. Like the rest of us, I suppose.

No, no, no, not in a million years! Empedocles would never take his own life. He loved himself too much! And me too. When we were having sex and I was doing something to him that he liked, he would say, "Don't pause, Pausanias, don't pause."[79] He thought he was being funny. What a sweetie he was!

But like I said, he might have cracked up and then run away. You know, from all the attention and always having to do things for people. Maybe he just needs some peace and quiet so he can think straight again. He has a cousin in the Peloponnese he's fond of. Maybe he went there. Deep down he probably knows fame isn't doing him any good. I mean, he did sort of think he was a god. No matter where he was, he was always the smartest guy in the room. But he really did believe in equality and care about people. Much more than he cared about money or fancy clothes.

I'm sorry, I can't help it.

Maybe he fell off a carriage and broke his neck. Or off a boat and drowned. Ugh, gives me the chills just thinking about it. But he never would have left without saying goodbye to me. I don't believe it. Do you?

Thank you.

I don't know what I'm going to do without him.

I'm sorry, I'm getting a headache, and I need to be alone. Write what you want, but don't you dare say a single nasty word about him, you hear?

You promise?

9

Democritus at 109

(460–351 BCE)

No one was as wise,
And performed a deed so great,
As the all-knowing Democritus.
When death drew near,
He kept himself at home for three days,
Breathing the steam of hot loaves. (DL IX.43)[80]

HE'S LYING IN BED, eyes closed, head propped by pillows. Translucent skin hangs loosely on his tiny, desiccated body. Two loaves of freshly baked bread sit on his narrow chest, their warm, moist vapors rising. He breathes, shallow but regular. He is Democritus, and he's 109. Look closely, and you'll see the faint shadow of a smile on his lips. He has no fear of death, none whatsoever.

He hasn't gotten out of bed for a month. Servants feed and bathe him, change his diapers, and he's rarely been conscious. But three days ago, he suddenly revived. That morning his sister, who is ninety-nine, told a servant she desperately wanted to go to the Thesmorphia one last time before she died. She complained she would be unable to do so because her brother was close to the end. Dutiful as always, she refused to leave his side for the three-day festival.[81] To everyone's amazement,

Democritus opened his eyes and, with some vigor, said, "Don't be silly! Of course you should go."

"Oh shush," his sister replied, annoyed with him. "I can't let you die here without me."

"Please," Democritus said. "Go. It will do my heart good to know you are there. And I promise I won't die until you return."

"Don't be ridiculous. You're not going to last three more days," she said, her irritation palpable.

"Of course I will." He grinned and for a moment looked like his much younger self, the one who laughed often. "Go, my dear, go worship your goddess. And be of good cheer."[82] He closed his eyes.

Although he has never said so in her presence, he finds her piety absurd. In his world, there are no gods, just atoms moving through the void. They scatter and merge, scatter and merge, and such is the whole of things. To beg Zeus for a favor, to fear retribution in the next life, or to look forward to a reward is sheer stupidity.[83] But his sister has taken care of him for years, and despite her foul temper, he is grateful.

The old woman snorted and pretended to protest, but she quickly relented. She ordered the servants to pack her belongings. Within an hour, the mule cart was on the road, carrying her to the beach at Myrodato where the festival was being held.

As soon as she left the house, Democritus opened his eyes once again. He instructed the servants to start baking bread and to keep doing so for the full three days she was gone. They were to place two loaves on his chest and to replace them immediately when they cooled. He reasoned that inhaling the warm vapors would strengthen his lungs and prevent the few soul-atoms he had left from escaping. He was confident the procedure would keep him intact until she returned.[84]

When the first batch came out of the oven and the loaves were brought to him, he said thank you, and then closed his eyes. He hasn't opened them since. Despite the servants' best efforts, he's taken no food or water either. He is concentrating the tiny bit of energy he has left on breathing. His sister is due home tonight.

He grew up in a wealthy household. So wealthy that his father once hosted the great king himself: Xerxes, son of Darius. That evening, nearly a century ago, when the adults were feasting in the main hall, Democritus, then only twelve, sat with the Persian's entourage around their campfire. There were Egyptians, who spoke confidently about life after death, and Chaldeans, who predicted the future, and Magi from Persepolis who regaled one another with stories of gods and stars, subjects as enticing to Democritus as the men themselves.[85] He spent the entire evening listening, enthralled.

One story in particular took hold: the naked wisemen of India. They live in the forest, subsist only on water, fruits, and nuts, and sleep on leaves. Accustomed to the opulence of his father's estate, he couldn't imagine someone not wearing clothes or eating honey cakes or sleeping in a warm bed. "What do they do," he asked, when it rains? "Don't they get sad?"

"No," a Chaldean explained, "the naked wisemen never get sad. They do not miss their previous lives, for in the forest they are filled with joy. They feel the deep peace of being at one with the universe, and compared to the universe, honey cakes are trivial. Cosmic consciousness, they call it, and to enter it they must leave everything familiar behind. And when they do, they move from less into more, multiplicity into unity, unrest into rest. No, nothing bothers the naked wisemen. Not even getting wet in the rain."

Since many things bothered the young Democritus—his siblings in particular—these words, even if their meaning eluded him, drilled their way into his memory. For years after Xerxes' visit, he tried to imagine sleeping on leaves and being at peace. His father's palace, which was not peaceful at all, began to feel like a prison. His brothers loomed as aggressive boors, his sisters intrusive chatterboxes. He even lost interest in the city of Abdera, which to his young eyes used to feel exciting. Seeds of discontent had been sown, and he longed to discover what lay beyond. When his father lectured him and his brothers about their responsibilities to family and city, Democritus would fantasize about the naked wisemen of India. He was a good boy who excelled in his studies and rarely retaliated when his brothers bullied him or his sisters teased him, but deep down a mighty restlessness was taking hold. Many a night his body refused to relax, and he could not fall asleep. His legs twitched and vibrated with pent up energy, and the only remedy he knew was to walk around his father's estate for hours on end.

When his father died unexpectedly, Democritus, then nineteen, chose to take his share of the estate in the form of twenty talents of silver. His brothers were delighted, since their portions of the land, animals, and houses were worth far more. They thought their brother a fool, but in fact, he knew exactly what he wanted. Money to finance his journey to India where he would, at last, meet the naked wisemen.[86]

He booked passage on a merchant ship headed to Naucratis in Egypt. As soon as it entered open water and he could no longer see the mainland he began to tremble with excitement. He breathed in the cool air, felt its salty particles tickling his throat, and smiled, ready to begin his own life.

When he arrived in Egypt, he was greeted by Pheros, a blind priest who had been in Xerxes' entourage when the great king had visited Abdera. A tall, thin elderly man with a gentle face, a shaved head, and blank eyes, he hosted the young Greek generously. He arranged for Democritus to be taken on tours of Heliopolis, Memphis, and Thebes. Every day something new grabbed his attention. Rather than burning or burying their dead, Egyptians embalmed them. They said nothing when they greeted each other on the street, but only bowed. In the markets, women did most of the buying and selling. "Where were the men?" Democritus asked Pheros. "At home, weaving," was his remarkable answer. In Greece, a family might wash their clothes weekly but the Egyptians he encountered seemed to wear a freshly laundered linen garment every day. Once a month, they purged themselves by means of vomiting and enemas. "Why?" he asked Pheros. "Because," the priest explained, "all human illnesses are caused by food." Democritus thought this might actually be true, since he never once saw an Egyptian fall ill. On the other hand, he reasoned, climate was a more likely explanation. People in Greece usually got sick when the seasons changed, while the weather in Egypt was remarkably steady.

He was fascinated by the crocodiles. With pig eyes, enormous teeth and tusks, and no tongue, these intimidating animals lived on both land and water. One day, he saw one with its immense mouth wide open, and a small bird, which Pheros called a plover, flew inside it. To his amazement, instead of swallowing it whole, the beast allowed the bird to peck around to its heart's content. Pheros explained that because the croc slept in the river at night, its mouth was full of leeches, which, for a plover, is a delicacy. The bird was feasting and the croc's mouth was being cleaned at the same time. Democritus had to suppress a smirk when the priest added that in their previous lives each of these animals had been the other, which is why they got along so well now. He was sure there was a better explanation.[87]

He was fascinated by the Egyptian obsession with tombs and wondered why they were filled with elaborate offerings of food and treasure. Pheros explained that human beings possess a life force that never dies. While on earth, it is nourished by food and drink and even after the death of the body it continues to require food, whose essence it can consume. It is thus incumbent on the relatives of the dead to ensure their loved ones are well equipped for the long voyage to the afterworld. Not only are they supplied with food, clothes and jewelry, but also small statues of human beings and astonishingly precise replicas of animals, both real and fantastic. Eventually the life force would return to the body, which is why the Egyptians mummified their dead.

Hearing all this, Democritus was reminded of the death of his own father. His funeral had been elaborate. First his corpse was washed and anointed with oil, and then it was placed on a high bed within the house. Family, friends, and the leading citizens of Abdera came to mourn and pay their respects. After that the body was placed into a deep grave on top of which a marble column was erected. Democritus understood full well that the ritual was for one purpose only: to ensure his father would not be forgotten. The only immortality he would receive would be metaphorical and located in the memory of those still alive. By contrast, the funerary business of the Egyptians was an entirely literal affair. Or so it seemed. These were very intelligent people, and Democritus found it difficult to imagine they took their stories seriously.

While in Egypt he did not miss Abdera or his family. There were too many dazzling, dizzying, delightful sights and sounds. Still, at night, alone with his thoughts in the darkness, he wondered: Were these Egyptians really as exotic as they seemed to be? Or were they no more than a variation on a theme? Yes, their language was different. But like the Greeks, they used words. Yes, their religion was different. But Greeks too had their gods. Egyptian customs struck him as deeply strange, but surely Greek culture was as equally strange to an Egyptian. Behind the surface sheen of difference, he wondered, might there lie a same, single reality?

One day, Pheros invited him to visit the temple of Thoth in Hermopolis. As soon as they arrived, the old man began chatting with an old friend, and so Democritus wandered on his own. Within minutes, a curious sight caught his eye. In the courtyard, a group of priests were standing in a circle and staring intently at something on the ground. His first thought was that it might be a dead animal. He approached cautiously, without drawing attention to himself, and managed to find a vantage point just outside the ring. And what he saw was another, older priest using a stick to scratch figures in the dirt beneath him. Democritus craned his neck to see what he was drawing. Carefully etched diagrams of circles, triangles, rectangles. While he was drawing, the priest, obviously a teacher, was explaining. Democritus understood not a word, but he listened carefully as if he could. For reasons he could not fathom, he found the mysterious lesson alluring. The diagrams seemed to hold promise, but of what he had no idea.

That evening, in the guest quarters they shared, he asked Pheros about the priests. They worked for the Pharaoh, the old man told him, and their job was to measure the plots owned by farmers in the Nile Delta and to keep meticulous records. This was important since walls and property markers, even trees, disappeared every year when the great river flooded, and only the priests' records made it possible to determine the location of the different plots of land when the water receded, and then to assess the amount of tax owed to Pharaoh. The priests did their work in the spring, when the river was at its lowest, and were free to spend the rest of the year as they wished. They lived together in the Temple of Thoth, which they rarely left. To the average Egyptian, they seemed indolent. These priests, however, were not idling away their many leisure hours. Instead, they were studying. Although Pheros did not know it, they were developing the science the Greeks would later call geometry.[88]

Democritus was intrigued, and he begged Pheros to convince the teacher-priest to take him on as a student. Pheros agreed, and as he often did, he smiled at Democritus as if he were a child.[89]

Although his knowledge of the language was minimal, he found the lessons riveting. He could sense that the teacher-priest was a master, and he strained as hard as he could to glean an idea or two. He had little success until, one day, the teacher-priest began the lesson by showing the students a cylindrical basket. He talked about it with great enthusiasm, and as he did, he moved his hands along all of its surfaces. Then, as usual, he sketched lines on the ground with his stick. For the first time, Democritus grasped what he was doing—teaching them how to calculate the surface area of a cylinder—and he focused on the diagrams in order to burn them into his memory.[90] That night, alone in his room, he took a spoonful of ashes from his fireplace and mixed them with water to create a paste, which became his ink. His stylus was a small piece of wood, and his papyrus was a scrap he had found lying on the floor of the temple. With these tools, Democritus reproduced the diagrams the teacher-priest had drawn in the temple. For hours, he repeated this exercise until, near dawn, he discovered the pattern. Using his own Greek letters, he wrote down a rudimentary equation. Despite his exhaustion, it delighted him, for with it, he realized, he could now calculate the area of any cylinder, regardless of its size or color or the material of which it was made; regardless of whether it was Greek or Egyptian.

Democritus laughed.

Within three months, he was not only fluent in the Egyptian language but able to tutor those student-priests struggling to understand their geometry lessons.

When they weren't studying, the priests would perform rituals, whose purpose, they claimed, was to maintain the order of the cosmos. If they didn't wash their hands properly before eating, the sun might not rise or the Nile might not flood. Democritus thought this was sheer nonsense, but the priests were such good company, so intelligent and friendly, he never mentioned his misgivings. Still, he started to get bored with them, and soon his old restlessness returned. At night, his legs throbbed with energy, and he could not lie still. Just as he had back in Greece, he needed to take long walks in order to calm down. He recognized the sensation as the harbinger of travel. One morning, having not slept at all, he decided to resume his quest. He would travel to India and find the naked wisemen.

He began by going south, to what the Greeks call Ethiopia but whose proper name, as he learned, was Nubia. There he met dark skinned, hospitable people, whose kings were tall and lived to a very long age. They used elephants instead of oxen and had devised ingenious ways of mining gold. One day, in the bustling city of Meroe, where stone pyramids popped up from the sand like gigantic mushrooms, he was invited to attend a religious festival in honor of one of their gods, Bromius.[91] At first, it was a familiar routine—chanting, recitations, flaming oil pots—and he found it tedious. But then ten half-naked men entered the temple. One was dragging a white goat with a rope tied around its neck, three were playing reed pipes, the rest were carrying large sticks. They formed a circle, undid the rope, and pushed the goat into the middle. The terrified animal tried to escape, but the men kept it in place by hitting it with their sticks. Then, with the pipes blaring, they began to grunt in unison. As the goat gradually weakened from the many blows raining down on its helpless body, they grunted louder and the pipes played even more intensely. Soon the animal fell to the ground and could not get back up. The men dropped their sticks and instruments and pounced upon it. They grabbed each of the goat's four legs, pulled with all their might, and tore the poor beast apart. One man took hold of its head and twisted until its neck was no more than a few useless strings. He then yanked it off and lifted it high in triumph. Another ripped out the heart, took a bite, and passed it on. They smeared blood on their arms and chests and bellowed in mad delight. Suddenly, the men fell silent. Each carefully placed the piece of the goat he was holding onto a pile. Then, facing the neatly stacked remnants of the dismembered corpse, they bowed their heads, as did all the Nubians who were watching. After a long silent moment, they walked slowly away and left the temple. When they were gone, an old man from the audience, who looked to be a chief of some sort, walked to the bloody pile. He was carrying an ornate golden vase from which he poured a thick liquid. He was handed a flaming stick, which he tossed onto the pile. The fire ignited immediately, black smoke billowed. In a few minutes, it died down, and the Nubian crowd quietly exited the temple.

Democritus, feeling nauseous, was appalled. Still, he managed to ask himself a question: with all that liquid inside of the goat, how, when it was alive, did it stay intact?

From Nubia he went east to the Red Sea. He had wanted to travel overland to his next stop, Persia, but was warned that Arabia, the southern edge of the inhabited world, was far too hostile an environment. So he took a ship north back to Egypt and then another to Sidon in Phoenicia, where he began the long trek east.

After traversing Syria and Babylon, which took him three hard months, he finally arrived in Susa. There he was welcomed by Artaxerxes, whose father, Xerxes, had been murdered by one of his own commanders. Remembering the hospitality Democritus' father had once shown to his family, Artaxerxes hosted him generously.

For seven days, Democritus, well tended by Persian slaves, recuperated. While he was grateful for the respite, as soon as he regained his strength, he sought out the Chaldeans and Magi who had visited his home years before. He wanted to hear more of their stories, especially about the naked wisemen. But for reasons he did not know, such men were no longer welcome in the Persian court. He became discouraged and felt no closer to India than he had been in Greece.

One day, when he was feeling particularly dejected and could do no more than doze under a tree, a fat old man approached him. He was wearing typical Persian clothes and a conical hat, and so Democritus was shocked when he addressed him in vulgar but fluent Greek.

"Hey there, good looking," he said. "What you got cooking?"

Utterly baffled, Democritus could not reply.

"What's the matter, sonny? Cat got your tongue?"

"No, no, I'm sorry," Democritus said. "I was just surprised you spoke Greek."

"Course I speak Greek, sonny. Born and bred in Athens, as a matter of fact."

"Really?

"You betcha."

"Then how'd you get here?" Democritus asked.

"Came over with Themistocles. I was a kid, no more than ten, when he hired me as his page. That was during the war. From the beginning he took a shine to me, and we stuck together for years. Man, we had some times. You know, Themistocles had to hightail it outta Greece way back when, and that's why he came here. Now you might be puzzled by that. After all, he whupped Xerxes and his crew pretty good. But the old bastard—the O.B. I used to call him—jeez Louise, he was smart. He actually persuaded the Persians he'd done them a favor by not destroying their bridges over the Hellespont, and when the O.B. was done, he had them Persians feeling grateful to him. Can you believe it?[92] Anyway, he stuck around here for a few years and then decided to take up residence in Magnesia. He invited me to come with him, but I didn't want to go 'cause I liked it here in Susa. The food is just so darned good. Best in the world is what I think. You tried their chicken stew yet? Onions, pomegranates, walnuts, and then all them spices they got here. Nothing like it, by Zeus! I have it just about every day."

The old man patted his ample stomach and laughed. Democritus, marvelling at his vivacity, nodded in return. He explained he was demoralized because he had no idea how to get to India, which was the goal of his whole long journey.

"India? Why you want to go there?"

Even though he felt embarrassed, he answered honestly. "I'd like to meet the naked wisemen."

The old man grinned, his eyes twinkling. "Well, well, well. You know, sonny, I might be able to help you out," he said.

"Really?"

"Yes sir. I've been in Susa for quite a while and, like I said, it's real nice. But a little trip wouldn't do me no harm. Me and the O.B., we were seafaring men. Anyway, I ain't been on the water for years, but if you're willing to spring for my fare I'll take you down to the Gulf and we can grab a merchant ship headed to the coast of Malabar. It's a long way off but plenty of ships go there 'cause that's where the spices are. I heard about those naked wisemen myself, you know, and I wouldn't mind meeting up with them suckers. What do you say?"

Democritus hesitated. The man was crude, sloppy, and fat, but his eyes were bright, and despite his girth, he was spry. The only other option facing him was to begin the long trip back to Greece, and he wasn't ready for that. So he agreed. The old man was delighted, and he extended his hand. "By the way," he said, "Dicaeus is my name."

They began their journey by hitching a ride with a caravan headed to the Gulf, and then, just as Dicaeus had promised, they booked passage on a merchant ship headed to the coast of Malabar, the spice garden of the world. Unlike his first voyage from Greece to Egypt, Democritus felt calm. Although he was not convinced Dicaeus would be of much use in finding the naked wisemen, he was glad to be on the move once again, and India, he had heard, was vast and teeming.

When they docked in the port of Muziris, Dicaeus hired a guide who would also be their translator, and soon they began sightseeing in earnest. One of their first encounters was with a tribe called the Jains. They refused to kill any animal, and they even wore elevated shoes to prevent them from inadvertently crushing an insect. Then they met another group called the Callatiae who ate their parents when they died. When Democritus informed them that in Greece people either buried or burned their deceased, they were appalled. Another tribe had intercourse in the open, and the guide told them that the men ejaculated seed as dark as their skin. Democritus did not believe it. In one village they saw cockroaches a foot long.[93]

Despite its startling array of people and animals, sights, sounds, and smells, India, unlike Egypt, did not excite him. While he felt a tingle of stimulation, one thought shadowed him constantly: variations on a theme. Like Egypt, India certainly seemed exotic, but perhaps this was no more than a façade behind which lay, not difference, but sameness. And so when he was being shown a temple or a spice market, he found himself thinking about geometry rather than what appeared before his eyes. Dicaeus, by contrast, was having a ball, fearlessly experimenting with every new food he was offered.

Democritus had their guide ask everyone they met about the naked wisemen, but no credible information came their way. Perhaps, he wondered, they were no more than a legend, like the Egyptian afterlife. After weeks of touring he felt sure this was the case and once again became dejected. Then, one morning at a market stall whose vendor was selling statues of gods, they met a man named Bhadrabahu. Plump and jolly, with a thick brown beard, he advertised himself as a scholar whose life mission was to record as many of the customs of his vast land as he could. He said he knew where the naked wisemen lived, and for a modest fee, he would guide the Greeks, whose language he somehow had learned.

A week later they were trekking through a forest dense with huge trees draped in moss. It was dark, but Bhadrabahu seemed to know where he was going. Sure enough, he found them. In a clearing, the naked wisemen were sitting on the ground, in a circle, eyes closed, legs crossed, holding their hands, palms pressed together, in front of their noses. For the first time in weeks, Democritus' heart beat fast.

After an hour of silence, the circle disbanded, the naked wisemen bowed to each other and went their separate ways without saying a word. Bhadrabahu approached one of them, a middle-aged, bone-thin man with crossed cloudy eyes and a drooping mouth, and convinced him to answer a few questions. When he was introduced to the two Greeks, he did not seem the least bit surprised or interested. Democritus peppered him with questions, which Bhadrabahu translated. Did he sleep on leaves? Yes. Did he only eat nuts and fruits from trees? Yes. Did he only drink water? Yes. Did he ever return to his village? No. Did he ever want to? No. What did he do when it rained? Get wet. Why was he naked? He shrugged. Did he feel one with the universe? Another shrug. Was he at peace? No response at all. Did he think the external world revealed through the senses was an illusion? Was it, he asked, using a word Bhadrabahu had taught him, nothing but *maya*?[94] The naked wiseman looked at Democritus, his eyes as blank as those of the blind Pheros back in Egypt, and said nothing.

Democritus felt as if he had been punched in the gut. The man may have been naked but he was a moron. The next day, he told Bhadrabahu to take him back to Mizuris.

During the weeks of travel it took to reach the coast Democritus rarely spoke. He was not surly, but he turned down Bhadrabahu's offers of a tour of this temple or that tribe. When they finally reached the port, he and Dicaeus booked passage on a ship bound for Persia scheduled to depart in three days. They bade farewell to Bhadrabahu and found rooms at a cheap inn. Dicaeus was delighted, for there was a brothel next door and a dozen food vendors on the street, and after frequenting several of the latter, he entered the former. Democritus chose to sit on the veranda. It faced west, into the blazing afternoon sun, but was well-shaded by a thatched awning. On the street in front of him, a raucous parade passed by. Men, women, children, talking, laughing, yelling all at once. A servant approached him and proceeded to ask a long question. Democritus listened courteously although he understood not a word, and when it was done, he nodded listlessly. The servant left but returned a few minutes later with a large cup containing a greenish liquid. Without giving it a thought, Democritus took a sip. It was cool, herbaceous, and bitter, like nothing he had ever tasted, but its tingles were strangely pleasant, and so he took another. He soon realized he liked the way it was making him feel; a bit like being drunk but instead of stupefying him, the way wine did, his mind was clear. He took a few more sips and the street in front of him became increasingly vivid. He saw waves of heat rising from the ground, individual beads of sweat forming on glistening foreheads, long dark eyelashes of smiling children. He heard a multitude of voices, and even though the words were meaningless to him, each syllable, like a solitary bell, rang clear and distinct. He smelled the pungent fragrances of the spices displayed on the vendors' tables and marvelled at the colorful clothing the women wore. He sat there sipping his drink, relishing its bitterness, transfixed.

There was a small stand of trees on the other side of the street. Directly behind it the sun was beginning to set. As it descended, the light on the veranda became complicated and demanded his full attention. Shadows cast by the leaves undulated on the wall behind him, and he turned his chair around to watch them properly. He laughed in delight and then turned his chair back toward the street. Then he saw the sunbeam. Emerging through an opening in the branches it reached the street as crisply defined as a white marble column. And in the sunbeam, as if in an illuminated chamber, a swarm of tiny gnats, hundreds maybe thousands, flying around madly, as if they had been injected with fire. He was mesmerized. And he wondered: were these gnats only in the sunbeam, attracted by its warmth? Or were they everywhere, but only visible in the sunbeam? Yes, he decided, it had to be that. Because they were tiny, outside of the sunbeam they were invisible.

When his eyes started to burn, Democritus turned away and looked at the rest of the street, but the people had disappeared and been replaced by a huge buzzing cloud, like a beehive gone berserk. He looked down at the table beneath his cup and saw through it all the way to the ground, but there was no ground, only an empty hole. Terrified, his heart racing, gasping for breath, he jumped up from his chair. The servant who had brought him the drink rushed to his side. For a good ten minutes, he patted him on his back, as if he were a baby. Then, after returning him slowly into his chair, he ran to the kitchen. When he returned he was carrying another cup. This time the drink was black and steaming. He helped Democritus take a small sip. It was as bitter as the green one, but not pleasant at all. He spat it out. Communicating with his hands, the servant insisted Democritus had to drink the whole cup. He complied, reluctantly, and within minutes, his heart slowed, and he was able to breath normally. He looked at the street, and the people had returned. He looked under the table, and the ground was solid. The sunbeam was gone.

Democritus sat on the veranda for nearly an hour, while the servant brought him cup after cup of the hot black drink. And then it hit him, like a slap to the head. They were *everywhere!* Not just the gnats glinting in the light, but tiny particles, an infinite number. When they bumped into each other they became entangled and formed a clump, which got bigger and bigger until it became, like the people on the street, an object visible to the human eye. And when those people died, like the goat he had seen sacrificed in Nubia, their insides would pour out and sink into the earth, but the particles of which they were composed would continue to exist. For they were uncuttable atoms and would never fall apart. Instead, they would scatter and eventually merge with other particles and a different something, a chair, a dog, a tree, a naked wiseman, would come into view. Oh, how much his theory could explain! What seems to be coming-to-be and passing away is no more than atoms merging and scattering and merging once more. What seems to be difference—this chair, that table, Egyptians, Persians, Greeks, sights, sounds, fragrances, tastes—is no more than surface sheen—what the Indians call *maya*—behind which there is nothing but atoms.

He laughed again. In their own way, the Egyptians had been right. There is no death. If only he had been able to think straight when he was back in Greece, he could have figured it all out on his own.

As the sun sets, he begins to wheeze. The servants are worried, so they put a third loaf of steaming bread on what remains of his chest.

The hours pass slowly. Finally, shortly before midnight, his sister arrives. When she sees her brother lying in his bed, eyes closed, with three loaves of bread on his chest, she is flummoxed. She examines him carefully and hears the slight sound he is making. As he promised, he is alive. She looks relieved, but certainly not happy.

Suddenly he awakens, opens his filmy eyes. He somehow has the energy to shape his mouth into a tiny grin. He tries to speak but produces only a whisper no one can hear. He tries again, but his strength is now completely gone. Unafraid, he breathes out the last of his soul atoms.

10

Socrates at Dusk

(469–399 BCE)

For truly did the god call you wise, and wisdom is a god.
For you merely received the hemlock from the Athenians,
But it is they who, through your mouth, have drained the cup. (DL II.46)

THE DAMNED ATHENIANS, YOU know, they put executions on hold during their annual Theseus fest, which is going on right now. It's their time to commemorate our local boy's greatest exploit: saving fourteen kids from the Minotaur. Every year they send a boat to Delos to thank Apollo. While it's sailing, they don't lay on a finger on their prisoners.[95]

A boatload of bullshit is what I think, but at least I'll have a few more days. They won't execute him until the ship returns, and I've heard it'll take about a week. Then he'll drink the hemlock and die what they say is a painful death. But if anybody can handle it, it's him. I'm telling you, the man's tough as nails. Years ago, we were on campaign in Potideia, and it was brutally cold. Like everyone else, I was bundled up head to toe with every piece of clothing I could muster. Some guys wouldn't even come out from underneath their blankets. But Socrates, my god, he was wearing his regular cloak and, as usual, no shoes, and he walked around as if he was taking a stroll on the beach! And then there was the time when our patrol was cut off from the rest of the army, and we ran out of food. Didn't faze him a bit, no sir. And how about that crazy party at Agathon's? They drank till dawn, and by then even Aristophanes, who can hold plenty, had passed out. But not Socrates. He just trotted off to the gym for his morning workout.[96] Of course, I didn't actually see him do it since I was one of the guys dead drunk on the floor. But my buddy told me about it the next day.

No, I'm not worried about how he'll handle the hemlock.

He's been in jail for a week, and I visit him every day. All I have to do is hand the guard a couple of coins, and he lets me right in. And more than once he's made it clear that if I slip him a few more he'll leave the door open at night, and Socrates can bolt. It wouldn't be a problem. I've got plenty of dough.

The truth is this is probably what the bastards hope will happen. You see, they don't really want to kill him. They're not totally stupid; they know in the long run it'll hurt their reputation. The only reason they asked for the death penalty in the first place was because they were sure he'd cop a plea. If he agreed to leave town, they'd have let him go, just like they did with Anaxagoras way back when. But, no, the old coot wouldn't play along. He was born in Athens, he said, and Athens is where he would die. When he refused to ask for exile, he forced their hand, which is why he's here now, waiting to drink the goddamned hemlock.

You know what I think? He enjoys making them squirm.

I love the guy, and I've known him forever, but I swear I can't figure him out.

This morning I got to the prison at dawn. When I went into his cell, he was snoring away like he didn't have a care in the world. It was a nice, gentle snore, right as rain, but it didn't relax me. No, I was on edge, and I paced around the room until he finally woke up.

"Hi there, Meg," he said.

Meg. He's been calling me that since we were kids. My real name is Megacles. Anyway, he sounded glad to see me. "How you feeling, pal?" I asked.

"Not too bad. Yourself?"

"Okay."

When the guard heard us talking, he brought breakfast. Bread, olives, some cheese, a cup of water. I can tell he likes Socrates. In fact, he's never said so, but I'm pretty sure he wants me to spring him from jail, and not only because he'd get a nice chunk of change.

Socrates thanked the guard and slowly nibbled on his food. He seemed to be savoring each bite, but the look on his face told me his mind was elsewhere. His is not a pretty face, not by any means, but it has its charms.

I popped the same question I've already asked a dozen times.

"Hey, man, why don't we take off tonight? The guard'll leave the door open. He'd be glad to do it. We can go to Thessaly. I've got friends there, and they owe me a favor. They'll put you up for a while, and then I'll get you your own place. We've got to do it quick, though. No more dawdling. Your ship's coming in soon."

I was pleased with the phrase. He likes that kind of stuff. This time, though, he didn't seem to notice. Instead, he just repeated my name, two or three times, and I could tell he was running out of patience. Then he took a deep breath, and I knew what was coming. Sure enough, he explained to me, yet again, why it's wrong to break the law, no matter how shitty it is. See, Athens never forced him to stay. He could have left town any time he felt like it, but he never did, which means he agreed to play by its rules. Plus, he was always allowed to vote in the Assembly, and so, like every citizen, he had his chance to change those rules, or propose a new one if he wanted. Persuade or obey, that's the city's motto. He called it the good loser principle. Win some, lose some, but always follow the rules.[97] So, no, he's not going to bust out of here. Even if the trial was a load of bullshit, which it was, the fact is that 280 jurors voted against him and only 220 for acquittal.

"But you set them up, Socrates!" I told him. "You knew they expected you to counter the death penalty with exile, and that's exactly what they wanted you to do. But no, you had to mess up their plans. I still can't believe you told them the only punishment you deserve is free room and board at city hall for the rest of your life![98] You didn't give them any room to maneuver, which is why we're waiting for their stupid ship to come in so the bastards can pour poison down your throat!"

I was getting worked up, but he didn't say a word. It's not like he was sympathetic or anything. The little smirk of his, which I've seen a thousand times, was on his face.

"Are we finished now, Meg? he asked me, and it was like he was talking to a kid. Damn, that pissed me off. But I calmed down quick when he got serious and started talking to me, you know, man to man.

"What did you expect me to do, Meg? I had to tell the truth, didn't I? They accused me of corrupting the young, and I did no such thing. In fact, it was the opposite. I tried to make my fellow Athenians into better human beings. Of course I knew free room and board was a long shot, but that's what we give our Olympic champions, isn't it?[99] The athletes make us feel good about ourselves, and it's great fun to celebrate when they win, but basking in the light of someone else's glory is a pretty lame version of happiness. Me, I pull people away from the crowd. I ask them questions, simple ones that they can understand. What is courage? What is justice? What is excellence? At first they're confident they know the answers, but in fact they're only repeating what they've heard from their parents, or the politicians, or the poets. But when I force them to explain why their beliefs are true, they come to see they have no idea what they're talking about, which means their lives have been predicated, not on knowledge, but on blind trust. When this realization sinks in, they feel shaky, but that's precisely when education begins. I want them to become suspicious of easy answers and for the familiar to turn strange. They think they understand what it means to lead a good life, which they equate with having money, power, or fame, but I show them this isn't true. I want them to care about *truth*, Meg, not just their reputations. It's not easy, but they have to learn that the unexamined life is not worth living for a human being."

Of course, I probably haven't remembered his speech right, and the fact is I like money myself, but it doesn't matter. The point is my buddy was back to his old self, talking up a storm!

But then something happened I'd never seen before. His head sank, and he put his hands over his ears. He's almost seventy, you know, but this was the first time he'd ever looked old. Of course, he does have trouble hearing, but then again, so do I, and I'm two years younger.

Anyway, he stared at the floor for what felt like a minute but probably wasn't. Then, without raising his head, he muttered, "Fucking Alcibiades."

I was shocked. I hadn't heard him curse in years. Of course, when we were kids, back in Alopece, which is a rough part of town, our language was downright dirty. Man, you should have heard his father. He was a stonemason, and when he and his pals were drinking, their language was raw. Socrates used to talk like his old man, but he changed after he studied with Archelaus. He didn't put on a fake accent or anything stupid like that, but he did clean up his act. Occasionally he'll slip into old-town talk with me, but it's been a while.

Anyway, I asked him, "What about Alcibiades?"

He didn't look at me, but at least he answered. "I think he was right."

"Right? Right about what?"

It was strange, him bringing up Alcibiades. Now, let me tell you, that guy was a piece of work. Good looking, smart as a whip, great on the battlefield, and he could make a hell of a speech in the Assembly, even though he did have a little bit of a lisp. Just the type you'd expect to make it big in Athens. And he did, for a while, but then it went to pieces. First, he convinced us to attack Syracuse, which turned out to be a disaster. Then, just before the fleet sailed, he was accused of mutilating the Herms—chopping their weenies off—a charge I never took seriously. After that he knew he was in deep shit, and so he bolted over to the Spartans. Still, the Athenians were willing to forgive him. After all, he was our best general by far and we needed him in the war. And when he finally came home—what was it, eight years ago?—we welcomed him back with open arms. Of course, it didn't last long. Oh man, I can't remember all the details, but for years Alcibiades was the talk of the town.

He's dead now, you know. Killed, somewhere up north, maybe by the Spartans.[100] But here's the thing: I think Socrates was the only person in the world who actually meant something to him. Alcibiades craved his approval because he knew the old coot never kissed anybody's ass, and so if he got a thumbs up from him, it would actually count. What's strange is that the feeling must have been sort of mutual.[101] The only time I ever saw Socrates cry was when news reached town that Alcibiades was dead. Man, what a pair! The swashbuckler, smooth as silk, and the old philosopher, who didn't even wear shoes.

Anyway, where was I? Oh yeah, Socrates said Alcibiades was right. "About what?" I asked him.

"He said I was ironic."

"Ironic?" I forgot what it meant.

"Yeah, ironic," he replied, and he finally raised his head and looked at me. "You know, not saying what you really think. It's like wearing a mask. Alcibiades said I pretended to care about other people, when truth was I didn't. He said deep down I thought they were trash, and I was just playing with them."

It came back to me. Yeah, that's pretty much what he said. It was during the party at Agathon's house. It happened before the drinking began and so I managed to retain some of it. I was shocked at the time, but Socrates didn't blink an eye when he heard him say it.[102]

Look, it's true he can mess with people. Like when he told that religious guy, what's his name?—oh yeah, Euthyphro—he wanted to become his student. That was nasty because even I could tell Euthyphro was a dope. Or when he sunk his teeth into Thrasymachus and wouldn't let go until the poor bastard blushed. He even turned on Aeschines once. Poor bastard didn't have a drachma to his name, and when he asked Socrates for advice, he told him to borrow from himself and cut his own rations.[103] That shit was cold.

Still, Alcibiades wasn't fair, and I tried to tell him this. "Come on, Socrates," I said. "Of course, you care about people. Why else would you be on the streets every day, talking to whoever walks by, and for free, when you could charge a pretty penny for private lessons? Or open up a school, like I always told you to do."

He shook his head and didn't say a word. It was weird. I've never seen him like he was this morning.

After a while, though, he snapped out of it, but it seemed to cost him. "I know some of the youngsters think well of me," he said, real soft. "Like that rich kid, Plato. If you asked him, he'd probably say I was the greatest thing to hit town since the olive. But what does he know? Truth is, other people bore me. Nine times out of ten I can predict what they're going to say before they say it. I tune out when they start talking but I keep the interested look on my face."

Whoa, that one made me feel uncomfortable. He kept going, though.

"I mean, good god, look at some of the morons I've talked to. Phaedrus, Euthydemus, Meno. Believe me, not the cream of the crop. Once I tried to explain my theory of recollection to Phaedrus, and you know what he did when I was done?"

I didn't want to, but I forced myself to ask. "What?"

"He changed the subject![104] It was as if what I'd said meant absolutely nothing to him. The same thing happened with Meno. I had this great conversation with his slave boy—a terrific kid, very bright—and I tried to explain to Meno how well it illustrated my ideas, but it was like talking to a wall.[105] I gave him the best I had, and he was bored. That's what happens when you care about people and hope you can make a difference in their lives."

He stopped, and it was like he was, I don't know, reconsidering what he'd just said. Whatever it was, he didn't look happy about it.

"And then there are the ones who are intelligent but can't be budged. Like Callicles. My god, I went after him with every argument I could come up with. None of them took hold, and I simply could not get that man to wonder about the choices he was making. After a while he became annoyed, and he stopped talking to me. I've got to say, though, I admired him for that. At least he understood there was no hope of us finding common ground.[106] And do you remember the night at Cephalus' place? You know, when I talked about justice for ten hours straight? You want to know why I did that?"

"Sure," I said, even though I didn't.

"Because I couldn't bear listening to anyone else talk."

He paused for a moment. Lost in thought, I assumed.

"Why do I bother?" he continued. Then he answered his own question. "Maybe to amuse myself or think out loud. Maybe I'd feel ashamed if I didn't try. I don't know."

He was getting kind of gloomy, so I tried to cheer him up. "What about that kid Theaetetus, the math whiz you've been hanging out with recently? He's a good one, isn't he?"

"For sure he's very intelligent," he said. "But as far as I can tell he still prefers geometry. He's a decent young man, but no philosopher."[107]

He fell silent. Then he took a bite of cheese.

"Alcibiades said I was hubristic."

Another word I couldn't remember. He could tell, so he helped me out.

"You know, arrogant, full of yourself, think you're better than everybody else."

I wondered about this because, fact is, he can be a bully at times. And it seemed he was wondering about it too because he stared at the ceiling for a while. Then he snorted and said, "I suppose he wasn't all wrong. I know I'm way ahead of a lot of people. Especially the know-it-alls. You ever see a politician stand in the Assembly and say, we need to talk more since I am not quite sure what is best? Of course not. They think they know the answers, and yet they never even bothered to ask the right questions. Compared to them I come out on top. Even though I don't have much by way of answers myself at least I don't think I know something when I don't. And I've certainly never felt contempt for an ordinary person who works hard and is honest about his own ignorance. Like the guard in this prison. He's a nice fellow, and we've had some pleasant chats."[108]

I was relieved to hear it.

He nodded like he was agreeing with himself. "I never told you this before, Meg, but there were plenty of times, usually late at night, when I walked around town thinking I was a fraud."

"A fraud?"

"Yes. Someone who puts on a good face but deep down is afraid."

"Afraid?" I interrupted. "Come on, don't be a jackass! Remember, I've seen you on the battlefield. Arrows flying, dead bodies on the ground, and you walking through it all without a tremble. Remember when Alcibiades got nipped in the shoulder by a spear and you carried him to safety? You were cool as a cucumber."

"You're right, Meg, I was good in those kinds of situations. But I don't think it had much to do with courage. Fact is, times like that I just went cold, and I don't know why. Maybe because when things got bad my worst fears were realized and it seemed familiar. You know, like someone who worries about the wheels of his chariot falling off even though they've just been checked by a mechanic. Only when a wheel actually does fall can he finally relax."

I didn't know what he was talking about, and so I asked him, "What is it you're scared of, Socrates?"

For a moment he looked puzzled. "Getting hurt, I suppose."

He took a sip of water.

"I know you think I'm tough, and I don't need anybody to take care of me, and in a way it's true. But it's only because I do a good job of protecting myself."[109]

"From what?"

"Other people."

"What the hell do you mean?"

"Like the way I kept my distance from politics all these years. I used to say it was because the city will crush anyone who actually cares about justice; the real thing, not the nonsense they peddle in the Assembly. But maybe I was just scared of getting hurt. You know, like a wrestler who's so afraid he's going to lose that he refuses to compete, and then rationalizes what he's done by calling the competition meaningless. Maybe that's also why I never wrote anything. I was afraid the critics would slaughter it."[110]

He shook his head, like he didn't believe what he was telling himself, and stared at the ceiling again. Then he resumed.

"My god," he said. "Look at us! Athens could have been a school for all of Greece.[111] Instead, we became crazed militarists hell bent on expansion, and we ended up killing each other in the streets. And now Polemarchus, Critias, Charmides, Alcibiades, they're all dead, and I didn't do a damn thing about it. All those years, I talked and talked, and the city didn't change. It's the same old shithole it's always been."

"But you tried," I told him.

He chuckled. "You know, maybe Alcibiades was right," he said. "I do play with people. But that's not me being arrogant, it's me protecting myself, because if I took them seriously I'd either go crazy or turn into a bitter old man. So I pretend to care, but I don't, but even more deeply I do. I'm in-between, on edge, fueled by perplexity, driven by love. Now, though, my irony weighs heavily on me, like a sweat-soaked cloak in the summer. I need to take it off, Meg."

I had no idea what he was talking about, so I asked him, "What about your crew? You know, Plato, Xenophon, Antisthenes, Aristippus, Aeschines. Those are good boys. You take them seriously, don't you?"

"My crew? Is that what they are?" He shook his head in disbelief. "I doubt any of them will amount to much."

"Well what about Xanthippe?" I said, desperate to change the subject.

For the first time he grinned. "Ah, Xanthippe. A tough old girl, mean as she can be. Almost as mean as me, as a matter of fact. Living with her has been a blessing. I don't need much coddling any more, that's for sure. Alcibiades once said she sounded like a goose. When I told him, it didn't bother me, he said, at least you can get eggs from a goose. Then I reminded him Xanthippe was the mother of my children.[112] That shut him up. And you know what else?"

"What?"

"She's never once complained about . . . about . . . about my lack of employment."

He gave me a nice look, which I appreciated. I make sure Xanthippe can pay the bills every month, and he knows I'll keep doing it after he's gone.

"And she never gave me any grief about spending so much time out of the house. In fact, she used to encourage me to talk with my friends. But the truth is, I don't know if I've ever had a real friend."[113]

That one hurt, but I let it go. "You loved Alcibiades, didn't you?" I asked him.

"Yes," he said, so quiet I could barely hear him. "And you know what? He broke my heart."

"When he died?"

"Long before. When I realized I would never turn him around. If I'd been able to get through to him . . . ."

He didn't finish the thought. He took another bite of cheese and chewed it silently. Then he said something I'll never forget. "I'm not like you, Meg. You're not afraid to love. You love your family, your friends, your horses, your olive trees. Which means you're not afraid to get hurt. I remember when you wept like a baby when your son was killed in the Piraeus."

I couldn't believe he said that! You see, my boy was killed by Critias and his filthy band of thugs who took over the city a few years ago. "The Thirty" they were called. My boy joined the resistance, and I was proud of him. And the bastards cut him down like a dog. Why Socrates had to bring him up I'll never know, especially since he didn't lift a finger during the war. As far as I could tell, he just stayed home when the fighting got fierce. Plus, in the old days he used to hang out with Critias, and he even said some nice things about him. And I think he was the one who encouraged that bastard Charmides to go into politics.[114]

"You're not afraid to make yourself vulnerable, Meg," he continued, and his voice was pretty strange. "Me, I can't do it. I spend my time formulating arguments, figuring out how to go from A to B to C without breaking stride. I ask questions about justice and beauty and courage, and tell people philosophy is not simply the study of nature, as Anaxagoras thought, or of Being, like Parmenides. It's a way of life.[115] But in the long run, what did I care about most? All my questions, all my talk; maybe I was just keeping myself safe."

He ran his hands through what was left of his hair.

"It's like Erinna put it in one of her poems: *the pulse, obdurate, keeps its rhythm. You think you cannot keep breathing, but your rib cage has other ideas, rising and falling, emitting sighs. You must thrive in spite of yourself; and so that you may do it, god takes out your heart of flesh, and gives you a heart of stone.*"[116]

"Who's Erinna?" I asked.

"A poet. From Lesbos," he replied. "One more thing, Meg."

"Yeah, what?" I said, and not in a nice way. He was starting to get on my nerves.

"I've been having a strange dream lately. Same one every night since they stuck me in this place. I hear a voice and it tells me 'to make art.' That's it, just make art. The first time I heard it I was sure I understood what it meant. It was telling me to keep doing what I've always done, which is philosophy, because it's the most beautiful art of all. But a couple of nights ago, when the dream came to me again, I started to wonder if I had it all wrong. What if it wasn't telling me to do philosophy but to practice another, more normal art? You know, like poetry or music, sculpture or storytelling. So yesterday, I actually scribbled some verse. It wasn't any good, but at least I managed to hedge my bets.[117] But I'm still troubled. What if I was right the first time and philosophy is a kind of art, and finally there isn't much difference between it and poetry? What if all these big ideas of mine about the Good—hell, what if truth itself, which I pretend to love—is no more than a fiction? You know I've always been tough on Homer, especially the *Odyssey*, but now I wonder if I'm more like him than I'd care to admit.[118] If so, my whole life has been a sham. And the worst part is that, even if it's good, art may be nothing more than a way of forgetting the human disaster for a while."

"Then get to work, my friend, and make your while worthwhile."[119]

He actually smiled. "I can't do it, Meg," he said. "I've had enough."

"Good! So why don't you try something new? Come with me to Thessaly. Find a real job." I was getting sick and tired of hearing him complain.

He gave me a funny look. I don't know, maybe it was affectionate. "I don't have the energy," he said. "My knees, back, hip, they all hurt. Pain trails me like a shadow, and I worry about how bad it's going to get."

He sighed, but then went right back to it. "Plus, I have to pee all the time, and my hearing is going. I'll probably start forgetting things soon, and it'll only be downhill from there. Why not quit while I'm ahead? Take the easy way out."[120]

"Hemlock ain't easy, you damned fool!" I screamed at him.

"A lot easier than a slow decline into oblivion. Like your grandfather. Remember when we were kids, he couldn't even recognize your mom? I don't want that happening to me."

"So what do you want?"

"To ponder death and not travel far. Take one swig and get it over with. I was never smitten by it, you know."

"By what?" I asked, totally confused.

"Life. Not all it's cracked up to be."

I was getting angry but I had no idea what to say. Suddenly there was a knock at the door. It took me a few seconds to realize how weird that was. We were in a jail cell, after all. It was the guard. "Excuse me, Socrates," he said timidly. "You have a few visitors. Should I let them in?"

"By all means, my good man" he replied, pleased as punch.

In walked Antisthenes, Aeschines, Cebes, Simmias, and a few others I didn't recognize. Socrates greeted them warmly. The guard brought in stools and arranged them in a semi-circle around his pitiful little cot. And then the old coot began to talk.

At first I could sort of follow what he was saying, but when they started yapping about The Form of the Equal, I gave up. Just words to me, but at least they were familiar, soothing, almost like the lullabies my wife used to sing to our son when he was small. Naturally, I dozed off. When I woke up, he was still talking. I swear he said something like, "if one man is a head taller than another, he's not taller by a head but by the Tall Itself, and if another is shorter he is not shorter by a head but by the Short Itself."[121]

I love the guy, but he's an asshole in more ways than one.

11

Aristippus and the Featherbed

(Aristippus: 435–356 BCE; Aeschines: 425–350 BCE)

Even amid Bacchic revel
True modesty will not be put to shame. (DL II.78)[122]

"YOU LOOK GOOD," I said to him. And I meant it. Aristippus was seventy-eight, and he was still burly with powerful shoulders. He walked slowly but was steady on his feet. As always in the summer, he wasn't wearing a shirt. While the hair on his head, which was thick, had gone gray, that on his chest remained black. Even though his wrinkles were etched deep, his cheeks were full and his large hands trembled only slightly. The thin line of a scar on his forehead, which he used to say had come from a Scythian's knife—but as he once confessed to me was actually the result of falling flat on his face when he was drunk—had kept its pinkish hue.

"Looks can be deceiving, amigo," Aristippus replied jovially. "Everything hurts. Hip, knee, shoulder, lower back. I have to pee fifty times a day, and it's no more than drip drip drip, and when I'm done, no matter how much I shake it, there's still some trickle. I get winded taking a short walk. Hell, I get winded just thinking about a walk. Can't see worth a damn, and even when I can make out the words in a book, I don't hold on to them for long. By the way, what's your name again, sonny?"

I smiled, relieved to hear the same joke he makes every time I visit him here in Cyrene.

"Well then," I replied, "how about a nip of wine? Maybe that'll refresh your memory."

He pretended to ponder the question. "Wine?" he asked. "Well, why not. But just a little one." The answer he always gives.

"You sit here, and I'll be right back," I said. I went into his kitchen and took two large cups down from the shelf. Into one I poured wine, into the other water. I brought them back to his room. Aristippus grinned when I handed him his drink. "Gracias, amigo" he said, and he raised his cup.

I did the same and replied, as I always do, "Vaya con dios." Neither of us could remember what these words meant, nor from whom we had learned them.

Our friendship began more than forty years ago, and not auspiciously. I happened upon him in the *agora*, and without even saying hello, I rebuked him for not having been with Socrates on the day of his death.

"You selfish ingrate!" I screamed. "Where were you? Oh, that's right. Aegina. And you couldn't come back to see him one last time? Simmias and Cebes came from Phlius, Euclides from Megara, but no, you couldn't make the trip! What, those Aeginean girls, just a little too pretty? Or was it their wine? You owe everything to Socrates, and you weren't even there on the day he died!"

"Plato wasn't either," Aristippus said, looking pleased with himself.

"Of course he wasn't, you idiot! He was sick. He couldn't get out of bed!"[123]

"Excuses, excuses. We all have them, don't we, Aeschines?"

"You're pitiful, Aristippus!"

"Watch yourself, young fella. I began listening to Socrates while you were still playing knucklebones with your pals."

"Well, you don't seem to have learned much. You're still chasing women and filling your belly with fancy foods. Don't you remember what Socrates used to say? The pleasures of the body are nothing compared to those of the mind. In fact, on that very day in his jail cell he reminded us that a real philosopher doesn't care a whit about the so-called pleasures of food and drink.[124] Oh, sorry, you missed that, didn't you, because you were in Aegina with one of your girlfriends."

"How do you know it was only one?"

"You're disgusting! Socrates should have shipped you off to Prodicus like he did with all the other losers! But, no, he let you stay, and look how you ended up. A sophist who takes money for his lessons!"[125]

He got annoyed. "You're a self-righteous young pup, aren't you?" he said to me. "Think you know all the answers. Well, if you're so smart then surely you remember what Socrates used to say about wisdom: namely, he didn't have any worth a damn, and he didn't kid himself into thinking he did either. Unlike you, the only gospel he ever preached was the sanctity of the question. He was a disruptor, a gadfly who pushed people to challenge their most cherished beliefs. And he did it by questioning them, not shouting from the rooftops the way you do. How you like them apples, you arrogant little slug?"

It stung, and I didn't know how to respond. My eyes fell to the ground. He sensed my discomfort, and he softened his tone. "Look, Aeschines, what Socrates wanted was for us to think for ourselves. He hated it when we repeated what he said. You know, like that runt, what was his name?"

"Aristodemus?"[126]

"Yeah, him. Went around barefoot, always trying, as he put it, 'to be like Soc.' Had the words *Question Authority* tattooed on his forearm and bragged that while most people live to eat, he ate only to live. What a moron! Come on, kid, lighten up. Have a glass of wine with me. Let's bury the hatchet and start over."

"I don't drink," I replied.

"Nonsense," Aristippus said. "You can't say no to a peace offering. Come on, have a sip. We'll raise our cups and become friends."

To my surprise, he seemed sincere. His voice was inviting, and although he was my senior by at least a decade, he had taken the first step. So I gave in. "Well then, by Hera, okay," I said. "I started this fight, but you're ending it."

"And starting our friendship, I hope," he said.

"You're a better man than I thought," I muttered.

And so it began, a long time ago.

He used to invite me to join him on his escapades. Once, when we were in Syracuse, he wanted to bring me to his favorite brothel. As usual, I declined. And do you know what he said? "Don't worry, old boy. The hard part isn't going in, it's not being able to get out." I remember blushing, even though I wasn't sure what he meant. And then there was the morning I dropped by his house. Naturally I thought he'd be studying, but no, he was at the table, feasting on grilled partridge, and there were two women sitting next to him. Did he feel embarrassed when he saw the look on my face? Of course not. Without hesitating, he rushed over to me, gave me a kiss on the cheek and told me I was right on time.

It took a while, but I came to realize there was a method to his madness. At first glance, he seemed to behave like any other dissolute aristocrat who did little more than frolic with the rich and famous. But as I gradually came to realize, his extravagant lifestyle was actually a kind of spiritual discipline. The challenge, he explained to me, wasn't to *abstain* from pleasure. It was to *master* it by enjoying it and keeping it at a distance at the same time. "Any dope with an iota of willpower can live without women," he once told me over a jug of wine. "The real challenge is to live *with* them. When I'm in bed with Laïs, I have her, but she doesn't have me. I may be having fun with a beautiful woman, but in the long run I couldn't care less. *Take it or leave it*, that's my motto. And it's equally true when it comes to the bad stuff. Like the time Dionysius spat on me. Most men would get riled up, but to me it only meant I got wet like a fisherman hauling in his catch. Truth is, it wasn't hard to deal with his spit. I just concentrated on the feeling—it was a little slimy—kept it at a distance and reminded myself I could take it or leave it. It's a lot harder to do when you're having a fling with a courtesan in a featherbed. Then the temptation is go back for a second helping, and then a third, and before you know it, you're thinking about how to make her yours. Resisting that, now there's a challenge. Compared to it, wiping spit off your face is a breeze."[127]

He took a long swig of wine, burped, and then continued. "Now, I'm not gonna lie to you, amigo. Give me the choice between a night with Laïs and one with Dionysius, and I'll choose the former every time. But, like I said, if she doesn't show up, I'll manage, no problemo."

I couldn't tell whether he was being sincere or just making excuses for his outrageous behavior, but I wanted to hear more, and so I asked him to elaborate.

"Look," he said to me, "when you boil down Socrates' teaching, it comes down to one sentence: the unexamined life is not worth living for a human being.[128] Resist easy answers, challenge your most cherished beliefs, never rest content. I call this the philosopher's conviction, and it guided Socrates throughout his life. This is why he was such a hard guy to be around. But here's the deal: consistency requires that the philosopher's conviction must itself be challenged. But how? By examining it philosophically? Of course not, because if you did then you'd be abiding by it, not challenging it. As the schoolboys say, you'd be begging the question.

"The point is this. Socratic self-examination is a problematic, and possibly even a self-defeating, because self-congratulating, game. The risk is becoming a moron like Aristodemus who runs around yapping, 'question everything!' No, the only way to authentically live by the philosopher's conviction is to jump into a featherbed with a voluptuous lady and see if you can keep your wits intact. And if you can do it, if deep down you know you can take it or leave it, then you've won."

I was confused. "But Aristippus," I asked, "how can you bear partying with guys like Dionysius? He's nothing but a tyrant."

"It's true," he said, with a grin on his face. "He liked me, though, and you know why? Because I wasn't afraid of him. Once, at one of his parties, he ordered me to explain a treatise I had just written. I told him not to be ridiculous. If you want to learn from me, I said, then you can't order me around. He didn't get mad. In fact, he laughed and passed me the wine. You see, Aeschines, it's possible to live in luxury and not lose your mind. But you have to be like a doctor."

"What do you mean?" I asked.

"A doctor spends time with people who are sick, but he's not sick himself. That's me. I eat at the tables of the rich and I wear fine clothes, but I could just as easily dine on cabbage and go in rags. I have fun in the featherbed, but here I am now, enjoying myself just fine talking to a scraggly little philosopher like yourself. I enjoy whatever comes my way. Wine water, sex no sex, wealth poverty, health sickness, life death, doesn't matter to me. Wherever I go, there I am. At home. And you know what this makes me, don't you?"

"What?" I asked.

"Free."[129]

I must have looked skeptical for he studied me carefully. "Look, Aeschines," he said, "Socrates didn't give a damn about money, power, or fame. He was an outsider, and his mission in life was to get his claws into the souls of the insiders, men like Alcibiades and Callicles, and turn them around, make them long for more than what the world could give them. And if he bruised them in the process, well, that was for their own good. I'm his student, and so that's what I'm doing as well. But in my own way. I work from the inside out. I party with the boys, but only in order to teach them that in the long run it doesn't matter. It's like charging my students tuition, which I know Socrates didn't do and you don't approve of. I do it for their sake, not mine, to show them what's worth spending their money on."

I was never sure whether he was toying with me or being serious, but as time passed I began to think that, in his own strange way, he was honestly trying to follow in Socrates' footsteps.

The other Socratics used to give him no end of grief. Xenophon in particular. At almost every symposium, he would remind the guests of the time when Dionysius ordered all the men in the room to put on women's clothes and perform a dance for him. Plato refused, but not only did Aristippus comply, he had a jolly good time doing so. And once he reprimanded Aristippus for living with a courtesan. Cool as a cucumber, Aristippus replied, "Tell me, my friend, would you live in a house in which other men have lived before you?"

"Of course," Xenophon answered.

"And what about a ship in which many have sailed? Would you have a problem with that?"

"None at all."

"So what's the difference with a woman?" Aristippus asked.

Poor Xenophon could only blush. When he recovered, he tried to counter. "And what about the woman you lived with last year? I hear she's pregnant and you won't acknowledge paternity. You gutless piece of Cyrenian trash!"

Aristippus didn't blink. "Ah, dear Xenophon," he said. "You know what happens when you walk through a patch of thistles? You get a few scratches. But you'll never know which thorn was the culprit."

Because he said such outrageous things, and with such palpable relish, he was labelled a misogynist. And yet, unknown to all but me, he was devoted to his daughter, and he conscientiously tutored her throughout her childhood. She became a first-rate philosopher in her own right.

"Aristippus," I said, "do you remember the trip we took to Corinth?"

"Corinth?" For a moment he looked lost.

"Years ago. We were on a ship and there was a fierce storm. You were seasick and frightened out of your wits. Do you remember?"

He grinned and nodded his head, as if anticipating a treat. "Yeah, sure do, Tell the story anyway," he said.

"A sailor made fun of you. He said, 'I thought you were a philosopher, but no, here you are, trembling like a baby, afraid you're going to die. While me, an ordinary man, I'm not scared at all.' And then you said, 'that's because you have nothing to lose and I do.' Then you vomited on his feet! Poor guy looked like he'd seen a ghost."

Aristippus chuckled. "When are you going to have a real drink with me, Aeschines?" he asked. "I'm an old man with one foot in the grave, so why not?"

"Oh, you know me. I prefer water."

"Never touch the stuff myself," Aristippus replied.

"Yeah, and look at the shape you're in," I said. "Every bone in your body hurts."

"Ahhh, who cares. I'm living in the lap of luxury. I'm here in my daughter's house, got my own room, and she takes good care of me. I can't remember if I've told you this before, but I've decided she's going to be the next head of the school."

"You have told me."

"Shoot," he said, shaking his head. "Well, truth bears repetition, and she'll do a damn good job, that's for sure."

"I imagine she will," I replied.

"So, yeah, no question, life is good. Especially when one of my old girlfriends drops by with a casserole."

As I have so often in his company, I laughed.

12

Stilpo's Daughter

(Stilpo: 360–280 BCE)

Surely you know Stilpo the Megarian,
Old age overtook him, and then disease,
A formidable pair.
But he found in wine a charioteer more powerful
Than that evil team. (DL II.120)

"FOR GOD'S SAKES, SHE'S sixteen!" Stilpo cried. "It's time for her to get serious and stop making all that awful noise with her friends. She needs an education, and I'm willing to give it to her. Do you know what an opportunity that is?"[130]

His mistress, Nicarete, who was lying next to him in bed, grinned. "Course I do, darlin'. But you gotta remember, I can't read or write, but far as I can tell I'm doing fine," she said as she stroked the hair on his chest.

"Stop it," he barked affectionately. "I'm being serious. I'm offering her something precious."

"To study with her father, the great philosopher, Stilpo the Megarian!" Nicarete slid her hand between his thighs.

"Correct," he said. "But all she wants is to go outside and play with the boys. She's very athletic, you know. You should see her run. But she's also incredibly bright. Any topic and she gets it fast. She's stubborn, and she argues with her mother all the time, usually about trivial matters, like when she should go to bed, but even then I can see how quick she is. If she'd stay out of trouble and focus on her studies, she could make something of herself."

"And she's gorgeous," Nicarete added. "My god, I'd die just for her hair, and she's so slender and tall. Trust me, men won't be able to take their eyes off her. It's obvious Simmias can't."

"Simmias," Stilpo grunted. "All the more reason why she should get to work now, gain some heft. There's more to life, you know, than having fun."

"Really?" Nicarete said mischievously as she increased the pressure.

Despite the fact that he was getting hard, Stilpo ignored her. "Socrates studied with a woman, you know. Her name was Diotima. And two women were students in Plato's Academy. Aristippus taught his daughter Arete, and she took over his school when he got old. Shows what a woman can do if she gets the chance. Callista is intelligent. She deserves an education, not a dope like Simmias."

"I don't know about that. He's awful good looking, and he's certainly not poor. She could do worse."

"That's what her mother keeps saying."

"And you always listen to her, don't you?" Nicarete said, barely able to stifle her laughter.

"It's possible for a woman to think for herself and not live for the sake of a man. My daughter deserves a chance."

"Okay already, I get it," Nicarete said as she nuzzled his neck. "Time to change the subject," she whispered.

As a tall, skinny, pimpled teenager, Simmias had been an enthusiastic wrestler, but not a good one. He was neither well coordinated nor particularly strong, and the other boys had little trouble pinning him. In defeat he would seethe with rage and then kick his next opponent in the groin or gouge his eyes. In the gymnasium such infractions were not tolerated, and revenge was swift. One day after practice, a half dozen boys beat him senseless. He never returned. Instead, day after day, month after month, he spent hours lifting weights by himself. He grew thick and strong. After a year, his past sins were forgotten, and his bulk coupled with a deep voice and salacious wit made him an imposing and popular figure. Even if he still couldn't wrestle.

Only twenty when his father died, his first impulse was not to mourn but to scheme. For years the old man had sold his modest harvest of wool, olives, and wine to a local merchant, a friend, who then exported it. Just two days after the will was read, and he officially inherited the farm, Simmias made an offer to buy the field next to his own. When it was accepted, he heard his father's voice—avoid debt like the plague—but scoffed and promptly borrowed more to pay for a flock of sheep. This was only the beginning, though, for his dream was to have his own ships and become an exporter himself. He was determined to depend on no one else to make his fortune. His uncle urged him to move slowly, but Simmias ignored him. It took more than a decade, a string of vicious quarrels with creditors and five lawsuits, but his work finally came to fruition. His was the first vertically integrated operation in all of Megara, and he prospered.

His next project was to get a wife and start a family. Since he was far and away the most desirable match in town he had his pick of marriageable women, but he made his choice quickly: Callista, daughter of the philosopher Stilpo. He first met her when she was sixteen and he thirty-four. It was a summer evening, not too hot, and he was leaving a meeting with a merchant to whom he owed great deal of money. Simmias had tried to convince the man to reduce the interest on his loan, but with no success. Flush with anger, he stormed onto the street where he crashed into Stilpo and sent him tumbling to the ground.

"Sorry," Simmias muttered, offering his hand.

Stilpo looked peeved and got up on his own without saying a word, which made Simmias even angrier. He was on the verge of shouting when he noticed her. Long neck, eyes open wide, silky red hair reaching to her shoulders, she carried herself like an athlete, but no one could mistake her for a boy. She looked at him as if fascinated by an exotic animal. He looked back, and his rage was transformed into desire.

"Are you okay?" he asked Stilpo, forcing himself to turn away from Callista and to feign interest in her father. "I'm really sorry, sir. I was in a rush and not paying attention."

"I noticed," Stilpo replied curtly.

Simmias put a massive hand on the philosopher's thin shoulder and gave it a gentle squeeze. "You're not hurt are you?"

"No," Stilpo said, taking the measure of Simmias' size. "But you'd best be careful in the future. You're big enough to do some serious damage."

"I understand. I'm sorry. Really."

Stilpo, unconvinced, sighed. "Well then, good evening to you."

"Thanks. Same to you," Simmias replied.

Stilpo extended his arm for Callista to take, which she did, and they walked off. They made an odd couple, for not only was she gorgeous, which he most certainly wasn't, she was taller.

For the rest of the summer, Simmias made sure to be in town whenever the evening was cool and his busy schedule allowed it. He would drink wine with other merchants, but his eyes were glued to the street. If he saw Callista strolling with her father, he would jump up from the table, approach them, politely say hello, and inquire about Stilpo's health. She never said a word, but she always met his gaze. Even with the distance between them, each could feel the other's heat. Finally, desperate to be near her, Simmias, who had not read a book since his tutors forced him to as a child, enrolled in Stilpo's school. He paid absolutely no attention, but thanked Stilpo profusely after every lecture.

After two weeks of self-imposed servitude, Simmias asked Stilpo for his daughter's hand in marriage. The philosopher looked horrified, mumbled something about having to discuss it with his wife, and abruptly walked away. "Do you promise?" Simmias asked him.

"Promise what?" Stilpo replied.

"To discuss it with your wife."

He did not answer, but when he turned around, he did raise his hand, a gesture that Simmias took to be a yes.

Despite not wanting to, Stilpo kept his word. His wife was delighted by the offer and wanted to ink the deal as soon as possible, but he insisted on discussing the match with Callista first. His wife protested that it was his decision to make, not hers, but he ignored her. That evening, on their stroll, they talked.

"Do you actually like this man?" Stilpo asked, his thin voice tinged with disbelief.

"I do, Dad," she replied.

"But you're so young. Do you think you're ready to make this decision?"

"It's your decision to make, Dad, not mine."

"True, but you know I won't do anything that goes against your wishes."

Callista grinned, eyes twinkling in anticipation. "Then, yes, I want to be married to Simmias."

"But you barely know him! In fact, you barely know any men at all. You have no basis for comparison."

"I know some of your students at the school, don't I? Metrodorus, Timagoras, Clitarchus."

He hesitated, unsure of himself. "But this man, this Simmias, well, he's different from them, isn't he? He's not . . ."

"Not what?" she interrupted. "A philosopher?" She giggled.

"It's obvious he's not—how should I put it—engaged in his studies. The only reason he comes to my lectures is to get access to you."

"Looks like his plan worked pretty well then!" she said cheerfully.

"I suppose he could be smart, in his own way. But that doesn't mean he has a good mind."

"You mean one like yours?"

"No, no. Um, he doesn't seem . . ."

"Seem what?" she interrupted again.

"Refined."

"What do you expect? He's a businessman. But if you think about it, what he's doing is impressive. Even if it's just for me, he's still coming to your lectures. That should tell you something."

"It does. He's a man who goes after what he wants and is used to getting it. The truth is, Callista, he doesn't care one bit about what I say or think about anything."

She looked at her feet. "I'm no philosopher either, Dad."

"But you're a thinker, even if you don't know that about yourself yet."

"It's true, I do like to think. About marrying Simmias and making sure you and Mama have plenty of money when you get old. And lots of grandchildren to take care of you."

He felt a jumbled mix of despair and pride. "You have an ear for ideas."

"I don't know what you're talking about, Dad."

"I remember once, many years ago, I came home from the theatre, Euripides' *Medea,* and I was telling your mother about it. You were only three or four, but you listened to every word and then you peppered me with questions. Why was Medea mad at Jason? And why was she so mean to her children? Somehow you'd gleaned the plot, and you badly wanted to understand it."

She laughed. "I don't remember a thing."

"Well, that's who you are, Callista. Someone who asks questions."

"My question now is this, Dad. When can Simmias and I get married?"

"How about you wait a year?"

Her body stiffened, her eyes turned cold. "Not a chance," she said. "You're prejudiced against him because he makes money."

"Maybe, but there's something else about him, something I can't put my finger on. Are you sure he's an honest man?"

"Of course he is. He says he loves me, and I believe him."

Stilpo's eyes tightened, and he tugged at his small ears. The look on his face suggested he was thinking about something far away. "And when exactly did he say this to you?"

Callista blushed. "Only once. You and I were walking, and you stopped to talk with Metrodorus for a while. That's the only time he and I were ever alone, and it's when he told me we'd get married."

"And he didn't think he needed to ask me first?"

"No."

"And what did you say?"

"That I couldn't wait."

"Before you talked to me?"

"Yes. Look, Dad, we're crazy about each other. It's simple, and it's wonderful. I feel like I'm flying, Dad. I'm sixteen, I'm ready to get on with my life."

He stopped, withdrew his arm from hers, and studied his daughter carefully. "And what kind of life do you have in mind? One like your mother's?"

"Don't start ragging on Mama again, Dad! She's very smart. Look at how she manages your money, and not just for the house but for your school too. I mean, come on, you wouldn't even have a school if she didn't keep the books. And Simmias told me he'll make a big donation after we get married."

Stilpo looked up at the pink sunset painting the sky. Even he understood how badly his school needed funding, and he struggled to keep this thought at a distance. "You learn nothing worth knowing by counting drachmas and haggling with merchants," he said. "Studying philosophy, thinking for yourself, not just doing what other people expect."

"Oh give me a break, Dad! I keep telling you I don't have your kind of mind."

"Yours might be better, you know."

"You always say that! But I'm not cut out for study, Dad."

"But you are cut out for marrying Simmias?"

"Yes, and that's final!"

Stilpo stroked his only child's cheek with a tender motion they both knew well. He wondered if his love had forged her iron will. He sighed and extended his arm for her to take. No longer perfectly comfortable, they continued their stroll in silence.

She wondered why the servant bothered to tell her Stilpo had a visitor from Cyrene. Philosophers from around the Greek world often came to Megara to attend her father's lectures, so, except for the fact that it was deep into the winter, this was hardly unusual. This visitor, though, was different. For she was a woman, and well, she looked a little strange. Callista's interest was piqued. Fortunately, Simmias was not home, and she did not have to ask his permission to leave the house. After giving the nurse instructions and kissing her two small sons a perfunctory goodbye, she walked quickly to her father's school.

The courtyard was empty, which meant Stilpo was in his study. Since he was always glad to see her, she entered without knocking. Her father was on the couch talking with someone. Yet another bald old man, she thought, disappointed. But a second look made her realize, to her amazement, the guest was indeed a woman. Her shaved head was a perfect glowing sphere, her lips were bright red, she was wearing silver hoops in her ears, and when she saw Callista, her wrinkled face burst into an exuberant smile.

Stilpo grinned awkwardly, as if he'd been caught in the act, and then stood up to greet his daughter. When the old woman followed suit, she moved with the ease of a dancer. "Callista, this is Arete. She's a philosopher from Cyrene." He gestured at the table and invited the two women to join him there. A servant brought a jug of water and a plate of cheese.

Arete's father, Aristippus, had studied with Socrates and after spending fifteen years in Athens, he returned to his hometown to open the Cyrenaic School of Philosophy. There he had educated his daughter, and when he died, she became head, a position she held for decades and from which she had only recently retired. Her son, also named Aristippus, and nicknamed *Mothertaught,* had taken her place. Arete was celebrating her retirement with a trip to see her philosophical friends, and had just arrived in Megara after visiting Xenocrates, Pyrrho, and Crates in Athens.

Callista politely asked about her travels, but before Arete could reply Stilpo suddenly excused himself. He said he needed to put the finishing touches on his afternoon lecture. Callista shot him a surprised look as he was leaving the room, for she had never seen him behave rudely before. Arete noticed, and after Stilpo closed the door behind him, she explained. "Don't worry, he's just giving us girls a chance to talk," she said, leaning towards her and confiding as if to an old friend. "He thinks I can be a good influence."

"Influence?" Callista replied.

"I know," she said, gently tapping the table twice with the palms of her hands. "Silly man, isn't he? I'm sure you've been doing fine without my help, or his, but don't be hard on him. He means well."

It dawned on her. Even though she now had children and was managing her husband's sprawling new estate, her father still believed she should study philosophy. For the first time in her life, she did not recoil at the thought, but it did make her sad. Arete read her face. "But you're not doing so fine, are you?" she asked gently.

Callista was stunned by the question and her mouth instinctively tensed into a defensive smile. But for reasons she could not fathom she felt the urge to tell the truth to this bald old woman she had only just met. "No, not really," she said, and began to sob.

At first, she explained, she and Simmias would make love every morning and every night, and if he came home for lunch, then too. She was in a constant state of flushed excitement. Eleven months after the wedding, her son Lycas was born. Simmias was delighted with the baby and at first was tender with her, but he wanted to resume having sex a week after the birth, and when she refused, he stormed out of the house. Since then he often stayed out all night, and when he was home, their coupling was brief and harsh. Things got worse after the birth of their second child, Androsthenes. The only time Simmias seemed to enjoy her company was when he occasionally took her into town for an evening stroll.

"He likes to show you off, huh?" Arete smiled sympathetically. Callista, puzzled, tilted her head. "Well, no surprise there," Arete continued. "You're beautiful. Which can be a problem."

"Problem?"

"For us. Men treat us like we're some kind of prize."

"How did you cope?"

"I was lucky. My father was a wonderful man, always cheerful, loved to talk, and he spent a lot of time with me when I was young. He got me ready."

"Ready for what?"

"To live like a human being, and enjoy it."

"Did he talk about philosophy?" Callista asked, sensing the onset of full-blown regret.

"Sort of. He would take me on long walks through the vineyards and olive groves. When we bumped into a farmer, he'd chat with him about the weather, and it was like he was gabbing with an old friend, even though he had never laid eyes on the man before. If we saw an animal, a mouse or a rabbit, even an insect, he'd stop, put his hand on my shoulder, and we'd both go still and stare. Then he'd give me a little squeeze, and we'd be off again. Sometimes he would gaze at a tree or take a handful of water from the river and splash it on his face and then break into a big smile. It didn't seem to matter what it was, he enjoyed himself. Once, and this was funny, a bird, and it must have been a big one, dropped a load on his head. And you know what he did? He pretended he was taking a bath, and he rubbed the shit through his hair, which was long and curly. And then he belted out a song at the top of his voice. *I feel poopy, oh so poopy, I feel poopy and loopy and gay.* I laughed so hard I peed myself, and when I realized what happened, I began to cry. My father rushed over to me and told me to close my eyes. Which I did. And then he asked me what the pee felt like on my skin. I was embarrassed, but I managed to say, wet, warm. Then he said to me, but sometimes it's nice being wet, right? Yes, I said. And sometimes it's nice being warm, right? Yes. Well, let's make this one of those times. Forget it's pee and you're a big girl who isn't supposed to have accidents any more. It's just wet and warm, that's all. And you know what we're going to do next? Go to the river and jump in. With all our clothes on. Come on, we'll get clean and it'll be fun." Arete was beaming at the memory. "Yup, that was my pop."

Callista thought of her own father. He too was a wonderful man, reliable, gentle, and kind. But he'd never been fun. "I thought the only thing philosophers liked to do was study," she said to Arete.

"Sure, my dad studied a lot, but for him philosophy wasn't simply an intellectual exercise. It was a way of life. He used to say that ideas by themselves mean nothing. They have to be put into practice. He got that from Socrates."

Callista wondered whether her father's philosophy was also a way of life. Her face felt hot when she realized she had no idea. "What was your father's philosophy?" she asked timidly.

Arete lightly stroked Callista's cheek. "Aristippus believed that pleasure is the highest good and what all human beings ultimately desire."

Callista hadn't expected such an answer.

"Now, by itself it's not a particularly original idea," Arete continued. "It goes all the way back to Democritus and, these days, this young fella Epicurus seems to be making it popular. But my father had a unique conception of pleasure. He thought it could only be found by being-in-the-present. This is what he was trying to teach me on our walks when I was a child. It didn't matter what the experience was—it could be smelling a flower or a bird shitting on his head—if it were taken in simply as present it would be pleasurable."

When Stilpo lectured her, she always felt ignored. Listening to Arete was entirely different, and Callista wanted to understand what she was saying. "I don't get it," she said.

"It's a strange, I know," Arete said with a mischievous grin. "Here's an example. Imagine two carpenters are building a house. One hates the work and is only doing it in order to get paid. He's always looking toward the future, and when he's doing one part of the job—say, laying stones for the foundation—he's already anticipating the next: building the wall. What he really wants is for the whole job to be over so he can go home, which is why he can't stop checking to see where the sun is in the sky. He's bored, and he doesn't pay much attention to what he's doing. The second carpenter finds the work engaging and is totally absorbed in every single task. When she's laying stones that's all she's doing, all she is. She doesn't glance at the sun, and so she's surprised when her shift is over. For her, time flies."

Her? Callista wondered.

Arete noticed Callista was perplexed. "Here's another example. Think of the difference between an Olympic wrestler and the amateur who only goes to the gym to enjoy a workout. The wrestler wants to win prizes and get famous, and so he trains hard every day and adheres to a strict diet. He feels terrible when he loses a match, and even after he wins, he begins preparing for the next one. His life is perpetual stress, for it is oriented to a goal beyond the activity itself. Now the amateur, well, she doesn't care about prizes, and there aren't any spectators watching her. She simply enjoys physical exercise as a refreshing interlude, a break from her ordinary life. When she runs a race, yes, of course she tries to win. But it's not victory she craves. It's the running itself that she loves."

For a moment Callista wondered whether Arete was talking about her. Did she somehow know how much she'd loved running when she was a girl? When she got older, the only thing that had ever matched it for sheer fun was having sex with Simmias before Lycas was born.

Arete interrupted her thoughts. "The point is this," she said, and for the first time she sounded like a teacher. "Two people can be doing the same thing, but one may experience it as pleasurable and the other as disagreeable. What differentiates them is the degree to which they are immersed in the present and lose track of time. This was my father's insight. What makes an activity pleasurable is not found in its particular content. It could be lying in bed with a beautiful man or wiping bird shit through your hair. No, what matters is only whether you're absorbed in the activity and not looking beyond it."

Callista wasn't sure. "I don't get it," she repeated.

Arete was glad to explain. "Look, sweetie, do you know what makes people miserable?"

Too many answers came to mind, so she shook her head and said nothing.

"They feel the passage of time in their bones, and it makes them restless. They know the present will become the past in the blink of an eye, and so rather than enjoying what they have, they worry about losing it in the future. They cling and scheme, try to hold on or get more, but of course this just makes things worse, and they end up a heaving mass of stress." Arete scoffed at herself. "Is this making any sense?" she asked.

Not confident it did, Callista nodded tentatively.

"There's only one path to liberation, and that's to step outside the flow of time; to be in the present."

The old woman took a bite of cheese, closed her eyes, and chewed it slowly. Then she took a long drink of water. "The more you think about this stuff, the more complicated it gets. My father never worked out the details in any kind of systematic way, and I was more concerned about teaching my students how to actually pay attention. It's my son who's doing the hard work of developing a theory. He's a marvelous philosopher, stronger than me or my dad, and he's doing great work at the school. I wish you could meet him."

"I wish I could too," Callista said. She wondered what sort of men her sons would become. Probably like their father. They'd make money and beat their wives. Her beautiful strong shoulders slumped, and she felt her future dissolve.

Detecting her mood, Arete changed the subject. "Your father's busy with his lecture, and I could use a walk. Why don't you show me around town. I've never been to Megara before."

After years of resisting her father's exhortations, she began to study philosophy, even though she was a wife, mother, and house-manager with little time to spare. Arete gave her a reading list. Its first item was a short scroll written by her father Aristippus: *An Invitation to Philosophy.* Next came Theophrastus' *Teachings of the Natural Philosophers,* a compilation of texts by the early Milesians. After that was Heraclitus' *On Nature,* Parmenides' *On Being,* Anaxagoras' *Cosmology,* Democritus' *On Atoms and the Void,* and Philolaus' edition of Pythagorean treatises. "When you're done with these," Arete told her with a grin, "you'll be ready to read a little Plato, which you're gonna love."

"What about your books?" Callista asked.

"Mine?" Arete chuckled, her eyes squinched, her cheeks ballooned. "I only wrote one and, truth is, it's no more than an application of my father's ideas. It's still pretty good, though. You can read it if you'd like."

"What's it called?"

"*The Therapy of Desire.*[131] But first things first, sweetie," she said as she pointed to the list. Callista looked worried. Arete clasped her hand firmly. "You'll find the reading to be tough going, but don't worry, you're smart. Start by skimming the text. Get a hang of the sentences and a sense of the whole, and don't even try to understand it. Then start over again, but this time stop when you bump into something you don't understand. Read the passage three or four times. Even better, copy it. Getting your body involved, even just your hand, helps loosen the mind. Most important, don't beat yourself up if you feel confused. Just slow down and try to identify what's confusing you. Maybe it's a word or a couple of sentences which don't seem to fit together. Formulate a question, jot it down, and we'll talk about it when we get together."

Callista nodded cautiously. "Which will be when?"

"How much free time do you have?"

She blushed. As badly as she wanted to, she could not bring herself to tell Arete it was far too risky for her to deposit her sons with their nurse and then spend time with her. If Simmias found out, he'd likely beat her senseless. "Not much," she replied, her voice cracking.

As usual, Arete grasped the situation. "I'll be in town for a while, you know. At least until the weather breaks and I can get a ship back to Cyrene. Come see me whenever you can."

"But don't you want to talk with my dad and the other philosophers?"

"No, sweetie, I want to talk with you!" Her bald head radiated warmth, and Callista was drawn like a moth to a flame.

"I'll find the time," she promised Arete, and herself.

She gasped when Simmias announced they were moving to Athens. Her mother had died the previous year, and the thought of her father being alone made her shudder.

"He's not alone," Simmias said bitterly. "He's got that fat bitch Nicarete with him day and night."

"But he needs me! And he likes being around the boys. He's been teaching Lycas his letters, and he wants to do the same with Androsthenes in a couple of years."

"Bullshit! The boys would rather be with me any day."

"We can't just yank his grandsons out of his life!"

"We can do whatever we damn well please," Simmias responded, the muscles in his face clenching.

"You mean whatever *you* damn well please," she said.

He grinned, his lips pressed together tightly, and then lectured her as if she were a child. Athens was booming. Its merchants were trading with cities across the Macedonian world. Only by moving there could his business expand.

"But you're already doing so well here in Megara," she protested.

"It's nothing compared to the big boys. Athens is where the action is, which is why we're going there. I've already rented a house in the Piraeus. Don't worry, doll," he sneered, "you'll like it. It has a view of the harbor."

Callista's eyes narrowed, her face turned to stone, and she declared that she was staying. But even her strong will was no match for Simmias' fist when it smashed her jaw.

That night, lying in bed, the pain radiating from her head down her neck and into her shoulders, she desperately tried to apply Arete's method—to concentrate on the throbbing, isolate it, and then push it into the distance—but to no avail.

She finally fell asleep, but only for a few minutes. When she awoke, the pain had subsided a little, which was enough for fear to creep in. How could she show herself to her servants and sons? Worse, what sort of story would she tell her father about yet another bruise on her face? Her mouth quivered, but it hurt too much to sob.

◇◇◇◇

"I'll never see him again," Callista said through her sobs.

"Nonsense!" Arete said firmly.

"No, it's not! How could I possibly go back to Megara. I'd be too ashamed."

"Nonsense!" she repeated. "Your father is a philosopher. He doesn't care what other people think."

"But I'm a bad woman. I left my husband and my sons."

Arete put her hands on Callista's shoulders and looked into her red eyes. "Listen to me! You're anything but a bad woman. You had to leave him. Your life depended on it, simple as that. And your boys will be fine. You told me that yourself."

"They will," she managed to say. "Simmias won't hurt them. He needs them too much."

"If they were girls, you never would have abandoned them. Not in a million years."

She nodded, reluctantly, in agreement.

"You would have stayed. Either that or you would have brought them here with you," Arete said, her familiar grin returning at last.

Callista nodded again.

"Darling, you're in Cyrene now. You'll be safe, I promise. And you are going to become the woman you were always meant to be."

"I am?"

"Oh yes. And you know what?"

"What?"

"You and me, we're going to have ourselves some serious fun."

Callista looked at her in amazement. "We are."

"You betcha! So, my dear, where should we start?"

"Start?"

"Reading. How about Heraclitus? He's always been one of my favorites, you know."

As the sun was dipping below the horizon, her cart arrived in Megara, and even before she reached the door of her childhood home, Nicarete came rushing out of it. Bursting into tears, she hugged Callista tightly and would not let go. Stilpo's mistress had aged but had kept her full figure and was still lovely. For once being in her presence caused Callista no pain.

"He's been sick a long time," Nicarete said, her eyes welling up again. "But lately it's gotten much worse."

"Where is he?" Callista asked.

"In the bedroom."

She separated herself from the older woman and began to march into the house, but when Nicarete said "Wait!" she stopped in her tracks. "It's not good in there."

"What do you mean?" Callista asked.

"It's not, it's not . . . you have to . . . ." She faltered.

Callista turned and nearly ran into the house, and then into her father's room. Stilpo, diminished almost beyond recognition, was in bed, staring vacantly at the ceiling, but she did not hesitate. "It's me, Dad," she said softly. "Callista."

The old man turned his rheumy swollen eyes to her, but was unable to focus. "Who that?" he slurred.

"It's me, Dad, your daughter. Callista. I'm here."

"Here?" he said, his voice nearly inaudible.

"It's been a long time, hasn't it, Dad?"

"Callista?" he said again, now studying her face carefully.

She squeezed his hand hard, wiped her tears away, took a deep breath, and steadied herself. She looked around the room, saw the empty jug on the table next to her father's bed, the cup on the floor, and red stains on his nightshirt. She suddenly realized the whole room smelled of wine. She was baffled since, except for her wedding feast, she could not remember ever having seen her father drink.

"Are you okay, Dad?" she asked.

He did not reply.

"Looks like you had a little to drink last night," she said, pointing to the empty jug and trying to sound cheerful.

"Hummm," he mumbled, sounding lost.

"Why didn't the servants clean this mess?"

He did not answer her question. Instead, he murmured, "Water."

She immediately stood up and, taking the empty jug with her, walked to the kitchen. She returned with a cup of water, which she handed to her father.

He took it eagerly, but before he could bring it to his lips, it fell from his trembling hands. His shirt and sheets were soaked, but he didn't seem to notice.

"Oh my," Callista said. "I'm going to get the servants. Be back in a minute."

"Hummm."

"What's going on, ladies?" she asked angrily when she confronted the two women working in the kitchen. During all her years in Cyrene she had never had a servant of her own, not even when she was appointed assistant head of the Cyrenaic School of Philosophy. Still, she effortlessly assumed a lady-of-the-house voice. "Why didn't you clean my father's room last night? It's filthy in there!"

"We clean, miss," the older one replied.

"Really? Then why is it such a mess?"

"He been drinking all afternoon and he don't want us when he drinking. Only time we can clean is when he sleep."

"All afternoon? What in god's name are you talking about?"

"He drink all day, miss, soon as he wake up."

"He drinks?" Callista said, flabbergasted.

"Yes, miss. He want to drink himself to death. That why he don't mix water in the wine. And he don't eat nothing either."

Her hands pressed hard on her cheeks. "What are you saying?" she asked.

"He drink himself to death, miss. He told us so. He been sick long time and don't want no more. He tell us bring him jug after jug of wine. We try keep things clean, miss, when he sleep, we do, but he piss himself regular. I'm sorry, miss. Your father been good to us."

Callista took a deep breath, tried to process what she had just heard, and said, "I see. And I thank you for your trouble. But I'll take over now. Where is the clean bedding? And he needs a fresh nightshirt. And some cabbage."

"Cabbage, miss?"

"Yes. It's good for hangovers."

"How I cook it, miss?"

"Keep it raw. Just chop it fine. And some flowers, if you can get them. Oh, and one more thing. Heat some water. Put in a small amount of honey."

Callista returned to her father's room. Stilpo had fallen back to sleep. She gently shook his shoulder, shocked at how brittle his bones were. He did not recognize her.

"Wha? Wha you doing?" he said groggily.

"It's me, Dad. Callista. You need to get out of bed for a few minutes. I'll help you."

"Don't wanna," he said.

"You have to, Dad. You're wet, I need to get you dry and clean."

When she took his arm to lift him out of bed, he offered no resistance. He was light as a child, and she helped him ease into his chair. She kissed him on his forehead and nearly recoiled at the smell. Then she went to work. Fast and efficient, she stripped and replaced the bedding. Then she turned back to her father, who had dozed off, and said, "Okay, now we do the shirt."

"Wha?" Stilpo looked at her uncomprehendingly.

"It's okay, Dad," Callista said. "I'll do it."

She managed to remove his nightshirt, towel him clean, and then get him into fresh clothes. When she was done, she carefully guided him back to bed, where she tucked him in.

"Are you warm enough, Dad?" she asked.

"Yeah," he said.

"Good. I'm going to get something from the kitchen. I'll be right back," she said.

"Okay," he replied meekly.

The servant had chopped the cabbage, found flowers for the vase and had a jug of warm honey-water ready to go.

"Ah, wonderful," Callista said gratefully. "I'll take the flowers. You can bring the rest."

"Yes, miss," the servant replied.

Stilpo was still awake when the two women, each about forty years old, returned to the bedroom. He looked at them and then, almost cheerfully, said, "You gals could be sisters."

For a brief moment Callista wondered if the woman standing next to her might actually be her sister. She learned that Nicarete was her father's mistress when she was a teenager. "Thank you," she said. "I'll take care of things now."

She spoon-fed her father. He offered no resistance but managed to swallow only a few bites of the cabbage. Most fell into the scraggles of his beard. He drank the honey-water more readily. When he finished his first cup, she poured him a second.

"Don't want," he said, his voice a little stronger.

"Sorry, Dad, you need to drink. It'll make you feel better."

He was compliant and drank most of the second cup.

"Gotta pee," he said.

She brought him the chamber pot, and as he was going she made sure nothing got wet.

"Feel better?" she asked when he was done.

"Yeah."

"Do you recognize me, Dad?"

It took him a few seconds, but then he smiled through his tears. "Callista. It's you."

"Yes, Dad, it's me. Now get some sleep, and when you wake up, we'll have a good long talk."

"Wine," he said.

"No wine, Dad."

His face collapsed in despair. "Wine," he begged her. "Please."

She felt like Simmias had just punched her in the face. "How about we drink some together when you wake up?" she managed to ask. "Sound okay?"

The old man looked peeved, but he closed his eyes.

Callista brought the dishes back into the kitchen and told the servant, "Come and get me as soon as he wakes up."

"Yes, miss," she replied.

Callista hadn't yet changed her clothes, which were filthy from travel. The sail from Cyrene to Athens had been smooth, but the cart that took her to Megara was rickety, and her body felt like it was still shaking. She went to her old room, which was ready for her. She washed herself with a cloth, put on a fresh peplos, and lay down, exhausted and in agony, on her childhood bed. Inconceivable! Her father, the most sober of men, was drinking himself to death. Well, she would fix that. She'd get him back on his feet, and when his head was clear, she'd ask about his work and then share with him how much she had learned during her years in Cyrene. He would be so happy. She would tell him about a treatise she was writing on Parmenides, explain to him that when she first read *On Being and Becoming*, she thought its argument was absurd, but now she realized it was really very powerful. She didn't have the energy to sustain this fantasy and fell fast asleep.

Two hours later she was awakened by a hesitant knock on her closed door. It was Nicarete, her face pale and expressionless. "He's gone," she said, barely audible.

13

Diogenes the Cynic

(404–323 BCE)

'Twas a dog's savage tooth that sealed his fate.
Holding his breath,
Diogenes ascended to heaven. (DL VI. 77)[132]

I WASN'T WORRIED, NOT at first. He liked to wander, and sometimes he'd disappear for days at a stretch. But one night, after not seeing him on the streets for more than a week, I got a bad feeling, and so I decided to check on him in the morning. I woke up at dawn and walked to the Metröon. He was there, in his tub, and, damn it, I was right. He was dead. After I puked, I looked at his body more carefully. Not many flies and the smell wasn't too bad, so I figured he must have died during the night. But his foot, oh my god, his foot was swollen twice its size. There was a note pinned to his cloak. "Throw corpse in ditch. Let birds have a go."

That's as close as he came to writing a will. He didn't own anything. Fact is, though, we couldn't bring ourselves to honor his last wish. Hegesias wanted to give him a proper funeral. A simple one, of course, the kind Cynics give. But Monimus objected. He said Diogenes once told him he wanted his corpse to be thrown into the Ilissus where it could at least be useful. For feeding the fish, I guess. We agreed to do it, and we did.

A month later I found out how it happened. I was in the Piraeus, picking up fish scraps for dinner, when I bumped into Onesicritus. He studied with Diogenes for a while, but gave up philosophy to become a sailor. He used to brag he'd been the commander of Alexander's fleet, but we knew he was, at most, a helmsman. Still, he wasn't a bad guy, and I liked him. He told me how surprised he was when he heard Diogenes was dead. "He seemed fine last time I saw him." I asked when that was. "A few days before he died," he answered. He told me the story.

He had been in the Piraeus for a few days and was sleeping in an empty shed on the docks. Onesicritus had been bringing him food. One day he gave him an octopus. Of course, Diogenes didn't bother cooking it. He cut it into pieces and ate it raw. He couldn't finish it, though, and he tossed the leftovers to an old dog who used to beg the sailors for food. It thanked him by biting his foot. Onesicritus wanted to kill it on the spot, but Diogenes told him to leave it alone. Said it was a kindred spirit. The wound wasn't too deep, but the next day it caught fire and turned bright red. Onesicritus offered to get a doctor, but Diogenes laughed him off. Said our ills are of our own making, and he'd be fine when he got back to Athens. He was in good spirits when he left the Piraeus, and only limped a little.

How he managed to walk all the way back to town, I don't know. He never wore shoes, and it's at least five miles. But I'm sure his mind was clear until the very end. He wanted to die in his tub, and I bet when the pain got bad he held his breath. I know he wasn't scared. He used to ask us, how can death be something terrible if we're not aware of it when it arrives?

Yes, Diogenes lived his life totally on his own terms, and he was determined to do the same when it came to dying. Like his hero, Socrates.

He used to complain about those guys who call themselves Socratics. Said they were phonies. They talk about virtue, but they live in nice houses and eat fancy food. Diogenes only ate what he could scavenge, and he slept in a tub. Well, everybody calls it a tub, but it's really a big wine jar. In the summer, he used to roll it in the sand to make it even hotter. Someone asked him why, and he said, despising pleasure can itself be pleasurable.

He used to love to taunt the rich and famous. One night, he was walking past a big house, and a loud party was going on. He walked in, like he was a honored guest. Of course, they all stared at him. Then some old man, probably a politician, picked up a bone from his plate and threw it at his feet, like he was a dog. Everybody in the room burst into laughter. Diogenes laughed too. And then he pissed on the bone.

Nobody could intimidate him. Once he was lying in the middle of the street, having a sunbath, and Alexander himself walked by. The great leader got curious and went over to take a look. He recognized Diogenes and asked how he could help. You know what he said? "By getting out of my damned light!"

He didn't care a bit who you were. If he thought you were a phony, he'd go after you. Especially philosophers. They pretend to be serious and to care about happiness, but what they end up doing is making life much more complicated than it actually is. He learned this when he was a kid. He wanted to study with Antisthenes and begged him to take him on as a student. He said no, but Diogenes wouldn't give up. Day after day he hounded him until Antisthenes finally blew his stack and threatened to hit him. "Go ahead," Diogenes said, "I deserve it." Strange, but that won him over. He didn't last long with Antisthenes, though, because he didn't want to waste his time on logic.[133] The last straw was when he had to study Zeno's paradoxes. You know, like the one about Achilles not being able to catch the tortoise. Diogenes thought the argument was ridiculous, and you know how he refuted it? By jumping up from his chair, wrapping Antisthenes in a bear hug and yelling, "See! I did it."

The guy who bugged him most, though, was Plato. He used to sit in on his lectures at the Academy just to give him grief. Once Plato told his students a human being is a featherless biped, and you know what Diogenes did? He put a dead chicken on his doorstep! When Plato called him a dog, he said thank you. And once he went to a symposium at Plato's house, even though he wasn't invited, and he didn't bother to wipe the mud off his feet. He got Plato's new carpet all dirty, and then he said to him, "Oh dear me, I'm stepping on your pride and joy, aren't I?" Plato had a good return, though. "You're the one who's proud. Proud of not appearing to be proud." Diogenes was impressed, but he pissed on the carpet anyway.

His best teacher, he always said, wasn't a philosopher at all, but a skinny little girl, a street urchin, no more than eight. He was giving a sermon in the *agora* when he saw her sitting on the ground. She glanced his way but was too busy eating to pay attention. No bowl, she was scooping lentils out of the pot with a crust of bread. She didn't have a cup either, so she used her hands to drink water from the fountain. This made him realize how little he needed, and so he threw away his own utensils. If I had an axe, he used to say, would my wrists be so strong?

He was right, you know. Society ruins you, it teaches you to compare yourself to other people and always to worry about how you look in their eyes, and then you end up losing sight of yourself and not being able to tell the difference between what you want and what other people want you to want. Of course, the only thing truly worth wanting is happiness, but you certainly won't find that in society. No, you can only get there by living like a dog. Natural, spontaneous, free, not giving a shit what other people think. People used to give him a world of grief for doing his business in the *agora*, but he only did it to make them wonder about how they're living. Shame turns you into a slave, he'd tell them, a slave of convention, and miserable to boot. The gods have given you everything you need to live well, and yet you always want more. Who needs a bed when you can sleep on the ground? Who needs a bath when you can stand in the rain? Don't confuse yourselves. Happiness is there for the taking if only you let yourself be.

He once lit a lamp in broad daylight and carried it all around town, and if somebody stared at him he'd say, "I'm looking for a human being; a real one, not a phony."

I'd be the first to admit, by the way, I'm not the world's greatest Cynic. I haven't been at it that long, and I'm still having a hard time with some of the exercises. I can handle begging, being dirty, sleeping on the street, and giving up wine, but when Diogenes told me I was ready to begin missionary work, I got nervous. The first time I tried to pee in public I felt people looking at me and I couldn't squeeze out a drop. But, as he used to say, freedom's just another word for nothing left to lose, so I got used to it. Even now, though, I can't bring myself to shit in the *agora*. Every once in a while, Diogenes would masturbate there. You know, to get people to ask themselves who gets to decide what counts as disgusting. I'm not ready for that. At least not yet.

14

Crates and Hipparchia: Cynics in Love

(circa 300 BCE)

As leaves on tree,
such is the life of men. (DL IX.67)

"Yo, DOG! METROCLES, WAIT up!"

"Menippus! Well I'll be darned. You actually came."

"Course I came. You think I'd miss the fun-and-all."

"The what?"

"The fun-and-all."

Metrocles' long face squinched.

"Come on, dog, you ain't no fool!" Menippus replied. "The funeral!"

"Ah," Metrocles said. He was relieved but did not smile. "Do you ever stop clowning, Menippus? Are you ever serious?"

"Serious? *Moi*? Never touch the stuff. On the other hand, I did hoof it all the way here to pay my last respects to Crates."

Metrocles finally smiled. Although Menippus frequently annoyed him, deep down he was fond of the younger man. Despite his steady stream of jokes, he was a genuine Cynic. He lived in a hovel, didn't wear shoes, hadn't cut his hair in years, urinated on the street, and scavenged for scraps when the vegetable market closed. He'd often spend a whole morning standing on a corner where he would shake his walking stick and spew invectives at the well-heeled folk who passed by. More than once he got a beating in return. Still, he reveled in his freedom and was always ready to laugh. And Metrocles could even forgive his terrible language. After all, Menippus' father had been a fishmonger; his mother, a prostitute.[134]

"So, what you been up to?" Menippus asked.

"Up to? The usual, I suppose," Metrocles replied.

"Sniffing around and laying down a trail of pee?"

Metrocles stiffened. "Menippus, please, this a funeral! Don't you ever let up?"

"Nope. And if you can't take a joke then you should hand in your dog collar, dog, and haul your ass straight to the Academy. No fun there, that's for sure."

Metrocles knew he was right. He smiled again, and put both hands on his walking stick.

"So what's up with this here fun-for-all?" Menippus asked.

"What you'd expect," Metrocles said. "Simple, no rituals, no reception. Just a grave, and we'll say good-bye to Crates."

"And Hipparchia? Will she speak?"

"Of course."

"Excellent!" Menippus said. "Your sister's quite a dame."

"True," Metrocles said quietly.

Hipparchia's sister invited her to join an afternoon gathering of her friends, but she didn't want to go. To avoid embarrassment, she slipped out of the house before the guests arrived. She didn't usually walk after lunch; it was too hot. But she made an exception. She didn't want to see the other girls in their fancy clothes, hear them giggle or suffer through their petty dramas, so she grabbed her wide-brimmed hat and a water-skin, and bolted out of the house. Despite the heat she felt lighter as soon as she stepped outside, and she began to run towards the olive grove at the northern edge of the estate. But before the house was even out of sight she found it hard to breathe and had to slow to a walk. When she finally arrived at the grove she felt faint and sought refuge in the shade of a large and ancient tree. She nearly collapsed onto the ground under its branches. After a few minutes and a long swig of water, her strength returned and she was able to sit upright.

Nearly six feet tall, slender, with long neck and limbs, tangled brown hair hanging low on her back, she was fourteen years old and had not yet grown into her body. She moved like a fawn unsure of where it's supposed to go. Deep down, though, Hipparchia was anything but unsure. She already understood that when she got older men would gaze at her with longing, but this fact, which would have made her sister deliriously happy, was repulsive to her.

Her mother, famous in the neighborhood for her cooking, regularly chided her for not finishing her dinner. Hipparchia would smile and say, "Okay Mom," but take nothing more than a bite of bread and a fig, and leave the lamb stew untouched. Her mother would lose patience and send her off to her room, which was just where she wanted to go.

After dinner, when her sister and two brothers played knucklebones, she would read her favorite book, one of the few her family owned. Homer's *Odyssey*. She had memorized most of it, but she still liked to see the words on the papyrus. Hipparchia adored Penelope and thought her every bit the equal of her husband. She especially loved the trick she played on him. After twenty years at war and sea, Odysseus had returned to Ithaka. But Penelope, exactly like her husband, was cautious, and even though she was confident the man standing in front of her was Odysseus, she had to make absolutely sure. So she told her maid to move her bed outside the house. When Odysseus heard this he went berserk. "Woman, you must be crazy!" he screamed. "Only a god could move that bed!" Odysseus had built the bed himself and its post was the stump of an olive tree rooted firmly in the ground. That it was unmovable was known only to husband and wife. Penelope had given Odysseus a test. When he exploded in anger, he passed.

Some day, Hipparchia thought, I'll have a husband and be every bit as smart as he is, and he will love me for that. Who knows, maybe he'll build our bed from this very olive tree sheltering me from the sun.

For several minutes she stared at the heat waves emanating from the grove. Then she poured some water into her cupped hand, and as she was wiping it on her brow a familiar sensation of well-being washed over her. She lay back down on the rocky ground and felt entirely at home. A moment before she fell asleep, she smiled.

◇◇◇◇

"You remember the symposium at Lysimachus' house?" Menippus asked. "Damn, old Crates sure shocked the town when he brought Hipparchia with him."

"Yes he did," Metrocles agreed.

"Man, what a couple! They waltzed in arm-in-arm, like it was their house. Your sister, young, tall, and beautiful, even though she was wearing rags and was skinny as a toothpick. Crates, small, bent, old. And neither had taken a bath in a good long while."

"They used to wait for it to rain," Metrocles added.

"I remember every word," Menippus continued. "She was the only woman there—except for the flute girls, of course—but that didn't stop her from laying into that rich dude, Pleonektos. You remember him, don't you? Fat, wore two or three rings, stank of perfume?"

"Yes."

"She went after him like the second coming of Diogenes himself. She began by buttering him up. 'Isn't it true,' she asked, 'that if Pleonektos performs an action, the action cannot be wrong?' The chump agreed, and so she kept going. 'And isn't it true that if Hipparchia performs the same action, it too cannot be wrong?' He hesitated, but then he agreed to that too. 'And isn't it true that if Pleonektos wants to slap his face it would be perfectly all right for him to do so?' By then even he could see what was coming and he clammed up, but she went for the kill. 'Therefore, it's perfectly all right for Hipparchia to slap his face too.'

"Man, I couldn't believe my ears, and I was on the edge of my couch waiting to see what would happen next. Sure enough, she walked right up to him and whacked him across the face! For a few seconds, the fat-ass was shocked into silence. Then he went nuts, lunged at her, tried to tear her clothes off! But, nope, didn't faze her a bit! She stepped back and glared at him. 'You filthy bitch!' he screamed.

"'You're right, Pleonektos,' she said, all calm and collected. 'I am a filthy bitch. A Cynic.' She turned around and walked toward Crates like she didn't have a care in the world. They linked arms and walked out of the house like nothing was strange. The men at the symposium were awestruck. Goddamn, your sister was true blue!"

While she was polite and always did her chores, Hipparchia avoided her parents, her sister, and her younger brother as much as possible. But she loved spending time with Metrocles, even though he was eight years older. He was serious and studious, and when she asked him what he was thinking about, he was always willing to explain. In simple language he would recount Theophrastus' latest lecture on plants or the winds. Metrocles told his little sister that he too would be a teacher some day, and she could be his first student. When she promised him that she would work hard, Metrocles said, "I know you will, Hippy."

The more Hipparchia thought about her future, the more pathetic her family's luxurious home seemed to be. She still spent as many hours at the loom as her sister, but her thoughts were far away. She felt like a ghost walking through the house. Accustomed to her distraction and silence, her family increasingly treated her like one. Eventually her mother stopped imploring her to brush her hair or wear a nice peplos.

"Yes, she was always sure of herself," Metrocles said. "Did you know Antisthenes would have approved of her becoming a philosopher?"

"No shit?" Menippus said.

Metrocles nodded. "He once said virtue is the same for women as for men, and those who are wise are allowed to fall in love. With each other, that is."[135]

"You're saying he would have been cool with Crates and Hipparchia getting hitched?"

"Most definitely."

"Guess they figured out a better way of handling their urges than Diogenes. At least they didn't have to jerk off in public. Although I once heard a story about them getting ready to do it on the Painted Porch, in broad daylight with a lotta people around, but nobody got to see because Zeno threw a blanket over them. What a chickenshit! He didn't realize Crates could care less."

The memory caused Metrocles to flinch, and he did not respond. Fortunately, Menippus changed the subject. "You gotta tell me one thing, Metrocles," he said, waving his stick at the older man's face. "How'd your sister meet Crates? And how the hell did she persuade your parents to let them get married? Not to be rude or nothing, but why'd she want to marry him in the first place? I mean, the man was bent over like a hunchback."

A late morning, she was seventeen and in the weaving room with her sister and mother when Metrocles burst into the house. Without a word he flew past them and into his bedroom. The bang of the slamming door shocked them, for they had never known him to be anything but quiet. Her mother jumped up and rushed down the hall. The two girls followed.

"Metrocles! What's wrong?" she shrieked.

No response.

"Metrocles!" she said, knocking hard on his closed door. "What in god's name is wrong with you?"

Again, no response.

"Now you listen to me, mister!" she yelled. "Open this door right now! I don't put up with such nonsense in my house!"

Silence.

As usual, her mother quickly lost interest in her parental duty, and with a disgusted shake of her head returned to the weaving room. Her sister followed. But Hipparchia stayed. She put her ear to the door, but recoiled when she heard her brother sobbing. She took a deep breath, exhaled slowly, and then sat down on the floor, her back against his door. She squeezed her eyes shut, summoned an image of Metrocles and concentrated hard on it. After a few minutes, he opened the door slowly.

"Go away, Hip. Please," he said soft and sad.

"No Metrocles, I can't."

"Why not?" he moaned.

"Because I can help."

He looked at her with pity in his eyes. "No, you can't. You're just a kid."

"Tell me what's wrong, Metrocles. You'll see, I can help. You know me. I'm good at everything."

He nodded his head gravely. "Sometimes it does seem that way," he muttered.

"So let me come into your room. Don't worry, no one will hear us."

For a long moment he didn't move. Finally, he sighed, turned around and walked back into his room. But he left the door open, and she followed him. He lay down on his bed, she pulled a chair next to it. For a long moment they didn't speak. Metrocles' hands were clasped behind his head, and his haunted eyes stared at the ceiling. Hipparchia stared at him.

Finally he spoke. "I'm going to starve myself to death," he said, his voice flat.

Hipparchia was relieved that she felt no panic. "Why?" she asked.

He didn't look at her. "I made a fool of myself," he said. "It was shameful."

"What?" she asked evenly.

"We were rehearsing our speeches in class. When it was my turn, everything was going fine and then . . ." He winced.

She did not push him to finish the sentence. After a painful pause he did it on his own. "I broke wind. Loud."

At first the words didn't register, but when she understood what he meant she didn't laugh. She simply asked, "Did it smell bad?"

Metrocles put his hands over his eyes and moaned, "Oh god, yes. And Neleus made fun of me, and now I can never show my face in public again."

Hipparchia was baffled. Her sister's friends often made fun of her. They called her the "stork" and made nasty comments about her tangled hair, plain clothes, and lack of interest in boys. In turn, she thought being rich had made these girls stupid, and their insults didn't bother her a bit. She was surprised Metrocles was so upset, but when she factored in how serious and reserved he was, and how averse to conflict, his reaction became more plausible. The first son and oldest child, he had always been responsible, hardworking, and obedient, an excellent student and a decent wrestler. Never once had he been a laughingstock.

"Would you go away now, Hip. Please. I need to sleep."

"Okay," she said.

Metrocles did not join the family for dinner that evening, and no one at the table mentioned his name. Nor did he leave his room for the entirety of the next day. That night, lying in bed, Hipparchia decided her brother might actually harm himself, and she vowed to act.

The next morning, after another silent breakfast without Metrocles, she left the weaving room. As usual, her mother and sister didn't look up from their looms. She grabbed her wide-brimmed hat, a waterskin, and a handful of figs, walked out the door without making a sound and began the trek into town. If her mother had known that she was on the road without a chaperone she would have flown into a rage, and her father might even have given her a beating. But she didn't care.

A couple of hours later, her face grimed by sweat and dust, her long thick hair matted and wild, she arrived in the *agora*. At first she was puzzled that no one was giving her a second look, but then she realized that in their eyes she was no more than a slave girl running an errand. They were half-right. She did have an errand. To find Metrocles' teacher,

Theophrastus. She knew the name of his school—the Lyceum—but not where it was. Fortunately, she saw a boy about her age walking towards her. He was slight, seemed distracted, and was carrying a scroll, so she approached him. As soon as she said, "Excuse me," he jumped back in terror. Not only was she a girl, but she was also a half-foot taller than he was. To his credit he recovered quickly, and when she asked him where the Lyceum was, he pointed her in the right direction.

A few minutes later she entered the Lyceum. A man she assumed was Theophrastus was giving a lecture. His large audience was, of course, entirely male, so she stood on the outskirts, where she could barely hear a word. When he was done, he took a few questions. The midday sun was starting to burn, and the crowd gradually dispersed as the men sought refuge from the heat. As soon as the last student said goodbye to Theophrastus, she made a beeline for him.

"Excuse me, Mr. Theophrastus," she said. "May I have a word with you?"

He was surprised, but did not seem annoyed. He studied her carefully. Her clothes, hair, and dirty face suggested slave, but her accent and poise suggested aristocrat. "Yes?" he replied.

"It's my brother. Metrocles. He's one of your students. You know him, right?"

"Metrocles? Of course I know him." Theophrastus stroked his beard. "And who are you?"

"I'm Hipparchia. His sister."

Theophrastus nodded. "I see," he said. "Metrocles has mentioned you. He said you might like to study philosophy some day. Is that true?"

She didn't answer his question. Instead she said, "I'm here about my brother. He's in a bad way."

Hipparchia told Metrocles' story with clinical efficiency. When she was done, Theophrastus put his hands on his cheeks and stared at the ground. Then he nodded and muttered something, which Hipparchia could not decipher. When he looked up, his face had brightened. "I know someone who might be able to help," he said.

"Really?"

"Yes."

"Will you ask him to do it?"

"Yes, I will," he replied. "Now, young lady, it's getting hot, and I need to go inside. You should do the same."

For a second Hipparchia looked worried, and Theophrastus, recalling that Metrocles lived on a farm outside town, realized she was far from home. "You can rest in my house, if you'd like. You should stay out of the sun for the next few hours."

"No thank you," she said firmly. "I can rest over there." She pointed to a small grove of trees. "I have water and figs."

Theophrastus studied her again, astonished that a wealthy young girl would eat outside and alone. Then he said, "Suit yourself," and walked away.

After her meager lunch and a long nap, Hipparchia walked home. She arrived just as the rest of the family, but not Metrocles, was sitting down for dinner. Nobody asked her where she had been or why she looked more disheveled than usual.

The next morning Metrocles still hadn't left his room. She was beginning to feel frantic when there was a loud knock at the door. She rushed to it, but one of the servants beat her there and opened it. A short man dressed in a filthy cloak, no shoes, skinny legs, and scraggly hair was standing on the doorstep. He was not terribly old, but his back was bent as if he were, and he was holding a walking stick. He greeted the servant with a cheerful smile and introduced himself. He was Crates and had come to visit Metrocles. When she heard her brother's name she pushed the servant away. "Did Theophrastus send you?" she asked.

"Send me?" he chuckled. "My dear, no one sends me anywhere. But Theophrastus did ask me to speak with his student. He thought I could be of some use, and when he explained the situation, I agreed. Even though he wastes his time studying plants, Theophrastus is actually quite a decent fellow."[136]

"He told you what happened?" Hipparchia asked.

"Isn't that what I just said?" Crates asked, without the slightest trace of annoyance.

"How can you help him?"

"By explaining to him there's absolutely nothing wrong with farting. It's perfectly natural."

Crates, still standing at the doorway, then cut a long loud one. He smiled and said, "Ah, the fava beans are doing their job. I'm here to show your Metrocles he shouldn't care a bit about what happened. Please take me to him right away. Before I run out of gas." He chuckled again.

Crates was ugly, dirty, and bent, but she felt happiness radiating from him and could not take her eyes off him. Mesmerized she neither spoke nor moved. Her trance was broken only when Crates waved his walking stick in front of her face and said, "Hello there! Anybody home?"

Awkwardly she ushered him into the house and then led him to her brother's room. She was about to knock, but with surprising quickness and strength Crates grabbed her wrist and said, "Allow me. They call me the 'door-opener,' you know."

"Why?" she asked.

"Because I can weasel my way into anybody's house. And once I get inside I give the inhabitants a tongue lashing for their vanity."

Hipparchia had no idea what he was talking about, but she loved the sound of his voice. "Okay," she said.

Crates released her wrist and looked at her carefully. "You're smart, aren't you?"

"Yes," she said.

"Very nice," he said. He tapped on the door with the handle of his walking stick. "Metrocles," he said firmly. "It's Crates. Theophrastus asked me to speak with you, which is precisely what I am going to do. Please open the door now, and we can begin."

As she hoped, desperately, a few seconds later Metrocles opened the door. Before he entered the room Crates winked at her.

An hour later, while she was squirming miserably on the couch in the sitting room, she heard his voice. "See you tomorrow then." A few seconds later Crates appeared before her. "You can go in now," he said. She jumped up and for a split second felt the urge to hug the bent little man. Instead, she caught herself and rushed to her brother's room. She was delighted when Metrocles greeted her with his familiar warmth and then told her he would be leaving his room soon. She asked him what Crates had said to him.

"He told me stories about Diogenes."

"Who?"

"He was Crates' teacher. He learned about the power of the dog from him."

"The what?"

"They're called Cynics—you know, dogs—and they have their own philosophy."

"What is it?" Hipparchia demanded.

"Simple. Happiness is living in accord with nature. The things most people want—money, power, fame, the usual stuff—just get in the way.

Diogenes knew how to live with the bare minimum, and never at the expense of others."

"Bare minimum of what?"

"Food, shelter, clothes. You name it and he did without."

"So did he get mad at you for living in a fancy house?"

"Not at all. Crates comes from money himself, but he threw it into the sea when Diogenes told him to."

"Wow!" she said quietly.

"He said the most important thing is to stop caring about what other people think of me. Just be natural, and if they can't handle it, too bad for them. Which means I was stupid when I got so upset for passing gas in Theophrastus' class."

"For farting," she said.

Metrocles grinned. "You know what he said? Better to fart and bear the shame than not to fart and bear the pain. And you know what he did next?"

Hipparchia was sure she did, but still asked, "What?"

"He farted! Really loud." Metrocles laughed again. "I was such a fool. I can't believe I spent all those years with Theophrastus and he never explained this to me. You know what I'm going to do tomorrow?"

"What?"

He smiled wide. "Start training with Crates."

The next day, after breakfast, which he wolfed down, Metrocles left the house and walked into town. He never returned. Three days later Hipparchia announced to her family that she too had made a decision. "I have fallen in love with Crates, his words and his way of life, and I will marry him. I want to be a philosopher."

Her mother screamed, her sister followed suit, her younger brother and father burst into laughter. Hipparchia looked at them in contempt and calmly said, "And if you refuse to allow me to marry him, I will kill myself." The table fell silent. They knew she was serious.

"What a dame," Menippus repeated.

"Yes," Metrocles relied. "My father begged Crates to dissuade Hipparchia and, god bless him, he tried. He told her he had no money, and only two cloaks, one for winter, the other for summer. He bathed when it rained, and for long stretches in the summer he smelled bad. He lived in a shack with almost no furniture and ate nothing but vegetables. His bones were porous, which was why his back was bent. He spent almost every day either teaching or proselytizing. Hipparchia's response to every one of his objections was the same: 'You are everything to me, and with you I shall spend my life.'"

"And what? Crates finally gave in?" Menippus asked.

Metrocles smiled. "Yes, but not before he made one last attempt. She had come into town and found a few of us begging on the street. She went up to Crates and told him, in a voice loud enough for the rest of us to hear, they should get married straight away. He grinned at her and began to undress. Right on the street, with dozens of people walking by. When he was totally naked he spread his boney little arms and said, 'Behold, your bridegroom. These are his possessions. Make your choice, and please understand that we will marry only if you will work with me day and night.'[137]

Hipparchia examined every inch of his crooked body and said, 'I do.'"

"Damn," Menippus said softly.

"They were inseparable," Metrocles continued. "She never complained about their poverty, even if their dinner was often no more than a discarded cabbage and water their only drink. She always declined our mother's offer to take her shopping. She wore exactly the same kind of cloak as Crates, and the only time they washed was when it rained. Then they would stand together in the street, hand in hand, and get drenched. She clung to his arm whenever they were in public, although as he got older, he was the one who needed support."

"How often do you think they actually did it?" Menippus asked.

"Did what?"

"You know, humpty-dumpty?"

Metrocles sighed, shook his head, and said, "If you want to know, you'll have to ask Hipparchia yourself."

"No way, José. She scares the shit out of me."

"Menippus, we Cynics are supposed to be fearless," Metrocles said.

"I hear you, but I'm making an exception here and now. Whatever Crates and Hipparchia did at night was their business. Not mine. They have a kid. Maybe the old man went one for one. Whatever. We'll just leave it be."

"Good idea," Metrocles said. "They used to finish each other's sentences, you know. Especially when they were giving lectures."

"I do know," Menippus said. "I heard them do it more than once."

Metrocles sighed. "When Crates was near the end, I asked my sister, rather stupidly, was he afraid? She replied as if I were a child, 'How can death be bad if, when it is present, we are unaware of it?' I asked her how she was holding up, and she said she was fine and that Crates was perfectly capable of taking care of himself. When the pain got bad he'd sing to himself—'You are departing now, dear Hunchback, and approaching the house of Hades, bent by age'—and a smile would appear on his face. My sister learned from the Master, and she'll carry on without him."

"What a bitch," Menippus said admiringly. For once he was completely serious.

15

Pyrrho and Philista

(360–270 BCE)

Who knows if to die is to live,
And what men believe to be life is death?
Thus spoke Pyrrho,
On the day he died. (DL IX.73)[138]

"I LOVE HIM, BUT he drives me crazy," Philista said.

Philo grinned, but then quickly put his hand over his mouth to conceal it. "I understand," he replied. "But I'm not sure now's the best time to talk about it."

The two old folks, both of them lean and standing straight, were sheltering from the sun in the shade of an enormous oak tree. Inside the house, Pyrrho, Philista's brother and Philo's best friend, was dying. He had been in bed for a week.[139]

"Oh, for god's sake, why not?" Philista asked. "What, do you think he'd get mad if he heard us? Don't be ridiculous, Philo! Nothing bothers him!"

Philo studied the sharp lines of her still handsome face, her thin straight nose and unyielding eyes, the simmer of impatience. He knew her well.

"I remember once, a long time ago, we were on a ship—I have no idea where we were going or why—and there was a storm. Huge waves, the wind was fierce. I was terrified, so were the other passengers and even some of the sailors. And my brother? He was staring at a little pig, locked in a cage. It was eating its supper without a care in the world. Pyrrho looked up, smiled, and said, 'A wise creature, indeed.' Of course, no one heard him except me."

Philo nodded. "I love that story," he said.

"What? I've told it before?" she asked.

"Yes, dear, more than once."

"Oh hell, who cares," she sputtered. "The truth bears repetition."

He sighed and then rubbed his eyes. "Well, then," he said, his patience restored, "explain it to me. Why does he drive you crazy?"

"Because nothing gets to him. Like the time he fell and broke his arm. The bone actually shot out through his skin. When the doctor set it back into place, he didn't flinch, even though it must have hurt like hell. I tell him to do the most menial tasks, like cleaning the house or bringing birds to the market, and he never complains. It doesn't matter what's happening or what he's doing, nothing upsets him."

"Okay, but remind me: Where's the problem?"

"Sometimes you should get upset! At the Macedonians, for example. Imperialist bastards! I used to tell Pyrrho we should join the resistance, but what'd he do? Nothing! And one time I heard him say to Anaxarchus that if we cooperated with them, Elis would be more secure and our economy would grow. Can you believe it?"

Philo, who could indeed believe it, did not reply.

"My brother! No matter what I say, he'll say the opposite, and when I get angry, he just smiles. He drives me crazy!"

"Come on, Philista, after all these years you must know this is the heart and soul of skepticism. We counter assertions but make none ourselves. Had you said Elis should make peace with the Macedonians he probably would have argued for war."

"He's a goddamn fence-sitter, Philo, and so are you!"

"Bad metaphor, dear. Try a scale instead. To every argument a skeptic will pose a counter-argument of equal weight. Macedonian imperialism is bad because it deprives Elis of its sovereignty. Macedonian imperialism is good because it fosters economic growth and security. The scale is balanced, judgment is suspended, and there's no need to quarrel. Stress disappears. *Ataraxia* follows like a friendly shadow."

Philista's eyes narrowed in protest. "And, what, you're not going to stand up for your rights? You philosophers are disgusting! You wall yourselves up, safe and sound where no one can touch you. Like your hero Socrates. The most self-sufficient man who ever lived![140] Or was that Diogenes? Oh hell, who cares! You think it's great not to need a soul. You know, sometimes my brother wouldn't leave his room for days at a stretch. He wouldn't talk to me or sit at the table, and I had to put his meals outside his door. Can you believe it? Other days, though, he'd spend hours wandering around town gabbing with complete strangers. I mean, the man was oblivious! I once watched him giving a lecture to somebody, and he didn't pause for a second, not even to catch his breath. And then, when the guy got bored and walked away, he just kept on talking. Same thing at home, especially in the kitchen, he used to talk to himself all the time. I asked him why, and you know what he said?"

"What?"

"He was training himself! Cripey! And then there was the time when Anaxarchus fell into a pond. Pyrrho was walking by and saw him, but he didn't lift a finger to help. It made me crazy, but Anaxarchus, he had no problem with it. In fact, he admired my brother, said he was thoroughly disengaged! Disgusting!

"Damn you philosophers! You call it indifference or apathy or self-sufficiency. Or maybe its imperturbability. Who the hell knows, but it's what you want out of life. And do you want to know why it sucks?"

Philo knew what she was going to say, but asked anyway. "Why?"

"Because it's inhuman. You philosophers turn yourselves into stones. You stay safe in your thought bubbles where nobody can touch you. And you know why you do it?"

"Why?"

"Because you're afraid."

"Of what, my dear?"

"Of getting hurt. You wall yourself off from other people because you're afraid they're going to reject you or disappoint you, or leave you."

"Or die," Philo whispered.

She heard him but did not reply. Instead, she sighed, her head drooped, her shoulders slumped, and she fell silent for a long moment. Then she straightened herself and spoke calmly, her voice tinged with sadness. "I don't think he ever got over our little sister's death. She was the youngest, and we all loved her the most. She was helping our mother with the vegetables, and she cut her finger on a knife. Two days later her whole hand was burning red and swollen. Then it spread up her arm. She was gone in a week. Pyrrho didn't say much, but I think he was shattered. I know our mother was."

Saying nothing, the two old friends began to walk slowly around the tree, their shoulders touching.

"I was a midwife for fifty years, Philo, and I can tell you one thing: women are not afraid to care because they're not afraid to suffer. My women loved their babies even though they understood perfectly well how vulnerable this made them. They embraced it! And during birth they felt pain the likes of which a man cannot imagine. And fear and anger and joy, and sometimes the worst kind of despair. But they never ran away from it, not like you philosophers. You think people make things worse, but you're wrong. They make it better, even if you do get hurt. You guys want everything to be clean, but it doesn't work that way, Philo. Life is a bloody mess, and it all starts at birth."

Although he was neither surprised nor irritated by Philista's tirade, he wondered, yet again, how Pyrrho had managed to live with this woman for so long.

"You have no beliefs," she said, oozing disappointment.

"Depends what you mean," he replied. "If I feel warm in the kitchen, then I believe I feel warm."

"Bully for you."

"What I don't believe is, even if I feel warm, the kitchen is actually warm. For it's entirely possible you may feel cold, and there's no reason why my feeling should be privileged over yours. The only rational thing to do is to suspend judgment on the question, is the kitchen actually warm? Which is why I won't argue with you about it."

"You sound just like him! He's always correcting me. If I say, 'Oh, this apple's really sweet,' he'll tell me, no, it's not really sweet, it just tastes sweet to me. Then he'll tell me to put a spoonful of honey in my mouth before I bite into the apple. See! It's not so sweet anymore. I say, big deal. I still love apples. And he does the same thing when it comes to serious stuff. Like Antigonus. He says he's going to legalize incest, and I don't care what you say, he's a stupid bastard and dead wrong!"[141]

"It's true, Greeks do believe it's unnatural for cousins to marry. Persians, however, do not."

"Well, we're right."

"Why? Because we're Greeks?"

"Yup! And because we're right."

"But isn't this exactly what Persians would say about themselves?"

"Who cares what they say! They're Persians! You skeptics are always giving the other side a chance to tell their story, even though they don't deserve it. Sometimes it makes sense to get good and angry and tell them to shut the hell up. But no, not my brother."

Philo chuckled. "Didn't we see him get angry once?"

She stopped walking, looked pensive. She knew he was referring to a festival decades ago when a drunken neighbor had assaulted her. Pyrrho punched the guy in the face and broke his nose.

"Yes," she admitted. "And do you remember what he said afterwards? 'It's difficult to completely stop being human.'"

She shook her head, incredulous.

"Certainly, Philista, you understand why Pyrrho might have had something positive to say about the Macedonians."

The memory annoyed her. "I know, I know," she said. "He went with Alexander's army to India."

"Which is where he met the naked wisemen. Just like one of his heroes, Democritus. They changed his life."

"You've told me this a million times, Philo."

"The truth bears repetition, my dear," he replied.

She did not smile.

"At any rate," he continued, "I knew he had changed as soon as he got home from India. It wasn't only that he gave up his painting. His whole demeanor was different. He was more relaxed than I'd ever seen him, and his eyes seemed brighter. Then he started going to lectures every day. Platonists, Aristotelians, Pythagoreans, even the Cynics, he listened to them all. What he really liked best, though, was arguing with them. No matter what they claimed, he would defend the opposite."

"Sounds peachy. I'm sure this did wonders for his popularity."

"Oh yes, he annoyed them, even though he never lost his temper or even raised his voice. He kept at it for years and then he began to develop his modes."[142]

"His modes!" Philista exclaimed. "Those damn charts hanging on the wall in his study. They're ridiculous! Like this one."

She picked up a stick, dropped to her knees—surprisingly nimble for a woman her age—and began scratching furiously in the dirt.

Hemlock → good for quail (H is G for Q)
Hemlock → not good for men (H is not-G for M)
No reason to prefer Q or M

Is H G or not-G?
Suspend judgment

"Well done, old girl!" Philo congratulated her. "You were paying attention after all."

"Of course I was. What do you think I am? A bag of dirt? I had to look at those damn charts on the wall every day when I brought him his lunch or cleaned his room."

"They're thinking maps. You can replace hemlock with incest, quail with Persians, and men with Greeks. Doesn't matter. Your brother's modes showed how it is possible to counterbalance any dogmatic assertion and then to suspend judgment and stop caring who's right. They may be strange but they're utterly brilliant."

"So why didn't he publish them and make some money? We've needed a new oven for years."

He laughed. "It all started with the naked wisemen, you know. He used to say his modes did no more than Hellenize their teachings."[143]

She scoffed. "You mind if we sit down? I'm getting tired."

"Of course," he replied.

When they both had made themselves as comfortable as they could on the hard ground, she said, "I've lived with him for a long, long time."

"I know."

"Did he ever tell you why I moved in?"

"Actually, I don't think so." He was surprised. He thought he knew everything about Pyrrho.

"My husband died when we were young. I had nothing but miscarriages and no children to take care of me. I would have been in a bad way, but Pyrrho invited me to stay in his house, and he did it so matter-of-factly, like it was totally obvious I should move in. And I never left."

She blinked back the tears. "I'll miss him," she said, her voice barely audible.

"I know," he replied. And he took her hand.

16

Cleanthes and the Soul of a Boxer

(330–230 BCE)

I praise Cleanthes, but praise Hades more,
Who gave him rest at last among the dead,
He who'd drawn such loads of water while alive. (DL VII.176)[144]

AFTER THE BURNING SUBSIDED and for the first time in weeks, his gums no longer throbbed. The doctor told him he could start eating again. But he didn't want to. He's had no food for three days, but feels no hunger. Now he's lying on his bed, and his mind is clear.

Like his beloved teacher Zeno, who fell and broke his toe and then, on the spot, decided to hold his breath until he died, Cleanthes has resolved to bring his long journey to an end. He will not eat another morsel. He is, they tell him, one hundred years old, and his death will be of his own choosing. A final affirmation of his freedom.[145]

He closes his eyes and, as he has throughout his long life, his first love returns to him. He is boxing. Hands up, feet dancing, eyes trained on the opponent, alert to his feints and jabs, poised to evade or strike, no thought, no words, utterly immersed in the fight, he is entirely his body at work. Even now, motionless in bed, he can feel himself moving.

When he broke an opponent's nose or crushed his ear, he felt no remorse. His own nose had been broken twice. Nor did he feel pleasure.

What mattered was only that he fought as hard and well as he could. For this was his duty. If his concentration wavered and an image of victory or defeat fluttered through his mind, he would swear an oath to Pollux, the patron god of boxing, and recite his coach's endlessly repeated admonition: *do your job*!

His best teachers were his opponent's blows. A fist would smash into his jaw, and his head would explode in pain. He could do nothing about this, but he learned that how he reacted to the pain was, in fact, up to him. If he kept it in its place, if he focused on it as if from a distance, then, yes, it would hurt, but this was no more than one sensation among many to be registered and disregarded. But if he faltered and allowed the pain to seep in, if he assented to it, he would identify with it, and then he was finished.

Boxing had primed him to become a Stoic. It taught him his only opponent was himself.

You cannot be conquered if you never enter any competition in which victory is not up to you. His teacher's words. He says them out loud, but they are audible only to himself.

He can feel his life force ebbing away, but he's not afraid.

He says more. *Things do not disturb us. Instead, it is our judgments about those things. Death, for example, is nothing terrible. If it were it would have appeared so to Socrates, which it did not. No, what is terrible is our judgment that death is terrible.*[146]

He is certain he would have loved Socrates. They both came from the working class and had thick, strong bodies.

He grins, barely.

At the height of his prowess as a boxer, he heard about the Zenonians, as they were then called, and for reasons he could not fathom at the time, he was gripped by the desire to meet them. He booked passage to Athens. Within hours of his arrival, he located the Stoa, the portico where the philosophers would gather.

Naturally, all unfolded according to Zeus' plan.

He was greeted by Zeno himself, a sullen man with a shriveled face. But Cleanthes was not intimidated and promptly announced his desire to enroll in the school. As he always did with prospective students, Zeno first asked whether he could pay the tuition. Cleanthes said yes, even though he had no money.

He took a job as a water-boy. Every night, he would haul two heavy buckets, yoked together and draped across his shoulders, from a well and into the garden of a wealthy farmer. For this brutal toil he was paid a minimal wage, from which Zeno, as was his custom, took a cut. But Cleanthes did not object. His was able to study during the day.

Because he could not afford papyrus, he had to write on shards of pottery and bones he picked up at the slaughterhouse. The other students would look at him, his filthy clothes, his workman's hands, his broad back, with amused contempt. It did not trouble him. Do your job, he told himself. Zeus takes care of everything else.

Fatigue was a constant in those days. He trained himself to fall asleep at every opportunity. He would doze for a few minutes while waiting in line to get his buckets filled at the well or nap in class before Zeno arrived at the speaker's platform.

Most days he did not feel his fatigue, but occasionally it would hit him as hard as a fist to the jaw. But this was familiar, and he managed.

Once he was summoned to the court to explain how, as poor as he was, he could be in such fine physical condition. The wealthy farmer for whom he worked testified on his behalf, and the judges' suspicions were removed. In fact, they were impressed. They rewarded him with ten minas. Zeno, however, would not let him keep the money.

He knew he was no genius and his mind worked slowly. His fellow students called him "the mule," and they were shocked when Zeno named him as his successor. Zeno explained to them that Cleanthes was like an old wax tablet. Hard to write on, but once inscribed even more difficult to erase.

Yes, he was a mule, which is why he was able to carry such a heavy load. For thirty years he was the head of the Stoic School.[147]

Unlike most teachers, nothing pleased him more than discovering a student smarter and quicker than himself. He enjoyed repeating a story about Sphaerus. He had been sent to Alexandria to tutor Ptolemy. One day, he was explaining that, because all his beliefs are true, a Stoic sage holds no opinions. Naturally, Ptolemy tried to prove him wrong. He had a servant bring a waxen pomegranate to the table. He asked Sphaerus whether he would like to have a taste, and when he said yes, the king shouted in delight that the Stoic had been fooled and now held a false belief! Nonsense, Sphaerus calmly replied. He did not believe it was a real pomegranate but only that, given the evidence of his senses, it was reasonable to assume it was real.[148] Cleanthes, never facile, knew he never could have come up with such a splendid rejoinder.

For a short while, Chrysippus, then only a teenager, attended his lectures, and it did not take Cleanthes long to realize the boy was far and away the most intelligent person in the school. Which is why he smiled when, after one of his lectures, Chrysippus told him he no longer needed Cleanthes to prove anything for him. "Just give me the doctrines," he said, without an iota of pretense or malice, "and I'll figure out the proofs for myself." Cleanthes knew this was true. Nor did he feel belittled when Chrysippus once came to his rescue. He was on the verge of being refuted by a visiting scholar, a terribly arrogant young man, when the boy intervened. "Stop distracting your elder from serious subjects," he screamed at the man, who became embarrassed and left the room.[149] Cleanthes was pleased.

Yes, all unfolded according to Zeus' plan.

He opens his eyes, but he's in a fog and discerns nothing. He feels like he's floating on air. Zeno's face appears, as unpleasant as ever, and then fades just as quickly. He sees himself lecturing to a large audience. Chrysippus, he notices, is sleeping in his chair. He feels his neck buckling under the weight of the two water buckets. He evades an opponent's blow and counters with a right jab to his jaw. The match ends, exhausted and drenched in sweat, he is victorious.

17

Plato's Last Dialogue

(428–347 BCE)

From a wedding banquet he has passed to that city,
Which he had founded for himself,
And planted in the sky. (DL III.45)[150]

HE'S IN BED, COVERED by a thick woolen blanket, up to his chin, but he's
still cold. Mostly he sleeps. When awake, he allows only a few of the many
people hoping to visit him to enter his room: his sister, Potone; her son
and his successor as head of the Academy, Speussipus; and Artemis, a
slave who has served his family for all of her fifty years.[151] She is the only
person with whom he actually converses. He only pretends to listen to
everyone else.

"Speusippus visits me every day," he says.

"I know," Artemis says.

"He's a dunderhead, I'm afraid. For years, he was too intimidated to
say much to me, but now he's a regular chatterbox. I suppose it's because
he's so pleased with himself. I've named him as my successor. He and my
sister know this, and of course you do too, but don't say a word to anyone.
I've written him into my will, and I want the announcement to be made
after I'm gone. Which will be soon."

"Got it, Chief," she replies without a hitch.

She's been calling him Chief for decades.

She was seventeen, slender and tall, almost gangly, with bright eyes. He was forty-eight, a broad shouldered man, as his old wrestling coach used to say.[152]

On a brutally hot summer afternoon, she entered his room. He typically spent this time of day talking with students in the courtyard, which is why she was surprised to find him sitting at his table, his head buried in his large hands. He looked beat.

"Are you okay, sir?" she asked.

He looked up, startled, and at first did not recognize her. "Oh, I'm sorry," he said, after examining her face for a long moment. "Artemis isn't it?"

"Yup, that's me."

"Is this your day to clean?"

"Yup," she said. "Same day every week."

"Right, of course. I'm sorry, I should have remembered."

He stood up slowly from his chair.

"Oh no, sir, no need! I can come back tomorrow, easy as pie."

"It's all right," he said. "You don't have to change your schedule. I'll leave for an hour or two."

"But you look tired, sir, and it's very hot outside. Why don't you lie on your couch, and I'll bring you some water. I can clean tomorrow morning when you're in class. Really, it wouldn't be any trouble."

"You're right," he sighed. "I am tired. Geometry was gruelling today. Thank god Axiotheos was there. He saved me from making a big mistake in a proof I was outlining, and after the lecture, he volunteered to help the students who were struggling, and I could get away. She's a blessing."

Her eyes narrowed, but she didn't say a word.

"You're absolutely sure it's no inconvenience to clean tomorrow?" he asked, slumping back down into his chair.

"No problem at all. It just means I'll have the afternoon off," she replied cheerfully.

Her smile, which revealed a narrow gap between her two front teeth, was effortless and radiant. She was gorgeous.

"And what will you do with your free time?" he asked. He wasn't sure if he wanted an answer or was only being polite.

"Oh, gosh, I don't know," she said. "Maybe take a walk through the olive grove."

"It's awfully hot, isn't it?" he asked.

"I don't mind. I'll wear a hat and walk slow. And bring a waterskin."

"I think the heat got to me when I was teaching," he said. "The ventilation is terrible in that room. After the first hour it was hard to breathe."

"And I bet it didn't smell too good either," she replied with a laugh. "All those sweaty boys!"

He grinned in surprise. "I didn't notice the smell, but I suppose you're right."

"I love smells," she continued. "Only the nice ones, of course, not the nasties, like stinky boys. Sometimes I ask myself, which is better? Taking a warm bath or smelling lilacs? And you know what I think?"

"What?" he asked, genuinely interested.

"Smelling lilacs, and you know why?"

"No, why?"

"The only reason my bath feels good is because I feel lousy before I take it. I mean, I'm pretty grubby after a day cleaning classrooms, and the bath refreshes me, but if I didn't get dirty in the first place I wouldn't need to take a bath at all. Same goes with food. I'm starving by dinner time and that's why it feels so good to fill myself up, but if I never got hungry I wouldn't like eating so much. Smelling's way different. I don't have to feel bad to enjoy it. A smell just hits me, and then, poof, it's gone. It comes by itself, for free. You know what I mean? And it's not like wine either because I don't feel bad afterwards. Anyway, that's why I walk through the fields in the summer. So many wonderful sniffs! Sage, thyme, boxwoods, crisp and dry."

Delighted by the free flow of her words, he listened carefully.[153]

"I'm sorry, sir," she said. "I'm blabbing." She did not, however, look the least bit apologetic. Instead, she seemed to be amused at herself.

"Not at all," he replied. "You cheered me up. And now I'll take your good advice and lie down for a while. Why don't you go on your walk, enjoy your free time, and come back tomorrow morning when I'm in class."

"Righto, sir!" she said. "Well, bye-bye, then."

"Bye-bye," he replied, his look lingering as she walked toward the door. "Then."

A few days later Plato fell ill. He was a strong man, but he had been working too much and sleeping too little. For the first time in anyone's memory he canceled his lectures and took to bed with a fever. Without being asked she tended to him. She wiped his forehead with a cool sponge. She freshened his bed, spooned him lukewarm broth, filled his cup with water. He smiled appreciatively but did not speak.

When she entered his room on the third day he was sitting up in bed reading a scroll. She blurted out, "You're better, sir!"

"Yes, much better indeed. You were an excellent nurse, Artemis, and I thank you very much."

"Oh no, sir, it was my pleasure. You know, if you don't mind me saying, you need to change a few things. First off, you work too much. You should take a nap in the afternoon instead of talking to your students, especially when it's hot. They can wait, and then you'll have more energy for the rest of the day. And you need to get some exercise. You should go to the gym at least three times a week. It'll help you sleep better at night. And make sure you eat balanced meals! Lots of greens with olive oil and not too much honey or wine."

He gazed at her, amazed. "Maybe you're right," he said. "Starting tomorrow I will take a nap in the afternoon."

"Promise?" she asked.

"Yes, Artemis, I promise."

"Well done, sir!" she said cheerfully. "You'll feel better, I'm sure."

The next day Plato told his students he would no longer be available for questions after his lecture. Instead, he would be returning to his room and did not want to be disturbed. He would, however, be glad to talk in the evenings when it wasn't so hot.

A few minutes after he settled on his couch for his mandatory nap, she entered the room. Without knocking. He was surprised, but not annoyed, to see her. She smiled at him. When she untied her headscarf, her thick brown hair tumbled down her breast. Then, without a moment's hesitation, she took off her clothes and walked to his couch. Her long arms and legs were elegant and her step as light as a dancer's. She was entirely comfortable in her own skin and when he moved over to make room she lay down next to him.

From that day on she always called him Chief, at least when they were alone. Which they were almost every afternoon for thirty years.

◇◇◇◇

"I'm right, aren't I? Speusippus is a bore, isn't he?" Plato asks Artemis.

His voice, which has always been thin, is now even weaker. She must lean close to him in order to catch his words. He's glad, for he can smell her hair.

"Not my place to judge," she says. "But let's put it this way. I wouldn't attend one of his lectures if you paid me."

He chuckles, which leads to a coughing fit. She helps him take a few sips of water, and after a minute it subsides.

"My nephew likes to gossip, and, I hate to admit it, it's weirdly soothing," he says slowly. "I don't have to pay attention. A lot easier than digesting a philosophical argument."

"Depends on the argument, doesn't it, Chief?"

"I suppose," he replies. "Anyway, Speusippus tells me the whole city is waiting for me to die. They're eager to find out who's going to be the next head of the Academy. He says rumors are flying."

"It's true."

"Apparently Philo is telling people I'm being devoured by lice. How ridiculous! Lice can't possibly kill a human being. It's probably more dangerous for a man to bite a louse than to be bitten by one."[154]

"Do you remember the louse-catcher in the *Sophist*?" she interjects with as much enthusiasm as she can muster.

He does remember. Vaguely.

For months he had agonized over the *Sophist*. His hope was for this dialogue to expose the limitations of technical thought. Or, as Artemis had put it, the limits of analysis. As much as he admired mathematics, the quintessentially analytic discipline, he was convinced it was incapable of addressing the most urgent of human questions, the ones Socrates taught him must be asked every day, even if they cannot be answered.

He created a character, a Stranger from Elea who is visiting Athens. A serious man and very much the professor, the Stranger practiced a method, which he called division. Take a concept, sub-divide it, and then sub-divide it again, until you reach an end and can define the concept. To illustrate, the Stranger began with an example: the fisherman. He is a skilled professional who has a kind of expertise. But what if, the Stranger asked, we don't know what expertise is? To find out we must perform a division. There are, he said, two kinds of expertise: some, like carpentry, produce objects other than themselves, while others acquire objects which already exist. The Stranger kept dividing, and when he was finished a reader could draw a diagram depicting his steps.

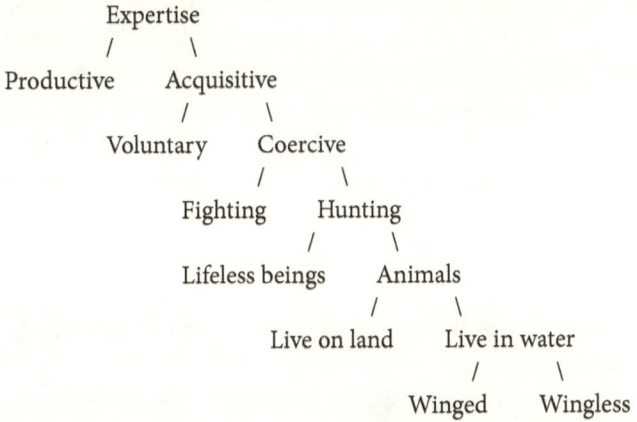

```
                    Expertise
                   /        \
         Productive          Acquisitive
                            /          \
                  Voluntary             Coercive
                                       /        \
                              Fighting           Hunting
                                                /       \
                                  Lifeless beings         Animals
                                                         /       \
                                          Live on land            Live in water
                                                                 /           \
                                                          Winged              Wingless
```

A definition had been reached. Fishing is a kind of expertise that hunts wingless water animals.[155]

Plato showed Artemis a draft of the passage, and as usual, she began asking questions before she finished reading it. As a definition of fishing it wasn't, she supposed, too bad, but it sure didn't tell her anything interesting about the fisherman. Why does he fish in the first place? For money or because he likes being out on the sea? How does he feel about killing innocent animals just so human beings can stuff their bellies? Do fish feel pain? And why, she continued, did the Stranger classify flying animals—which some of us call birds, she said with a wink—under animals that live in the water?

Plato beamed. He explained to her he wanted his readers to challenge the Stranger, and his method, by asking precisely such questions.

"And read this," he said, pointing to a passage later in the dialogue. Here the Stranger was discussing what he called the distinguishing expertise. Again, he began by dividing it into two kinds. In the first, like is distinguished from like. For example, two oaks trees are like each other, but they can be told apart on the basis of where they are located or how old they are. In the second, better is distinguished from worse. This, the Stranger said, can be called purification, which he then sub-divided: there is expertise in purifying inanimate objects, which is what the fuller does with wool, and expertise in purifying animals. Purification of animals he sub-divided into those performed on the body and those on the soul.

"You see," Plato said to her, his excitement mounting, "the reader is going to be curious about what purification of the soul is. They might even guess this is where philosophy will be located. But I'm going to give them examples of bodily purification first. There's the doctor, of course, who purges his sick patients of bile through a bloodletting, but there's also the bath-keeper, who is an expert in sponging. He rids the body of its dirt."

"An expert in sponging?" she asked with alarm. "Are you kidding me?"

"Keep reading," he said, his eyebrows arching.

She did.

After a couple of minutes she looked up and nearly yelled, "Wow! You nailed it!"

"Maybe," he said cautiously. "I'm worried it might be heavy-handed."

"Nope!" she said confidently. "You made the Stranger show his cards, and then hang himself in the process!"

She read the passage out loud.

> *My method of argument treats both the expertise of medicine and of sponging as the same. For both are forms of purification, even though the former benefits us greatly, while the latter only a little. The goal of my method is to gain insight about what is alike and what is not alike in all forms of expertise, and for this reason it honors them all equally and does not treat some as more ridiculous than others. For example, if someone, in trying to clarify what hunting is, uses the example of generalship, the method does not count the general as any the more dignified than the louse-catcher.*[156]

"The louse-catcher! Now who the hell is an expert in catching lice?" she said, trying to stifle her chuckle. "I mean, the only people I've ever seen doing it are nurses taking care of children. Or mothers."

Plato grinned mischievously.

"I get it!" she said. "The Stranger doesn't see any difference between human beings and lice. You nailed him, Chief. He's a bloody dehumanizer!"

Recollecting the various moves he made in the *Sophist* is far too difficult for him, and he gives up quickly. "I don't know what I did to offend Philo,"

he mutters. "Maybe it's because I once reprimanded him in a class. He was loud and he interrupted other students, and he'd been answering my questions before I'd even finished asking them. It's behavior I detest, and I lost my temper. 'Can you please let someone else talk!' I barked at him. He didn't say another word."

"Sorry, Chief, it wasn't Philo you barked at. It was Philippus. When you told me the story, you were nearly trembling with rage."

"Philippus? Really?" he asks. "Doesn't matter. Whoever it was, he must have been seething all these years, and now he's getting his revenge. Imagine, telling people I'm being devoured by lice."

"Guys like him are a dime a dozen," she says.

"Indeed," he agrees. "Here's another one. Hermippus claims my stomach is killing me because I ate too much fish at a wedding. Well, I did go to a wedding just before I got sick, but I don't remember whose it was. Maybe my niece's daughter? She's a nice girl, isn't she? And I probably did eat some fish. But I only took a few bites."

"As usual, Chief," she says gently, as she takes his hand. "And, yes, it was your niece's daughter, Archeanassa."

He gazes at her hand with such longing she wants to cry.

"Hermippus resents me," he says. "He's a poet, or at least he wants to be, and he thought I was making fun of him in the *Ion*. But it wasn't me who said those nasty things about poetry. I gave those lines to Socrates. But like most readers, Hermippus assumed Socrates was nothing more than my mouthpiece. Which he wasn't. He was a character in a dialogue. The fools don't bother asking themselves why I wrote dialogues in the first place. They don't wonder why I never wrote a treatise in which I straightforwardly articulated my own views. When they don't like something in a dialogue, they automatically attribute it to me."[157]

His voice is sputtering.

She has heard this complaint many times, especially during the past two weeks when he has been bedridden. Still, she squeezes his hand more tightly, as if to give him the energy to repeat it again.

"I know you don't hate poetry, Chief."

He nods. "As usual, Aristotle got it right. He said my dialogues were in-between poetry and prose. And Olympiodorus compared my dialogues to swans, flying from tree to tree, eluding their hunters."

He pauses, looks thoughtful, more like his younger self. "But you know what?" he asks.

"What, Chief?" she asks, her voice soft and loving.

"I've never seen a swan in a tree. Have you?"

"No," she chuckles. "But I do remember one afternoon when you woke up wild-eyed from a dream. You told me you had just seen a baby swan in your lap, and it suddenly sprouted feathers and with a sweet little cry flew away."[158]

"I don't remember," he said, annoyed with himself.

She chuckles again. "Well, I sure do. The symbolism wasn't exactly subtle. You had a quite an erection, my friend."

"I did?" he asks, amused.

"A mighty oak!" she says, this time with a full throaty laugh.

He laughs too, but his cough quickly overwhelms him. When it finally dies down, he whispers to her, "Stop with the jokes, would you please."

She grins. "Not sure I can promise you that, Chief, but I'll try my best."

He nods.

"Boy, you sure didn't do much laughing when we first got together," she says. "You were one totally serious guy."

"Either that or maybe you weren't funny back then."

She snickers. "Sorry, Chief, but I've been funny since I was born. It's how I charmed your father. Even when I was only three or four, he thought I was marvelous. I had so much energy. I was either talking or running. He was tightly wound, your father, but I could always make him laugh. He gave me the name Artemis and made sure I learned how to read and write."

Plato grimaces when she speaks of his father. "Do you think Hermippus said I ate too much fish at a wedding because he wants to remind people I've never been married? That bothers a lot of folks, you know. They think the job of a good citizen is to produce more citizens, which I haven't done. In their eyes, this makes me suspect."

"Well, they're not all wrong, are they Chief?" she asks gently.

For a brief moment he looks sad.

"Or maybe he wants to suggest I'm impotent," he continues. "They used to tell a terrible story about my father. They said he forced himself on my mother but was unable to complete the act. That night Apollo appeared to him in a dream and the next day she was pregnant. So I was the result of a coupling between an impotent rapist and a virgin."[159]

"People don't know what to make of you. You're too much for them."

"But not for you?"

"No, but I'm special."

He smiles, almost.

"Apparently," he continues, "Molon is saying I had affairs with all sorts of men. Aster, Alexis, Phaedrus, Agathon. He even claims I wrote love poems to them."

"Little do they know," she says.

"Indeed," he replies. "I've always preferred women, both in bed and everywhere else. I had two as students, you know."

Of course she knows.

"And one of them, Lastheneia, helped me a lot when I was writing the *Symposium*. I asked her to become my co-author, but she refused. She wouldn't even let me dedicate it to her."

He pauses, lost in thought, before he continues. "I made Speusippus promise me she can keep studying in the Academy after I'm gone. He didn't look happy, but he said he would do it."

Now it is her turn to grimace, but she does not say anything. Although they've never discussed it, she knows he has granted her freedom in his will and provided her with a comfortable income. On the one hand, she doesn't care. Her life has been good. On the other, she is relieved. She won't have to take orders from Speusippus.

"And Axiothea is a terrific geometer," Plato continues. "She thinks she has me fooled, you know. She calls herself Axiotheos and dresses like a man, but I've known for years."

He pauses again, closes his eyes, looks into himself for a long moment.

"Molon is an idiot," he continues when he returns. "Still, what he's saying about me and Dion is painful. For it's true, I did love him."

Now a surge of energy, pitifully slight, runs through him.

"I know," she whispers.

"He was the best of the best.[160] Intelligent, hungry to learn, full of energy, bursting at the seams. And he cared, oh my, did he care. And not just about philosophy, but other people too. He wanted to make a difference in his city, and he believed, he actually believed, he could put my ideas into practice. He thought the two of us together could teach Dionysius how to be a good ruler. He convinced me to go to Syracuse with him to try. And I did go, two or three times, even though I hated sailing. Deep down I knew it was crazy. My ideas aren't meant to be applied, at least not the way Dion thought they could be. My city was strictly in speech, a paradigm, laid up in heaven, not here on earth.[161] But Dion, well, he could charm a snake. It's not enough, he told me, just to talk. We have to do more than understand the world, we have to change it. He made me feel selfish. Like my father used to do. Which is why I sailed to Sicily that last time. Sick to my stomach the whole trip, I did nothing but lie on my cot, only getting up to vomit. Just to gratify Dion. Huge mistake."

He shakes his head, looks exhausted, but manages to continue. "Karudendra, the poet from Lesbos, once said my *Phaedrus* was inspired by Dion. She said I changed my ideas about love because of my infatuation with him.[162] Nonsense, of course, but I did love him. And who knows, maybe I did have sex with him. But I doubt it."

"It's easy to forget that stuff, Chief. A few minutes of friction and that's it."

She chuckles. He does not.

"My god, they cut Dion down like a dog. Which is why I had Socrates say no one who really cares about justice will survive for long if he goes into politics. No, the best thing is to find a quiet place to talk with a few intelligent people about justice and beauty and the good, and you certainly can't do that in the Assembly."[163]

"A place like the Academy," she says.

He does not register her remark. His wrinkled old face is flushed.

"My father would have been appalled, you know."

He's been talking about his father a good deal recently, and often his deep past is more vivid than what happened minutes ago. This leads Artemis to wonder. Is memory connected to a part of the body that deteriorates when we get old? Maybe it's like a piece of wax that becomes hard and can no longer absorb a new imprint. She tells herself to ask Aristotle what he thinks.[164]

"My god," he barks, interrupting her thoughts, "he was furious with me when I started spending time with Socrates. He called him a parasite who does nothing for his city except take. Every night at the table, he would remind me and my brothers we were descendants of King Codrus and it was our duty to serve Athens."

He looks troubled. "My father was mean," he says, "but he never hit us. Except for his lectures about the city, he never talked to us either."

He sighs and she wonders if he's fading, but he surprises her yet again. "My brother had it worse than me, though. I could always escape into my books or my daydreams, but Glaucon couldn't. I would sit at the table, tuned out, not saying a word, but he would challenge our father, just to get him mad, and the two of them would end up screaming at each other. My father held Socrates personally responsible for turning Glaucon away from politics.[165] He probably would have voted guilty had he been on the jury."

His eyes flutter, but they do not close. "He died, and I don't remember what I felt. I suspect it wasn't grief. We weren't close, my brother and I. He had a hard time at the end, didn't he?" he asks her.

She knows the answer is yes, but does not reply.

He waits for a few seconds and seems to understand. "It's good the old man is gone," he continues. "If he could see what I've become, if he could see me with a woman like you, he'd think I was trash, irresponsible, selfish, no true Athenian. And maybe he'd be right."

He looks deflated.

"Come on there, buck up, buckaroo," she says softly. "Being selfish isn't necessarily bad. It depends on your conception of the self, and your version is interactive and dialogical. You've spent your life teaching and talking to other people, especially to young folks, and even to women. No problem if a guy like you is selfish because you've got a darned good one. You followed in Socrates' footsteps and . . ."

"I never liked him, you know," he interrupts, his energy suddenly restored.

She is exhausted but still manages to grin. "Really?" she says, feigning surprise.

He does not register her irony. "You know why I wasn't with him in his jail cell on the day he died?"

She does.

"I was home, sick, but the truth is I wasn't that sick, and the jail wasn't far from my house, and I could have gone. Aeschines and Antisthenes were there, Cebes and Simmias too. And, of course, Megacles, his great buddy. But not me, and you know why?"

"Why?" she asks.

"I didn't want to."

He falls silent for a long moment. Again, she fears she is losing him, but he resumes. "I don't understand what he saw in Megacles," he says. "I think he made his money in leather. I overheard them talking once, and you can't imagine how crude their language was. And the way they laughed together! Like swineherds! Well, Socrates himself didn't come from much of a family either. His father was a stoneworker, and his mother a midwife. Still, why did he like Megacles more than me? Because I came from a privileged family? Was he jealous of me because I was rich and young?"

"And handsome, with the broad shoulders of a wrestler," she says, pretending to be merry.

"My god, he was fierce!" he says, ignoring her. "He'd sink his teeth into a question and not let go, and if he needed to talk all night, that's what he do. Totally focused, nothing else mattered. But he was a bully. You either played by his rules or you didn't play at all. Such a hard man! If you weren't a philosopher, he thought you were a nobody. He really meant it when he said the unexamined life is not worth living."

He begins to cough, but the spasm doesn't last long.

She asks him, "Did he actually say that, Chief, or did you put those words into his mouth in the *Apology*?"[166]

He is befuddled. "What?" he asks.

Although she genuinely wants an answer, she does not repeat the question.

He tries desperately to collect his thoughts. "He turned me around, though," he finally says. "Before I met him I assumed I'd be like my father and spend my life in the Assembly and on the battlefield. But after listening to him, and watching him tear people to shreds, I realized I didn't know a thing. It felt like the ground under my feet was shaking. *Aporia* he called it, perplexity, impasse, and he convinced me it was an achievement. I hung on to his every word, and he made me want to be a philosopher. But not like him. No, from the beginning I knew I couldn't possibly be like him. He had huge hands, a stoneworker's hands, and a thick strong body. I was strong too, but my body was gym built. His was just his."

For a long moment he massages his eyes. "I was a good wrestler, you know," he says, suddenly springing back to life. "But not as good as some people think. They say I competed in the Isthmian games. Flattering, but not true. Yes, I was strong and quick—hard to believe now that I'm peeing into a diaper and can't move my legs—but I didn't have the killer instinct. The great ones, like Socrates, they hate to lose. Not me. Still, I loved wrestling. I learned more about religion from it than I did from all the silly ceremonies."

She has no idea what this means, but she fears asking him would scuttle his jumpy monologue.

"When I was young, I wrote plays," he continues. "People say I burned them after I heard Socrates for the first time, but I don't think so. They're still somewhere in the house. Maybe you know where they are. I think they might have been comedies."

"I bet they were funny, Chief."

"I doubt it. I wrote them before I met you," he says. His cloudy eyes mist with tears.

"Right," she says, blinking back her own. "They probably weren't funny at all. But your dialogues do have their moments."

He does not hear her.

"Like when you had Socrates say Meno was surrounded by virtues like a swarm of bees. That was pretty funny. I mean, everyone knew he was a creep. Or when those guys were pushing each other to make room for Charmides to sit next to them on the couch, and one of them actually fell off! My favorite, though, was those two buffoons in the *Euthyde-mus*.[167] Crazy stuff. You had some juice back in the day, Chief."

"Socrates never wrote a word, you know," he says. "As if his thoughts were too precious to go on papyrus."

"But you nailed him in the *Phaedrus*!" she cries. "I love that dialogue, especially when you have Socrates criticize writing.[168] Fantastic! Only you could have dreamed it up. The best critique of writing ever written!"

She squeezes his hand. He wants to do the same, but has no strength.

"Socrates didn't have a drachma to his name," he says, as if she weren't there. "Megacles paid his bills. And he was never home for Xanthippe and his children. No, I didn't like him, and that's why I didn't go to the jail cell. Not because I was sick. You can tell him, if you want."

He places the index finger of his right hand against the bridge of his nose.

She waits patiently.

"My father was wrong," he says. "Socrates wasn't the parasite. I was. I took all I could get from him and gave nothing back. I didn't go to his jail cell because I didn't like him. But I did respect him, which is why I made him young and beautiful in my dialogues.[169] If Speusippus manages to preserve my writings, he'll be remembered. Thanks to me. Not Megacles."

"And not Xenophon either.[170] You may not have liked him but, my god, you sure did right by him. Your dialogues are fabulous."

He makes a sound which could be either a grunt or a chuckle.

"How'd the writing go this morning, Chief?" Artemis asked, as cheerfully as usual.

"Not too bad," Plato replied.

"Still working on the *Agathon*?"

"Yes."

"Well, I'm going to say it one more time, and I don't care if it pisses you off. You should change the title. Agathon doesn't deserve top billing, and you know it."

"But I love the play on words. *To Agathon*. The Good. Of course, Agathon's not good at all, which makes it perfect."

"I get it, but he's not the key to this dialogue. No one else is, really, not even Socrates. I mean, you gave Aristophanes pride of place by putting him smack in the middle. You know, fourth of the seven speakers."

"He represents a serious challenge."

"And he's funny as hell," she said. "And then you had Alcibiades crash the party and put the kibosh on Socrates' ascent passage."

"Diotima's ascent passage, please," he said.

"Whatever. The point is, this dialogue is not like the *Euthyphro* or *Crito* where there's only one guy he's talking to. Or like the *Laches* or the *Lysis*, where the title points to Socrates' target. No, it's more like a chorus. Seven speakers, each of contributing to the whole. Please don't call it the *Agathon*."

He looked thoughtful. "What should its title be then?"

"Why not call it the *Symposium*. I mean, it's a drinking party after all."

Out of nowhere he says, "Tell him it was for his own good." His voice is barely audible.

"Tell who?" she asks.

"Aristotle. I did it for his own good. He should do things his way, not mine, maybe start his own school. I had to push him out of here. He and Speusippus don't get along. Tell him he should move on."

"Of course I will," she says softly.

◇◇◇◇

Although he was over sixty, Plato was still a vigorous lover, at least on those rare occasions when he was in the mood. Which he had been that afternoon. Afterwards they were lying on the couch, their shoulders touching, their eyes fixed on the ceiling.

"You should see this kid, from up north somewhere," he said. "He's something special."

"Yeah, how so," she asked reluctantly, as if she did not want to awaken from a pleasant dream.

"He gets everything, and fast. He's only been here a few months and he's already read my dialogues. And he's been asking me questions about them. Respectful, but I can tell he wants to sink his teeth into me."

"Just like me," she said as she yawned.

"Yes, just like you," he said, and he kissed her on the cheek. "No, I take it back. No one's like you. You're sui generous."

"What's that mean?"

He chuckled. "One of a kind," he said.

"Sweet," she replied.

"But this kid, Aristotle, he's only seventeen . . ."

"Same age as me when I met you."

"I suppose. Anyway, I get the feeling he's going to do something special."

"What?"

"Anything he puts his mind to. He's studying astronomy, geometry, anatomy, Sophocles, and the Athenian constitution."

"And your dialogues," she interjected.

"Yes, those too. You should see him when he's reading. He's completely still, and his eyes never turn away from the book. I've never seen anybody so comfortable sitting in a chair. And I've heard from other students that he stays up most of the night reading. I'm sure his mind is more powerful than mine."

"Calm down, Chief. The kid's got plenty of time to go bad."

"Maybe, but I'm pretty sure he's the real thing. On my walk this morning, I saw him standing next to a plant. Hyacinth, I think. Full bloom and bees buzzing like mad in the flowers. He was staring at them, and he was still there when I returned. Just looking. I coughed to get his attention. He was startled, but when he saw it was me, he nearly ran to my side. Without saying hello, he asked me if I'd ever noticed that bees are continually crossing their legs. I certainly hadn't but before I could say a word he began explaining it to me. He said they're cleaning their eyes, which are hard and weak. Amazing, no?"[171]

"I guess," she said, completely uninterested.

"When he's not busy in the field or with his books, he talks up a storm. I'm going to have to put a bridle on him at some point.[172] But, my god, what wonderful energy he has! There's something about him I can't quite put my finger on. He seems to be, I don't know, interested in absolutely everything."

"Cool," she said, wanting him to stop.

"I could never do what he does. I'm not comfortable sitting, and I can't stand still for hours on end, like he does when he's watching bees or dissecting cuttlefish. I'm too restless and always a step ahead of myself."

"Even with me right now?" she said, as she nuzzled his neck.

He chuckled. "This is as close as I come."

He began to tickle her in the ribs.

"Hey, quit it!" she said, genuinely annoyed.

He stopped.

"Do you remember the time when you had students at the house for a symposium?" she asked, now fully awake. "It was a nice party, but after twenty minutes, you snuck into the kitchen to hang out with me. You sat down at the table and started planning your next symposium, even though there was one already going on! I couldn't believe it."

"I used to hate myself for being like that. You know, always looking to the future. I knew I was missing out on the present."

"But you're easier on yourself these days," she said as she nibbled on his ear. "You're more comfortable. Thanks to me, of course."

He fondled her breast affectionately. "It's true. I stopped beating myself up for not being here and now—as that numbskull Aristippus likes to say—when I came to understand there is no 'now' for us to be in. Time flows from future to past and the present is no more than an indivisible gateway between the two. We're temporal beings, Artemis, at our core, and painfully aware everything we love, including ourselves, is passing away. No wonder we're restless. I guess you could say I've become more comfortable with my discomfort."

"At home with being homeless," she said, and chuckled.

"Writing, you know, is what saved me."

"How so?" she asked.

"When I was a kid, I'd drive my tutors crazy because I couldn't sit still. All I wanted was to wrestle or run around with my friends. And even as an adult, I always read too fast and my concentration would waver. Everything changed when I started taking notes as I was reading. I remember the first time I worked my way through Parmenides' poem. I'd copy a line and then try to explain it in my own words. It helped me pay attention better. Writing gave my hands something to do. It relaxed me, made me a much better reader. Truth is, writing made me a thinker. Without it I wouldn't be able to concentrate."

"Burn it," he says.

His body is inert, except his desiccated lips, which are twitching. His voice is nearly inaudible. She places her ear close to his mouth in order to hear.

"Burn what, darling?" she asks softly.

"The *Laws*. It's boring."

She does not disagree. It is boring and far too long. In fact, she likes, and has memorized, only one passage in the whole of it. 'Let us be serious with the serious, and playful with the playful, and by nature only god is worthy of complete seriousness. And we humans? No more than playthings of the gods, and so let every one of us, man and woman alike, spend our lives playing as beautifully as we can.'[173] But she doesn't tell him this. Instead, she says, "Oh hush. Get yourself better and we'll spruce it up."

She thinks he has understood, for he looks at her sadly. Then his eyes glaze over. She grips his hand even more tightly, as if trying to squeeze the last bit of vitality out of his aged shell.

"*Metaxu*, me and you. Remember, Chief?"

He says nothing.

"Our special word. *Metaxu*. You know, in-between."

He is blank.

"It's how Diotima describes Eros in the *Symposium*."

She wants him to nod, but he can't. "A powerful spirit, a *daimôn* in-between the mortal and the immortal, binding them together into a whole.[174] A beautiful line, among your very best. I only wish I understood it better."

She cannot tell if he is breathing.

"*Metaxu* me and you. We used to say that, remember? You know, when we wanted to go to bed. I loved it. You could be so silly, at least when you were with me. But that was a long time ago."

He stuns her by managing to whisper, "No such thing."

"No such what?" she asks.

"Long time." He closes his eyes.

"Right," she says, understanding what he means. Time, he once wrote, is the moving image of eternity.[175] "We have so much to talk about,

Chief. It feels like we just got started." She begins to weep. "I don't know what I'll do without you," she says through her tears.

A thought, dark and wildly unfamiliar, flits through her mind. Maybe she should plunge a knife deep into her chest and lie down next to him. But it leaves as quickly as it had entered.

"Don't worry," she says. "I'll figure it out."

18

Lastheneia and Axiothea Reminisce

(circa 300 BCE)

Cruel their reward,
For loving wisdom so well.[176]

"You're here," she said, her fragile voice equal parts pleasure and surprise.

"Of course I am."

"I'm dying," she said.

"I know. Why else would I have dragged these old bones all the way from Mantinea to Phlius? I don't care if you're dying. You can still be reasonable. Think for yourself, Lassie, think for yourself."

Axiothea tried to smile. Lastheneia was reprimanding her with the very words Plato had often used during their tutorials, when he was talking only with them, the two women studying at the Academy. He would never allow them to parrot something he himself had written or said. Or to mouth a platitude or use technical jargon when simple words would do. Think for yourself, Lassie, he'd say, the statement meant for both of them, even though in those days Axiothea went by the name Axiotheos and was dressed like a man.[177] She hadn't fooled Plato, of course, although he never said a word to anyone in the school.

◇◇◇◇

When Lastheneia arrived at the Academy, about a year after Axiothea, she caused a stir. Twenty years old, tall, stately, with perfect posture, she walked up to Speussipus, Plato's nephew and personal assistant, and announced, in a strong clear voice, that she wished to speak with Plato. The dozen or so students milling about in the courtyard stopped dead in their tracks and looked in astonishment. At first, Speusippus was flustered, but then he managed to say, "Uh, he's busy, taking a nap and, uh, he doesn't like to be interrupted."

"I see," she said skeptically. Then she told him she would like to apply for admission to the Academy and asked how she should go about doing so.

The students nearly gasped in unison, and they stared at Speusippus, eager to see how he would respond. Naturally, he was fueled by their attention. "You're joking, right?" he grunted, guttural and fierce, his eyes narrowing, nostrils flaring. "What, did you get drunk at the Thesmophoria last night with the other ladies? Or did your husband fuck your brains out this morning? Or maybe it was the carpenter. Did he hammer you too hard? Go home. This is a school, not a kitchen."

Several of the young men in the courtyard, but certainly not Aristotle, giggled nervously. They were accustomed to Speusippus' tantrums, but never before had they heard anything quite so vile. Axiothea, then known as Axiotheos, stood silent, horrified by what was unfolding before her eyes.

Lastheneia's face tightened, but did not quiver, and she calmly replied, "Please tell Plato a prospective student from Mantinea has travelled all the way to Athens specifically for the purpose of meeting with him, and she would be terribly disappointed if he didn't at least give her the courtesy of a greeting. And I would prefer you do this sooner rather than later."

Speusippus was nonplussed. This was the first time a woman had spoken forcefully to him since he was twelve and his mother Potone, Plato's sister, yelled at him for throwing the family's dog into a well.[178] But he recovered. "Didn't you hear me the first time? He's taking his bloody nap! So, get lost, you stupid bitch!" Glancing at his expectant audience, he burst into laughter, utterly fake. He bent over, put his hands on his knees, and howled.

At just that moment Plato entered the courtyard, and everyone fell silent. He was nearly seventy, but with his broad shoulders he still looked like the wrestler he had once been. After surveying the scene before him, he said to his nephew, "What's so funny?"

Speusippus straightened up immediately, like a soldier whose commander had found him asleep at his post. For the third time, he became flustered, and he blurted out an incoherent string of words. Plato grew impatient quickly, and he turned to Lastheneia. "What brings you here?" he asked.

"I've come to study philosophy."

"Really?" he said, and then fell silent. All eyes were on Plato, but his were on the sky above. After a long moment he came back to earth and said, "Let's go to my room." He and Lastheneia walked away.

An hour later Plato escorted her back into the courtyard. He instructed a slave to get a room prepared for his new student. After doing so, he caught Axiothea's eye. A nearly imperceptible smile appeared on his lips. "And pair her up with Axiotheos. He needs a new study partner." He walked away as if nothing strange had happened.

"I knew you were a girl the first time we studied together. And I knew you knew that I knew. You remember, don't you?" Lastheneia asked. "We were reading Theaetetus' treatise on oblong numbers.[179] You helped me enormously, you know. Your geometry was superb."

"I was pretty good, wasn't I," Axiothea replied, her voice soft but assured. "My father studied in the Pythagorean school for a while here in Phlius. Then my brother as well. Of course, I wasn't allowed anywhere near the place, but when my father tutored my brother at night, he'd let me listen."

Lastheneia snorted. "I'm guessing you were better at it than both of them," she said.

"I was. My brother will confirm that, by the way. Ask him yourself. He'll be home this evening."

"I don't need to ask him a thing. You were a whiz, and geometry came easily for you. It was the opposite for me. In fact, the only reason I survived the Academy was because you helped me with my homework."

Axiothea's head sank deep into her pillow, and she did not respond. Her face was much the same as it had been when she was a student. Thin lips and a prominent nose, big ears, narrow puffy eyes. But the rest of her body, once thick, had shriveled. She looked exhausted, but managed an appreciative grin.

After waiting a moment for her old friend to catch her breath, Last-heneia said, "He must be a good man, your brother."

"He is," Axiothea replied. "And his children too. I helped raise all three of them after their mother died, and now they take good care of me."

A fiercely hot day cooled only slightly after the sun set, and so most of the students were outside, talking or reading. Axiothea was no longer wearing men's clothes. For years Lastheneia tried to convince her that a community of free-thinking philosophers would accept another woman, just as they had, however reluctantly, accepted her. Axiothea saw the logic in her friend's argument, and she knew Aristotle, far and away the strongest student in the Academy, would not complain. No, what she worried about was Plato. She feared that he, her beloved teacher, would be hurt if he learned of her deception, and this she could not bear. Lastheneia was sure Plato already knew and told Axiothea this many times, but she was adamant. She would remain clothed as a man until the day Plato died. And so it was that only after his funeral did she come out as a woman. To her relief, the other students were too consumed by grief to pay her any mind. Plus, they were preoccupied by the question looming over the Academy: Who would take over as head? Most assumed it would be Aristotle. A week after his death, however, Plato's will was read, and the successor turned out to be his nephew, Speusippus. No one could fathom the decision. Yes, he was his uncle's faithful disciple, but he was hardly a thinker in his own right. And his character couldn't have been more different than Plato's. Where the Master was even tempered and spartan in his habits, Speusippus was prone to anger and couldn't resist pleasure. Some students speculated that Plato's sister had pressured him into naming her son as his replacement. Others thought, however brilliant he may have been, Aristotle was unsuited to take over the reins. For at heart, they said, he was a zoologist. No one will ever know why he was not chosen. But this much is certain: two days after Speusippus was inaugurated as head, Aristotle left the Academy.

Within a week, life in the school returned to normal. Most students simply resumed their research. There was, however, one change in their curriculum. Speusippus required all of them to attend his weekly lectures on Plato's unwritten teaching. It soon became famous as the most boring course in the history of the Academy, for Speussipus was a walking oxymoron: a dogmatic Platonist.[180]

During this period, the two women were almost completely ignored by their fellow students. Speusippus had not said a single word to Lastheneia since she began her studies years earlier, and the only time anybody talked to Axiothea was when they needed help with a proof in geometry.

On that hot summer evening, Axiothea was sitting next to Lastheneia on a bench near Plato's tomb.[181] They were talking about the divided-line passage in the *Republic*. Axiothea was explaining how mathematical objects could be understood as images of Forms.[182] Lastheneia soon became fatigued by the effort required to follow her. "I'm tired," she said. "I'm going to my room. Want to walk back with me?"

"No," Axiothea replied. "I think I'll sit here a while longer. I want to finish the thought, and I like being near him."

"Good night, then," Lastheneia said.

Axiothea sat alone, using a stick to scratch diagrams in the sand below her feet and rubbing her forehead when she was thinking hard. An hour passed. Then she heard footsteps. Before she could even see his face, she knew it was Speusippus.

"Well, well, well. And how are you this evening, my deary dear?" he asked, speaking to her for the very first time. Overweight and hobbled by arthritis, he walked slowly, and when he stood in front of her, he shuffled his feet and smudged her carefully drawn lines. "Who are you, anyway? Axio something, right? Thea, Theos, Theon? Can't keep track. Confusing, isn't it? Identity, that is."

He sounded jolly, and she knew he was drunk.

When she said nothing in return, he asked, "And what are we up to this lovely evening? Matters geometric, I presume." He looked to the ground. "Oh my, seems I stepped on your nice little diagrams. So sorry, very, very sorry." He scoffed. "Why don't you draw them again for me, and you can explain the theorem as you go along."

Axiothea remained seated on the bench. Speusippus inched toward her, until his legs touched her knees. "Come on, sweetie pie, draw me a triangle. Teach me something. You're the Pythagorean from Phlius, aren't you? Show me what you can do, you scuzzy little cunt."

Axiothea, paralyzed, didn't say a word.

"Come on now, I'm asking nice," he snarled. "But you know me, don't you? Head of the Academy, took over after my uncle kicked the bucket, and when I tell a student to do something they damn well better do it and pronto, and if they don't, well, let's just say I will be a tad displeased, and you sure as hell don't want me to be a tad displeased, now do you?"

She did not respond. Then he kicked her right shin, not hard, but enough to register. She flew up from the bench in a rage and screamed, "Don't you dare touch me! Do you know where you are? You're standing next to Plato's tomb! Don't you dare desecrate his memory, you filthy little man!"

Speusippus slapped her hard across the face. "Bad girl," he said. "But you're right. Sacred space and all that. But I only want a little geometry lesson before I go to bed. Nothing wrong with that, is there? Just one proof and, I swear to Apollo, I'll be happy as a clam. Show me what you can do, girlie girl. Shake your booty and draw me a tooty." He giggled stupidly.

Axiothea, her face burning, hesitated. She hated the idea of humoring him, but there was no rational alternative in sight. She picked up the stick and began to scratch the divided-line in the sand. Her plan was to explain, as fast as she could, how to prove that the two middle of its four sections must be equal. She was bent over, sketching on the ground, when she felt his hand on her neck.

"You stupid cow!" he roared. "If I really wanted a proof, I'd do it myself. What do you think I am? A bag of dirt? Get your fat ass back on that bench," he ordered her. "It's a beautiful night. Let's you and me just sit here and listen to the harmony of the spheres. What d'ya think about that, chickie pie?"

She could not say a word. Instead, she voiced her contempt by standing up as straight as she could and looking him in the eye. Speusippus was furious. He put his hands on her shoulders and tried to wrench her back down to the bench. Operating on pure instinct, she rammed her stick into his groin. He let go of her, clutched himself, and bleated in pain. Axiothea ran and didn't stop until she had reached Lastheneia's room.

The next day both women left the Academy, never to return.

"He was a pig, wasn't he?" Lastheneia asked.

"Who?"

"Who? Speusippus of course."

"Oh, him. Well, he got what was coming."

"What do you mean?"

"You never heard? He woke up one morning paralyzed from the waist down. Every doctor in Athens examined him, but they couldn't find anything wrong. He even had a cock sacrificed to Asclepius. Eventually he became so depressed he killed himself. Poor bastard."[183]

"How'd he do it?" Lastheneia said.

"He forced one of his slaves to cut his throat."

"Typical. But I have to say, Axiothea, this doesn't make me feel any better."

"I know," she said.

"We never would have escaped without Artemis' help."

"Who?" Axiothea asked.

"Artemis. You remember her, don't you? Plato's servant. Beautiful, friendly woman, must have been about fifty at the time. She let us hide in her room when Speusippus was trying to hunt us down. If he'd found you, he'd have killed you on the spot, that's for sure. And then she managed to hire a wagon and smuggle us out of town."

"Ah, yes," Axiothea said, "I do remember. She was kind."

"Funny," Lastheneia said, "I used to think she was sleeping with Plato. I mean, I saw her come out of his room dozens of time."

"She was probably cleaning."

"Maybe."

Axiothea did not seem interested, so Lastheneia dropped it. Both of the old women yawned and soon they dozed off. A minute later, Lastheneia woke up and, without noticing her friend was still asleep, said, "You know, if Aristotle had been head we could have spent our whole lives in the Academy, doing what we were meant to do. Studying. Teaching. Talking philosophy day and night. We'd have made some team. You doing the math, me the soul. Instead, you've been holed up here in Phlius and me in Mantinea all these years."

Axiothea, barely awake and guessing at what had been said, replied, "I've helped raise three wonderful children, and I always had time to myself."

"Did you ever do any writing?" Lastheneia asked.

"No. Proofs were enough for me. What about you?"

"I never wrote anything either. It made no sense. Not after Plato published the *Symposium*."

Axiothea nodded. Only she and Lastheneia knew Plato had modelled his character Diotima on her. Most readers, including all the male students in the Academy, assumed she was pure fiction. It was already hard enough for them to understand why Plato had given the most important speech in the whole dialogue, the one most closely aligned with his own views, to a woman. It would have been impossible for them to conceive of a Diotima in flesh and blood.

Plato chose Lastheneia to be his sounding board. By his lights, he told her, the human soul had three distinct parts: reason, desire, and a third, which he called "spirit." When it was functioning well, reason would issue commands—drink only one glass of wine with dinner—and desire would obey. If needed, however, spirit would assist reason by providing the muscle to keep desire in its place. You damn fool, it would shout, put that cup down right now! The miracle of the human soul: it can talk to itself.

From the beginning, Lastheneia was unhappy with Plato's burgeoning theory. She resisted the conception of the human soul as a static thing divisible into distinct parts. This, she thought, would turn it into a lifeless abstraction, which she knew it wasn't. Think for yourself, Lassie, Plato had often said to her, and she was not afraid to challenge him.

"I wonder if I might ask you a question," she said to him one afternoon.

"Of course," he replied.

"If I understand correctly, you're saying that when the human soul is functioning properly, then desire is controlled by reason. Right?"

"Yes," he said.

"Which implies the two are different. Right?"

"Yes."

"But doesn't reason itself have to be animated by desire?"

"What do you mean?" he asked.

"Well, for example, Axiotheos is a fine mathematician."

"Yes, he is," Plato replied.

"He, we might say, loves mathematics. Especially geometry. He loves the formal relations between lines and figures, which is why he spends so much time studying them."

"True."

"But doesn't this suggest that, in fact, reason and desire are not separate from one another? Without being impelled by desire, reason would be inert. But it's not. It's active and alive. And what else is philosophy, the pinnacle of reason, other than *longing* to know? Striving to understand, philosophers *yearn* for truth."

"I don't follow," he said.

"You've seen animals in mating season, haven't you?"

He flinched. "Of course," he said cautiously.

"They're wild, and nothing can stop them from going after what they want. Aren't philosophers like that when we're hunting down an idea? We want to learn, desperately, and we put all of ourselves into inquiry, which is why we sometimes forget to eat or drink. No wonder we call it love of wisdom, for that's precisely what it is. Erotic."

Plato looked thoughtful, but did not reply.[184]

Now fully awake, Axiothea said, "I still don't understand why he didn't give you credit. I mean, he was the least egotistical man I ever met."

"No, don't blame him! Blame me," Lastheneia replied. "He asked me if I wanted to write about Eros myself. He said he would make sure it got published. I told him no. I wasn't a particularly good writer, and he, as you know, was spectacular. Then he invited me to co-author, but I refused. My contribution would have been minimal. Truth is, writing always came hard for me. No, what I loved was talking."

"You still do, as far as I can tell."

Lastheneia grinned. "And you know what else Plato did? He offered to dedicate the *Symposium* to me. I didn't let him."

"Why?"

"I didn't want the attention. Don't you remember how good things were in the Academy back then? The boys left us alone—Plato made sure of that—we were able to pursue our studies, and you and I talked day and night. And, of course, our tutorials with him, when it was only the three of us, were absolutely wonderful. Highlight of my life, really. No, attention was the last thing I needed. So I insisted he keep me out of it entirely."

"Interesting," Axiothea said, her voice a whisper.

"But Plato, god bless him, did give me a nod."

"Diotima of Mantinea. Same as you." Axiothea nodded, pleased she was in on the secret.

"Of course, none of the boys ever figured that out." Lastheneia shook her head in disbelief. "They could debate like champs and trot out proofs by the dozens, but put a piece of literature in front of them, and they couldn't make heads or tails of it."

She fell silent, embarrassed at what she had just said. "I'm sorry, Axiothea."

"It's okay," she said. "I was a proof gal myself and not at all literary. Not like you and Plato."

Lastheneia snorted and once again closed her eyes. Axiothea did the same. Soon the two old women were snoring. They both woke up ten minutes later.

"We could have been teachers, you and me," Lastheneia said, without an iota of regret. "Maybe we could have started a school just for girls."

Axiothea looked skeptical. "I wonder if we should have gone back to the Academy after Speusippus died and Xenocrates took over," she said. "He seemed like a decent guy."

"He was, maybe. But, boy, he was as cold as a statue. Plato once told him to make a sacrifice to the Graces."

Axiothea did not understand.

"He needed to, you know, lighten up."

Axiothea tried to remember, but could not.

"At any rate," Lastheneia continued, "I never could have gone back to the Academy. Not with Plato gone. Besides, by then I was married and settled in Mantinea. My husband was a widower, and his daughters needed tending. I owed him since he saved me when we escaped from Athens. Gave me a home, servants, time to myself. He was a good man, like your brother. Left me some money. I live comfortably, which, I have to admit, I enjoy."

"You're right," Axiothea said. "We could have been teachers, had a school of our own. For girls."

"Wasn't meant to be," Lastheneia said.

"Sad."

"But true."

"Could have been worse."

"I suppose. We kept our wits and didn't have to wash dishes. And no man ever beat us."

"Even if Speussipus tried."

"We thought for ourselves."

"Did our best."

"Worked hard."

"Always."

"Learned a lot."

"Forgot more."

"It's been a good run, then, hasn't it? For both of us."

"Miraculous, but it seems to have turned out that way. So does that mean we're ready to die?"

"Don't kid yourself, dearie."

"What about Socrates? When it came time he was ready, wasn't he?"

"Only if you believe the story Plato wrote about him."

"You think he might have wavered at the end?"

"Oh my, I don't know."

"What about Plato?"

"No one saw him at the end. Well, no one except Artemis. You know what I think?"

"What?"

"Life is sweet."

"Maybe, but didn't Socrates say real philosophers spend their lives preparing for death?"[185]

"Hogwash."

They both nodded.

"What say we do a little preparing right now?" Lastheneia asked.

"Good idea," Axiothea replied, and she closed her eyes. Lastheneia followed suit. Once again, the two old women began to snore, this time in unison.

19

Polemon Falls for Xenocrates

(Xenocrates: 396–314 BCE; Polemon: 345–270 BCE)

Stumbling over a bronze vessel and breaking his head,
He cried "Oh" and breathed his last;
Xenocrates, that matchless ideal, a man in full. (DL IV.15)

HE WAS AWAKE, BUT still in bed, when there was a loud knock on the door. A servant entered and the look on her face told Polemon to expect the worst. Sure enough, the news she delivered, her voice sputtering, was awful. While walking in the courtyard last night, Xenocrates tripped over a washbasin and broke his neck. He was dead. Polemon nearly screamed, but he caught himself by biting his bottom lip. Without hesitating, he thanked the girl and told her to leave. He held his breath until she closed the door behind her, and only then did he finally exhale. He wiped the blood off his mouth and chin with his blanket and lay still, his mind a blank. Several minutes passed before he got out of bed, and when he did, he felt woozy. He bent over, placed his hands on his thighs. It took several deep breaths before he could stand up straight.

The blow was staggering, and not only because he had suddenly lost his beloved mentor. Equally terrible was the way he had died. Tripped over a washbasin![186] Xenocrates was the most dignified, thoughtful, and moderate of all men, the best of all Platonists. If he believed in the gods, Polemon would have been sure they were playing a cruel joke. Since he did not, he had no idea what to think. Nonetheless, he made a promise to himself: his voice would not waver, and he would shed no tears. In the inaugural address he would give after he was named head of the Academy, which he knew was inevitable, he would deliver one message: business-as-usual. Classes would resume, study groups would reconvene, and the evening lecture series would go on as usual. Because he had been Xenocrates' assistant for the past three years, he knew exactly what to do.

Before leaving his room to meet with his staff, and to get to work, Polemon splashed water on his face. As he was toweling it dry, a memory, as vivid as it was unexpected, surfaced. Years ago a mad dog bit him on the back of his thigh. The other students were frantic and begged him to summon Xenocrates. Even though the wound was deep and his face had gone pale, he refused. It was mid-afternoon, the time of day when Xenocrates would retreat to his room for one hour of silence, and Polemon insisted he not be interrupted. He was adamant, and his steely glare quieted the young men hovering around him. Within an hour, the color was back in his cheeks, and he was walking normally.

Such, he vowed, would be his bearing in the difficult days to come.

Twenty years earlier, the prospect of Polemon becoming the fourth head of Plato's Academy would have been inconceivable. For back then, he was a hellion.

One night, as he was returning home from a banquet in the Piraeus, he happened upon Phryne, one of the most beautiful courtesans in all of Athens. He didn't have a single drachma in his pocket, and she never allowed her clients to run a tab. He pleaded, but to no avail. Just as he was beginning to accept his sad fate, he suddenly remembered he had stashed a few coins not far from where he was standing for precisely this sort of occasion. They were hidden behind the herm in front of a large house. He retrieved them, paid his fee, and purchased several hours of her company.

The next day he slept until mid-afternoon, took a bath, then sauntered into his favorite tavern. His friends were already there, and they chided him for being late. It was hot, and unscathed from the previous night's debauch, Polemon convinced the group to walk to Colonus, where they could take a swim in a cool stream. Because they were not yet entirely drunk, the young men agreed. Before they reached their destination, however, they stumbled upon another tavern, this one with a nicely shaded veranda. Naturally, they decided to stop, and in no time they polished off several jugs of strong wine. Their table was raucous, and no one was listening to anyone else, until Callicles stood up.

"Yo, Polo," he blared. "See that thing over there?" He pointed to a large rectangular structure across the street.

"Course I see it," Polemon replied.

"Know what it is?"

"A brothel?" he yelled. He jumped up from his chair, lost his balance, and fell into the lap of his friend Aristodemus. The boys exploded in drunken laughter, as the few older men sitting at other tables looked on in disgust.

"No brothel, bro. It's the Academy."

The only thing Polemon knew about the Academy was that it was a school someone named Plato had started, and its students were notorious for being dull as dirt.

"So, Polo," Callicles continued, "I'll bet you don't have the balls to go inside."

"Go inside?" Polemon asked, slightly dazed and still sitting on Aristodemus' lap.

"Yeah, bro, like right now. Walk inside. I dare you."

"But don't they have classes or something? They'd look at me like I was a drunken fool."

"That's 'cuz you are a drunken fool, bro! Come on, Polo, you'll have some fun."

"What kind of fun?" Polemon asked, genuinely puzzled. He managed to extricate himself from Aristodemus, stood up straight, and brushed off his cloak.

"You'll get to see the look on their pasty little faces," Callicles said. "You know what they do all day? Read write talk, read write talk. No parties whatsoever. When they see you, they'll freak out. They might even piss themselves or scream like girls who see a mouse. Especially if you're wearing this."

Callicles displayed a laurel wreath he had somehow convinced the owner of the tavern to give him.

"If it's so much fun, why don't you do it yourself?" Polemon asked.

Callicles turned to the others around the table. "Behold, my friends, this man Polemon. He talks the talk but can't walk the walk. Come on, buddy! Put this wreath on your head, and you'll look like a champ. Then haul your sorry ass over there in style."

Polemon, debating with himself, did not reply.

"Come on, Po," Callicles implored him. "Tell you what. You go in, and tonight, if Phryne is available, I'll pick up the tab. But only if you pay those losers a visit and then tell us what happened."

"Really?" Polemon asked, his interest piqued.

"Yup. All you gotta do is walk in, say hello and, you know, stir things up a little bit. See what happens, have some fun, come back with tales."

And so it was that Polemon, a laurel wreath on his head and rather drunk, entered Plato's Academy for the first time.

As he walked through the gate and into the courtyard, which was surrounded on three sides by a colonnade, he looked around nervously, but didn't see a single soul. He passed a cistern and then a pedestal on which stood nine statues of the Muses. Behind them was a building. He was stunned when he entered its large central room, for on all three of its walls were shelves filled with papyri neatly stacked, one atop another. At the rear was a door and as he approached a sound became increasingly audible. When he put his ear against it he could hear a man's voice. He sounded serious, but Polemon could not make out the words. He was tempted to turn around and leave. After all, he had kept his side of the bargain, however minimally, which meant Callicles now owed him a night on the town. But he couldn't bring himself to be small-minded, and so he took a deep breath, opened the door as quietly as he could, and inched forward. Suddenly he found himself in the front of a lecture hall all of whose seats were filled. On an elevated platform to his left stood a tall thin man, bald with a neatly trimmed beard. He stopped talking when he spotted Polemon, but only for an instant. Then, unperturbed by the presence of a drunk with a wreath on his head, he said, "young man, you may stand in the back of the room if you wish."

Polemon could not move a muscle. The tall man waited a moment, then shrugged his shoulders, turned back to his notes, and resumed his lecture, as if Polemon was not only frozen, but invisible.

He longed to bolt, but forced himself to stay. He knew Callicles would expect him to make some noise, or a spectacle of himself, anything to disrupt this all too serious crowd, but he couldn't. Strangely, though, he found himself listening to the man's sonorous, confident voice, and not wanting him to stop. He spoke deliberately, as if nothing in the world was more important than getting it right. His topic was *sōphrosynē*, a word

Polemon had not heard since he was a kid and his grandfather reprimanded him for lacking it. Moderation, continence, temperance, whatever it meant, he had worried, even back then, that the old man might
have been right.

He managed to make sense of only a tiny fraction of the lecture.
Sōphrosynē, it seemed, had something to do with self-mastery, when a
person's reason controls their desire for pleasure. Those who have it suffer
no mental conflict since every part of their soul sings the same tune in
unison. Sōphrosynē is a virtue that must be cultivated if you wish to be
truly happy and free.

An hour later, when the tall thin man concluded his lecture and
opened the floor for questions, Polemon, no longer drunk but still standing next to the door, dashed out of the room. He yanked the wreath off
his head, threw it on the ground, raced through the library, the courtyard,
and the gate, and looked for his friends in the tavern across the street. He
was relieved to see they were no longer there since, for the first time in
memory, he wanted to be alone. He needed to think. What in the world,
he asked himself, had riveted him and made him feel both excitement
and shame? He had no idea, but he badly wanted to find out. And so the
next morning, after a long sleepless night, he returned to the Academy.
He walked through the gate and saw four students, all a bit younger than
Polemon, standing near the Muses, talking amiably. To his immense
relief they did not seem to recognize him as he approached. When he
asked, as politely as he could, who gave the lecture yesterday afternoon,
they looked at him, surprised by his ignorance. For it was Xenocrates
himself, the head of the Academy. And, they told him, he was in luck.
There were still a few seats available for Xenocrates' introductory course,
which would begin the following week. If Polemon wished, he could register for it on the spot.

He did.

In his first month as a student, Polemon, who had never voluntarily
opened a book in his life, was shocked to discover he actually enjoyed
reading. Xenocrates had assigned several of Plato's dialogues, and even
though they were more complicated than anything he had ever read
before, Polemon couldn't put them down. Somehow they spoke to the
elusive longing that for years had driven him to drink, scream stupidly,
dance madly, and invariably end up in bed with women whose names he
could not remember. They brought to the surface questions buried deep

inside him. Why, no matter what he was doing or with whom, was he always uncomfortable? Why was he so restless? What was he looking for?

Polemon stopped going to the tavern with his friends. Instead, he stayed home at night, alone, and tackled his homework. Naturally, he still felt the urge to join the party. At first, this was hard to resist, and when he struggled to do so his concentration faltered. But as the weeks passed, and he began to feel healthier and more energetic, the lure of the tavern receded. He came to relish the early mornings, which he had always detested. Instead of a leaden head and lethargic legs, he woke up with a clear mind, eager to jump out of bed and get back to work.

The best part of his day, though, was the afternoon, for that's when Xenocrates delivered his lectures. Each had a title and a single theme. *On Prudence, On Friendship, On the City, On Fate, On Death, On Memory, On the Emotions, On the Writings of Parmenides.* So much to learn, so much to read, Polemon was consumed and soon became the hardest working student in the Academy.

He enjoyed the company of his fellow students, especially when they were talking philosophy and not just gossiping, which they did too often. The only stories he ever paid attention to were the ones about Xenocrates. Once he was a member of the Athenian delegation charged with negotiating a settlement with Philip. All of his colleagues quickly agreed to the Macedonian's terms, but Xenocrates refused. As punishment, Philip did not invite him to the banquet he threw to celebrate the signing of the peace treaty, and when the delegation returned to Athens, Xenocrates was mocked as having been a useless annoyance. The truth, however, eventually emerged. He was the only Athenian who could not be bribed. On another occasion, Philip's son, Alexander, presented him with a bag of silver coins. Xenocrates kept three thousand drachmas and returned the rest. In his thank-you letter he explained he was only a teacher, while Alexander, who had to take care of vast numbers of people, surely needed the money more than he. Then there was the time when a sparrow, pursued by a hawk, took refuge in his cloak. Xenocrates gently removed it, stroked it, and let it go, saying no one seeking sanctuary should ever be denied. Once Bion was poking fun at him for being so serious, and his only response was to say, cheerfully, tragedy does not deign to answer the mockery of comedy. The story Polemon liked best, though, was about the time Plato and Xenocrates visited Syracuse. Its ruler, Dionysius, furious that Plato would not flatter him, threatened to cut off his head.

Xenocrates intervened. Should anyone, he declared, try to lay a finger on Plato, he'll have to kill me first.

Polemon's moment of truth came on a wet winter morning a year after he had entered the Academy. He was on his way to a geometry class and was walking by Xenocrates' room. Suddenly a woman cloaked in a luxurious purple robe rushed out the door. She looked angry and for a moment glared at him. Then they recognized each other.

"Phryne!" Polemon said, his mouth dropping open. "What in god's name are you doing here?"

"I might ask the same of you, Polemon," she replied. "What are you doing here with all these eggheads?"

For a moment he was flummoxed, but, as Xenocrates had taught him, he kept his cool. "I'm a student," he said.

"You!" she gasped. "You gotta be kidding? How can you stand it here? These, these, these what? Philosophers? They're like the walking dead!"

"Why are you here, Phryne?" Polemon asked in a steady voice, now completely in control of himself.

She flashed her familiar mischievous grin. "I made a bet with Laïs. She said no one could seduce Xenocrates, the famous scholar, and I told her I could."

"And did you?" Polemon asked, even though he knew the answer.

"No," she replied, looking dejected. "Tried my best, but got nowhere. I knocked on his door, pretended to be scared, said I was being pursued by a drunk intent on having his way with me. I even broke into tears. He invited me in, gave me warm water mixed with honey, and told me to lie down on his couch. Which, after I took off my clothes, I did. Then I pretended to shiver, told him I was freezing and needed him to lie down next to me to make me feel safe. He looked puzzled. He had a nice voice, though. Calm. Even. Anyway, he didn't get undressed, but he did lie down next to me and then, well, I went to work."

Polemon nodded and pursed his lips to make sure he did not smile.

"But it was all for nothing," Phryne continued. "Even when I stroked his member and it became hard, he remained absolutely still. I've never seen anything like it. I mean, you were a normal guy, Polemon, and when you got hard, all you wanted was action. Xenocrates, well, his body may have been next to mine, but he wasn't there at all. He's made of marble, Polo, not flesh!"

Polemon felt a surge of pride in his mentor, and he did not hesitate when Phryne said to him, "Well, my friend, what are you up to right now? I have some free time, if you'd like to have some fun."

"No, thank you," he said. "It's a kind offer but I've changed my ways."

"What? You're not one of them, are you? Another statue?"

"No, I am a philosopher, and happier than I've ever been."

At that moment Polemon understood he would never again touch Phryne or any other woman. No, he would follow Plato, of blessed memory, who, according to Xenocrates, had renounced the pleasures of the flesh. He would emulate his master in everything he did.

20

Aristotle, Master of Those Who Know

(384–322 BCE)

He was born, he worked, he died.[187]

"PLEASE, THEOPHRASTUS," HE SAID, his face flushed with excitement. "You gotta take me with you! I've never been on a ship before, and I've always wanted to meet Aristotle, and I promise I won't be any trouble. Come on, you know I'm good company!"

Theophrastus grinned because Menander, abundantly confident as usual, was right. Exceptionally bright and energetic, his high spirits were infectious. And he could be hilarious, especially when performing impressions. He had a knack for imitating the voices and mannerisms not only of his fellow students, but also local merchants, slaves, and even Theophrastus himself. And, for all his hijinks, he was always respectful in the classroom. Still, Theophrastus knew Menander was no philosopher. There was no fire in his belly when it came to truth. He had a promising future ahead of him, but what it would be his teacher could only guess.

Two days earlier, Theophrastus had received a letter informing him that Aristotle was seriously ill and probably failing. Could he come to Chalcis as soon as possible to assist in the management of the Master's affairs, and to keep an eye on his children and Herpyllis until Nicanor returned from the army? Theophrastus, Aristotle's favorite student, closest friend, and successor as head of the Lyceum, immediately booked passage on the next ship sailing north. Now he had to decide whether to take Menander with him. While having a cheerful companion would no doubt make the trip more pleasant, he worried it would distract him from the gravity of his task. He wanted to reflect on the many years he had spent with Aristotle, not laugh at Menander's jokes. On the other hand, as he had to admit, even if he were to travel alone, he likely wouldn't spend all, or even most, of his time thinking about his teacher. No, he would be busy observing fish, birds, winds, and stars. Like Aristotle, he loved to work. Perhaps, he wondered, having Menander around might actually help him stay focused. He could give the boy a lecture or two on the Master's physics.[188]

"It's a long way, Menander," he said, stalling for time. "Probably take a week to reach the harbor in Aulis, and that's only if the winds are right. And then we'll have to hire a cart to get to Chalcis. Who knows what shape he'll be in when we arrive, and whether he'll even be able to talk with us. The letter said he wasn't doing well."

"I know," Menander replied. "But that's why I need to go. I only got to hear him lecture a couple of times before he left Athens, and, oh my god, he was fabulous. I want to ask him some questions. You know, like face to face. That would be awesome! I mean, Aristotle knows everything, doesn't he? I'm sure just being in the same room with him would teach me a lot. Even if he's sick."

"You don't learn by osmosis, Menander. It's hard, slow, sometimes painful and tedious work. Being smart isn't enough. You need patience and perseverance."

Menander sensed the affection in Theophrastus' voice. "Perseverance? Come on, I have that in spades!" he said. "Like, when two years ago I sat through the whole *Oresteia*, all three of those really long plays, and then I stayed for the satyr show too, and it was hot as hell in the theatre, and I forgot to bring food or water, and I wanted to leave, but I didn't get up from my seat, not even to pee, but, oh my god, was it worth it! I loved the last scene of the *Eumenides*. Didn't you? It was like a big party!"

"Maybe, but I'm guessing you enjoyed the satyrs best of all," Theophrastus said.

"Yeah, so what? Come on, I'll work hard as a silver miner if you take me with you. Anything you want—carry your bags, wash your clothes, catch a fish—it'll be done before you finish asking. You'll see, I won't let you down. Plus, we could have some great talks on the ship. Maybe we'd see some dolphins. I heard they suckle their babies like cows but do it underwater, and they're friendly to people! I've never seen a dolphin before. Please, let me come with you!"

"If I let you come," Theophrastus replied, struggling not to grin again, "you'll do exactly what I tell you. And when we get to Chalcis, you will speak only if you are spoken to."

"Aye-aye, captain!" Menander burst into a smile and saluted. "I'll go home right now and pack."

During their first day on the ship, Menander would occasionally glance at the sea, hoping to see dolphins, which he never did, and by the afternoon, he was bored. Theophrastus tried to get him interested in the fish the sailors were catching: mullet, bass, grouper. He even dissected one and gave the boy an anatomy lesson. Why don't fish have breasts? Because their offspring neither develop within the female nor are suckled. Note that the fish takes in water through the mouth and then expels it through the gills. Some fish have only a few gills, others many, but whatever the number, it will be the same on both sides. There are both single and double gills, but the last one on the body of every fish is single. The eyes of a fish are fluid.

"And do you know why?" Theophrastus asked.

"Why what?" Menander replied.

"Why fish have fluid eyes."

"I don't know. Because they live in water?"

Theophrastus, an experienced teacher, shook his head. "Not quite. Because they have to move great distances in order to get their food and they must be able to see things far away. Now, when land animals do this, they are looking through air, which is transparent, but fish move in water, which impedes vision. To counteract its opacity, their eyes are fluid in composition. Plus, water contains fewer sharp objects than air, which is why fish don't need eyelids. They wouldn't have any work to do. Always remember, Menander, nature does nothing without a purpose."

The boy, barely paying attention, nodded dutifully.

"Here's another example," Theophrastus continued. "Fish are saw-toothed. Do you know why?"

"No."

"Because they invariably take in water when they consume their food, and they have to expel it as quickly as possible. The slower they grind their food, the more water comes down their gut. This is why their teeth are sharp and well suited to cut up food."[189]

"Cool," Menander said, even though he wasn't impressed.

"There's one exception. The parrot wrasse."

"Never heard of it."

"It's rare, and why it has flat teeth I don't know."

"Why don't you ask Aristotle, Master of those who know?" Menander said, his eyes bright with mischief.

Theophrastus, realizing his student had no interest whatsoever in comparative anatomy, shifted gears. "You know when Aristotle was happiest?" he asked, hoping to recapture the boy's attention.

"When?"

"During our time together on the island of Lesbos. We went there after Plato died."

"Oh man," Menander interjected, "I bet he was pissed he didn't get the job! You know, head of the Academy. I mean, he was smarter than what's his name—oh yeah, Speusippus. Wasn't he?"

"Of course. He was far and away the strongest student in the Academy, and he had studied with Plato for twenty years, while Speusippus is not—how shall I put it?—the brightest of flames. Plus, he has a terrible temper. Aristotle certainly did not want to work under him, but as to whether he was angry about not becoming head, I couldn't say."

"I heard he once got into a fight with Speusippus," Menander said. "About a woman who was studying in the Academy. Speusippus wanted to sneak into her room and put a dead lizard in her bed, or something, but Aristotle stopped him."

"I never heard that story," Theophrastus said. "I suppose it might be true, but I doubt it. I can't imagine him getting into a fight."

"What about you? Would you have fought him?"

"Me? Gosh, I never asked myself that question."

"I would have punched him in the nose, just like Aristotle!"

"Good for you, my boy," Theophrastus said, amused as usual. "But let's get back to business, shall we. As I was saying, after Plato's funeral, we went to Assos, where Hermias hosted us for a while, and then to Lesbos, which is where I grew up. A wonderful place! A huge lagoon splits the island in two, and it's teeming with fish and birds. Perfect for studying animals. Every day we stumbled on a different species. We dissected and . . ."

"I heard Aristotle used to—what do you call it when you cut up an animal that's still alive?"

"Vivisection?"

"Yeah, that's it. He wanted to see the heart pumping, blood flowing and everything. Man, ripping them apart when they were still alive! That was cold!"

"No it wasn't," Theophrastus said sharply. "Aristotle respected and admired animals more than any philosopher who ever lived. Which is why he needed to identify their parts and learn how they worked."

"How they worked together, you mean," Menander said cheerfully.

Theophrastus shook his head, annoyed. "Always remember this, Menander."

"What?"

"We too are animals."

"Yeah, but, like, way different from frogs and fish. We're the only animals with *logos*," the boy said proudly.[190]

"Correct. But do you know what this means?"

"We talk a lot?"

"What makes us unique is our capacity to reason."

"Oh," Menander said. He was disappointed.

Theophrastus, lost in memories, gazed blankly at the sea and sighed. "You know what's most wonderful about Aristotle?" he asked.

"What?"

"He's interested in everything."

"Really? He sure didn't seem interested when I heard him lecture. Actually he seemed sort of bored, like he was doing us a favor just by talking."

"You heard him near the end, only weeks before he left Athens," Theophrastus said sadly. "He was under a lot of pressure then. Demochares was calling him a Macedonian sympathizer, and he had started to receive death threats. Trust me, you didn't catch him at his best."

"Are all women on Lesbos lesbians?" Menander said suddenly. "You know, like Sappho."[191]

"Don't be ridiculous! The women on Lesbos are like females everywhere. The vast majority couple with males. Which means that, like other animals . . ."

The boy grinned. "Gotcha!"

Theophrastus felt a tinge of embarrassment, but it passed quickly.

"But then tell me this," Menander asked. "Why is the sea salty?"

Theophrastus assumed he was being duped again, but he ventured an answer nonetheless. "The salt in the sea comes from the land. Imagine the soil is breathing . . ."

"Soil breathes? I can dig it!" Menander said loudly.

Theophrastus, exasperated, shook his head and glared at him. "As I was saying before I was so rudely interrupted," he continued in his most professorial voice, "the soil exhales salt which rises to the sky and is then carried down again in the rain.[192] Which is why the sea is salty."

Menander nodded, trying, but not succeeding, to look appreciative. Theophrastus gave up. "You'll have to excuse me," he said. "I'm getting tired. I think I'll lie down for a while."

A cool breeze was blowing from the west and the sunset was glorious, so everyone, sailors and passengers, even the captain, was on the deck. Theophrastus was tempted to lecture Menander on the nature of wind, but he knew the boy would be bored. Instead, he said this: "See those two men sitting next to each other?"

"Which two?" Menander asked.

"Over there," he pointed. "The two having an argument. One is big, fat, looks sloppy. The other is skinny as a toothpick."

"Okay, got it."

"Now, watch closely and you'll see the contrast extends to their characters. The fat one, he's what's called a sponger. He'll do anything to get something without paying for it. I've actually seen him take a piece of bread from someone else's plate. Remarkable! When he's home I'll bet he grabs the meat for himself after he performs a sacrifice."

"But why are they arguing?"

"Because yesterday the fat one asked if he could borrow some salt. The skinny one gave him five spoonfuls and now he's saying he wants it back with interest! He wants six spoonfuls! Can you imagine anyone being so small minded? He's what we call a penny-pincher."

"How do you know so much about them?" Menander asked. For once he seemed genuinely impressed by his teacher.

"I study them. I look and listen carefully."

Menander nodded.

"You see, both men are cheap, but in different ways. The sponger takes as much as he can from others, while the penny-pincher keeps everything he has for himself. Yesterday, the captain dropped a bowl of nuts, and they scattered all over the deck. The penny-pincher spent twenty minutes on his hands and knees retrieving as many as he could, even though they were dirty. He moved barrels, anchors, ropes, just to get a nut or two. But my guess is he'd never let anyone pick up an olive that has fallen from one of his own trees. Also notice how his head is badly shaved. He gives himself a haircut so he doesn't have to pay someone else to do it. And if you get close to him, you'll notice how awful he smells. That's because he uses rancid oil, which the cook throws away, to rub himself.

"Trust me, Menander, before we reach Aulis, maybe even tonight, these two will come to blows, and even though he's the smaller man, the penny-pincher will land the most."

Menander was paying attention like never before.[193]

"Or look at the sailor standing near the stern," Theophrastus instructed him. He was beginning to enjoy himself. "You see him?"

"Sure."

"Can you guess why he's alone?"

"No."

"Because the other sailors avoid him."

"Why?"

"Because he's garrulous."

"What does that mean?"

"He talks constantly. Watch him, you'll see. He likes to tell people what they're doing wrong. Yesterday I saw him explain to another sailor how to swab the deck properly. And as soon as he was done, he began to prattle on about how bad Aristophon's military strategy was. He didn't let him get a word in. Finally the guy just dropped his mop and walked away. Look at him now. He's scanning the crowd, trying to find a new victim. Why, he might even talk to a slave. But he won't get anywhere with that one over there."

He pointed to a man dozing on the deck. "He's a grouch. I've watched other slaves try to talk to him, and he won't say a word. Once someone offered him a fig, just to cheer him up because he looked so miserable. He took it but didn't even say thanks. Another time someone accidentally spilled water on his feet, and he flew into a rage. Imagine! Complaining about getting wet on a ship! The grouch asks nothing from anyone, not even the gods. Do not, I warn you, go anywhere near him."

"Okay, I won't," Menander said reluctantly.

"And the passenger over there, the one who looks rich. He's what we call a jerk. Watch him, and you'll see why. He'll go up to somebody, doesn't matter who they are or what they're doing, and tell them a dirty joke. And if he's not getting enough attention, he'll belch or brag about how much wine he brought with him on the ship. I won't be surprised if he exposes himself to the women who are waiting at the harbor when we dock."

"You're kidding!" Menander said.

"Have you noticed anything odd about the captain of the ship?"

"I don't know. He seems pretty serious, I guess."

"Keep an eye him, and you'll see. He's superstitious. Can you tell what he has in his mouth?"

"No, I can't. Let me go take a look."

Before Theophrastus could stop him, Menander was walking over to the captain. He said hello but got only a nod in response. When he returned, he reported that the captain had a toothpick in his mouth.

"It's actually a sprig of laurel," Theophrastus said. "He brought it with him from Athens, and he keeps it wrapped in a small linen cloth."

"Why?"

"Because it's sacred to Apollo. He keeps it wrapped in linen and he always washes his hands before he puts it in his mouth or takes it out."

"Really?"

"Yes. The other day he and I were talking on the deck, and a sea-snake swam by. The captain looked like he had seen a ghost. Then he closed his eyes and muttered a prayer to Dionysus."

"Wow!"

"And you, my friend, had better pray we don't run into a big storm. For if we do, the captain will sacrifice one of his passengers to Poseidon, and I've heard he prefers young men."[194]

Menander's eyes widened.

"Don't worry, I'm just kidding," Theophrastus said quickly.

The boy looked miffed and snapped, "Leave the jokes to me!"

As he was lying in his hammock, unable to sleep, Theophrastus mulled over his conversation with Menander. To his delight, he realized it was more than an entertaining way for him to capture the boy's fickle attention. In fact, it was an intellectual exercise, one not so different from his work as a botanist. He remembered when, years ago, an old farmer had shown him the differences between fir trees. Prior to that, they had all seemed the same to his untrained eye. But the old man explained that the Corsican was straighter and taller, and had thicker needles and bark than the Aleppo. It also produced more pitch, which was thinner and darker, and different cones too. The Aleppo's were round and split easily, the Corsican's were longer and green.[195] Thus began Theophrastus' lifelong inquiry into trees. He liked nothing more than observing, identifying differences, classifying. And this was exactly what he had been doing on the ship's deck, but with human beings. The sponger, the penny pincher, the grouch, all of them, however unique they may feel to themselves, are actually no more than tokens of a type.

"Maybe," he said to himself, "I should write this up when I get back home."

When they arrived in Chalcis, Herpyllis, a pleasantly plump, middle-aged woman, greeted them warmly. Theophrastus introduced her to Menander, who was exceedingly polite. She had servants carry their luggage and escorted them to their room.

"You must be exhausted. Why don't you freshen up and rest a while," she said.

"Thank you," Theophrastus replied, "but actually, I'd like to see Aristotle right away, if you don't mind."

"Of course," she said, tears welling. "But he's probably sleeping. That's about all he does these days."

He sighed. "So unlike him, isn't it?" he said. "In the old days, he'd stay up half the night reading."

"I know," she said. "I used to hear his bronze ball."

For years, when Aristotle read late into night, he would clench a bronze ball in his left hand. If he dozed off and his grip loosened, it would fall into a metal pot. The clang would wake him up, and he'd get back to work.[196]

As soon as Herpyllis left the room, Menander blurted out his question. "Who the heck is she? His wife?"

Theophrastus did not respond.

"Come on, please, tell me!"

"Stop it, you silly boy! Why do you care about such trivial matters?"

"Because I want to learn about the Master. So tell me. Who is she? Nicomachus' mother?"[197]

Theophrastus looked at the boy and, as usual, succumbed. "When Aristotle's wife died, Herpyllis was a widow, and she moved in with him. They have been in a perfectly proper relationship for years and, yes, she is Nicomachus' mother."

"Was she poor or rich?"

"I don't know," Theophrastus replied. "She may have been a servant at one time. I never asked. The only thing I'm sure of is they are close, and she has been exceptionally good to him."[198]

"Not much of a story," Menander said, his disappointment palpable.

"It gets worse, at least for you, Menander. Aristotle was devoted to his wife Pythias. In fact, I've been told his will stipulates that her bones be transferred to Chalcis and placed next to his grave when he dies."

"You sound like a rumor-monger to me, Theo!"

Theophrastus snorted. "For once, please, do shut up!"

"Sorry," he said, a sly grin on his face.

"I'm going to visit Aristotle now. You stay here. You can read a book."

"Nah," he drawled. "I think I'll take a nap and, you know, see if I have any interesting dreams."

Theophrastus gasped when he entered Aristotle's room. He was sound asleep, lying on a couch, no blanket, and he looked to be little more than skin stretched thin on bones. His face was ghostly white, his hands clasped atop his chest. Thankfully, he seemed to be breathing regularly.

Theophrastus glanced at the floor, but he did not see the metal pot and the bronze ball. He pulled a stool close to the bed and sat down. Exhausted by the long trip from Aulis to Chalcis, he too fell asleep.

An hour passed. Aristotle was the first to awaken.

"Eh? Who's that?" he said groggily. "Is it you Nicomachus?"

Theophrastus was startled. "Aristotle," is all he said.

"Eh? Who's that? Is it you Nicomachus?"

"No, it's me. Theophrastus."

"Ah, Theophrastus," he said, relieved. "You came at last."

"Of course I did."

Suddenly his eyes lit up with alarm, and he lifted his head from the pillow. "Plants, Theophrastus, plants!" he said.

"What about plants, Aristotle?"

"I didn't put enough time into them."

"What do you mean?"

"I didn't take them seriously enough. I thought they were inferior to animals."

"But they are inferior to animals. They don't have sense organs."

"True, but they're alive and as beautifully organized as any animal. They nourish themselves and reproduce, just like the rest of us. I'm sorry I didn't study them carefully. Promise me, Theophrastus, you'll do it. You'll study plants, won't you? I know you like trees."

"Of course, I will."

In fact, Theophrastus had already sketched a book he planned to title, *An Enquiry into Plants*. Its first chapter was an analysis of their parts; both the posterior—leaves, flowers, roots, stem, seeds, fruit—as well as the interior elements of which these are composed—sap, fiber, veins, flesh.[199] He had devoted years of research to this project, and he understood it would take many more to complete, but the prospect of work stretching far into the future pleased him. He looked forward to taking small steps on a long journey, and hoped one day his botanical work would stand beside Aristotle's zoology on every philosopher's bookshelf.

Aristotle relaxed, his head slumping back down into the pillow. "How was your sail from Athens?" he asked.

Theophrastus, glad that the Master still had the energy to be interested, answered, "Excellent. Moderate winds the whole way, and it cooled off nicely in the evenings."

"And did you see anything interesting?"

"As a matter of fact, I did. I got a good look at the tongue of a bass. It was bony and fused to the floor of its mouth, which I found strange."

Aristotle perked up. "Not hard to explain," he said. "The fish's food must enter the stomach quickly or else water would get in. As a result, it perceives little by way of taste. For this reason it does not need its tongue to do much work, which is why it lacks articulation."[200]

Relief coursing through his veins, Theophrastus smiled.

21

Demetrius in the Desert

(350–280 BCE; Overseer of Athens, 317–307 BCE)

> *An asp, full of gummy venom,*
> *Killed wise Demetrius,*
> *Not light, but black Hades,*
> *Darting from its eyes. (DL V.79)*

ALONE IN THE DESERT, he had to work hard to keep himself intact. He would sleep during the worst of the heat, which meant most of the day. Even though his decrepit hut felt like an oven, at least it protected his skin from being scorched. As soon as the sun went down, he would wake himself up and prepare a pitiful little meal, usually no more than lentils and a few dates. Except for a straw mat, there was no furniture, and he had to sit on the floor. There, for an hour or two, he would read one of the two scrolls he had managed to hide under his cloak a moment before the soldiers had ushered him out of his house: the *Pentateuch*, whose translation from Hebrew into Greek he had commissioned for the Library of Alexandria. He had never read it before, but this wasn't why he took it. No, in his haste, he had simply yanked it off the shelf without looking at its title. Now, though, he was glad to have it with him. For it was a book seared by the desert. Like the Egyptian sun, the God of the Judeans would incinerate the eyes of anyone who dared to look at Him. Nonetheless, His

181

commitment to His chosen people was unshakeable. And unfathomable. Why did God spare only Noah and his family from the flood? Because He regretted having created them in the first place. But how could an absolute Being regret, and what reason could there possibly be for the slaughter of countless innocents? Why did God test Abraham by commanding him to sacrifice his only son? Why did He harden the Pharaoh's heart when Moses begged him to let his people go? So many questions but, like the desert, the *Pentateuch* gave no answers. Strangely, though, its silences made perfect sense to him. During the past two years, he had read a portion every evening and was now close to finishing it for a second time.

He had no lamp, so when it got dark he had to put the scroll down. Then, if it was not too cold and there was enough moonlight for him to avoid stepping on the fat-tailed scorpions burrowed in the sand, he would wrap himself in his one thin blanket and walk. Fearing he would become disoriented in the vast empty land, he would orbit his hut, making sure never to lose sight of it. When his legs began to ache, he would return and sit on the floor. There he would doze, dream, and remember until dawn. When the morning light grew strong enough, he would read his second scroll, Aristotle's *Nicomachean Ethics,* until the sweat began to seep into his eyes and his head felt like it would explode from the escalating heat. Then he would step outside to stretch before lying down on his mat and putting himself back to sleep, or its restless semblance, for the remainder of the long day.

During this morning's stretch, he realized that, having used his last drops of water to rinse his face, he had to retrieve one of the clay jugs stored in the shed behind his hut. It was already filthy hot, and he didn't want to walk even such a short distance, but he forced himself to do so. Before he got there, however, he felt woozy and paused. The empty jug he was carrying slipped through his fingers, but did not break when it hit the ground. He bent over, put his hands on his thighs, and stared at it. Yet again he asked himself how much longer he would be able to endure the solitude. The only people he saw were the guards who arrived on their camels and brought him supplies once a month. They were kind-hearted men who were always relieved to see he was still alive, but they did not speak Greek, and he had never bothered to learn Egyptian. He knew he was tough, but not whether he was tough enough.

◇◇◇◇

Demetrius liked Alexandria. Even if it could hardly match the theatres, temples, and schools, the crystal blue skies and brilliant light of his native Athens, its summers were mild and its cuisine excellent. Of course, what he liked best was working in Ptolemy's new library. After years of rapid-fire political maneuvering and crowded rooms, the quiet business of books suited him. Since he was free to keep any scroll on his table for as long as he wished before it was catalogued, he never had to rush his reading. He once spent weeks working through an excellent copy of Aristotle's *The Art of Rhetoric*, delighted once more to be in the presence of the Master, whose lectures he had attended when he was young. For the first time since he was a child, he read the entirety of Homer's *Odyssey*. As he ran his finger over its lines, which he read out loud, he could feel their steady rhythm. He had long believed the *Iliad* was the deeper of the two epics, but in Alexandria he realized how wrong he had been. He labored through Aeschylus' *Oresteia*, admiring the trajectory of its massive plot and rejoicing in its celebratory finale, but suffering through the choral odes whose dense imagery he could barely decipher.

Even though he was over fifty when he was appointed as head librarian, he felt as if only then had he become the man he was meant to be: a philosopher. He read voluminously, advised Ptolemy on what books he should purchase, commissioned translations of works not written in Greek, took long walks, stared at the sea, argued with visiting scholars about Aristotle, and wrote. And he did it all on his own time.

On occasion, especially when it rained, he missed the zing of his political days back in Athens. As Overseer, the highest ranking non-Macedonian in the city, he had amassed great power. His job was demanding, the challenges he faced daily required quick decisions that had flesh and blood consequences. He figured prominently in the lives of many, and he was never bored. Still, even back then, he often wished everyone around him—secretaries, bodyguards, ambassadors, generals, petitioners, and most of all his Macedonian overlords—would disappear and he could retreat to his office with only a scroll for company. Except for occasional dinners with Menander and Theophrastus, his best friends from the Lyceum, he rarely talked to anyone about anything except how to manage the latest crisis.

Sometimes, but rarely, he even missed the parties he used to throw. Because he could not slow the torrent of thoughts racing through his mind at night, he needed to drink heavily in order to sleep. At least twice a week he would bring together as many people as he could into the banquet room of City Hall and feast them with lavish servings of food and wine. Of the latter, he would consume more than any of his guests.[201]

"Gentlemen, we have agreed that the best human life requires sustained, excellent activity. Naturally, this raises a question: What sort of activity is most excellent? You're well raised and thus you know that for a serious man there are only two possible answers: the practical life of political engagement and the life of theoretical inquiry. The former plants us squarely inside the city, while the latter requires us to separate ourselves from it. For philosophers need distance in order to see the world as it really is. We are, and must always be, outsiders. As Aristippus said, 'Everywhere I am a stranger,' and on this point, if no other, he was not entirely wrong."[202]

As he often did during his lectures, Aristotle grinned.

"I implore you, gentlemen, not to be dismayed. Yes, the philosopher says farewell to those most familiar of human gratifications: power, wealth, and glory. Nonetheless, his is the best and happiest of lives. For only theoretical activity is chosen simply for the sake of itself, which, as we have discussed, is the hallmark of the highest good. By contrast, everything the political man does is in response to external demands and aims to attain a goal other than itself. Shadowed by exigencies, interrupted by emergencies, burdened with responsibilities, the future is ever on his mind. Bereft of leisure he cannot pursue a line of thought, or read a book, or dissect a cuttlefish, simply because he finds it interesting to do so. In short, gentlemen, the political man is not free. This privilege, and pleasure, belong to philosophers alone, for they are the most self-sufficient of human beings."[203]

Without looking at his audience or saying another word, Aristotle gathered his notes, turned abruptly, and made a beeline for his room in the Lyceum. The small group of students fell silent until Theophrastus, the oldest and most respected among them, opened the discussion. Gentle but commanding, he reminded them that Aristotle kept his lectures lean in order to force them to think through the argument on their own. "You can't simply write down what he says. No, you must question him every step of the way. It's the same with his books. You have to work your way through them, and it can be difficult. It *has* to be. He's training you to be philosophers."

Even though he held Theophrastus in high regard, Demetrius was barely listening, for he was distracted by another voice in his head, equally insistent. It belonged to his older brother, Himeraeus. A political man from head to toe, a patriot and a lover of freedom, he had resisted Macedonian rule since Demetrius was a child. Even after the crushing defeat at the hands of Philip at the battle of Chaerona, Himeraeus refused to relent.[204] With his tattered band of survivors, he fled to Cape Sunion. There, in the shadow of Poseidon's Temple, the Athenian resistance movement was born. For years, its sole purpose was to torment the Macedonians and make their stay in Attica as costly as it possibly could.

Demetrius was only twelve at the time of Chaerona, and he could not understand why his brother suddenly disappeared once again only days after he returned home from the war. For the next ten years, he barely saw him. His few visits, always unannounced, came after midnight, and he would depart before dawn. He would silently enter Demetrius' bedroom and nudge him awake. The brothers would talk for hours. Mostly, they would argue.

For Himeraeus, the story was simple. The Macedonians were no better than the Persian barbarians who had invaded Greece a century and a half earlier. And just as the Athenians had defeated their enemy and won their freedom once before, they could do so again.

Demetrius reminded his brother that conditions in Athens had improved greatly since Philip died and his son had taken command. Alexander had granted the city a significant measure of political autonomy. Athenians were allowed to make their own laws and manage their internal affairs. Yes, their foreign policy was subordinated to Macedonian interests, but the economy was booming as never before and daily life was proceeding much as it had in the old days. The city was wealthy, stable, and at peace.

Himeraeus snorted in contempt. No one on earth, he bellowed, allows Athenians to make their own laws! Freedom is our birthright! Maybe Alexander feeds you well, but there's more to life than a full belly. The Athenians may be wealthy, but they are also indulgent and self-absorbed. Soon the glorious word *Marathon* will be forgotten entirely.

Demetrius responded by pointing out that Athenian culture was thriving. Huge crowds flocked to the annual dramatic festivals, the Lenaia in the winter and the Dionysia in the spring. The Academy was bursting with students, and in the Lyceum, where he himself was studying, Aristotle was transforming the way Greeks understood natural science. And don't forget, Demetrius reminded Himeraeus, Aristotle once tutored Alexander. The great leader actually respects philosophers. Athenian culture can survive, he pleaded, but only if you and your movement put down your arms and make peace with the Macedonians.

Himeraeus didn't budge. He thought philosophers were eggheads who talked and talked but never did a thing. They call it being rational, but in reality they were but rationalizing their own selfishness. In particular, he despised Aristotle, who in his mind was no more than a Macedonian lackey. But he loved his little brother and knew how greatly Demetrius revered the Master, and so Himeraeus said nothing nasty about him.

Shortly after Alexander's death at the age of thirty-three, one of his generals, Antipater, became governor of Athens. Determined to suppress the resistance movement once and for all, he imprisoned anyone who publicly criticized the authorities, and he executed many without giving them a trial. He relentlessly hounded Demosthenes until the great champion of the city's independence finally committed suicide. Demetrius sent a message to his brother in Sunion warning him the city had become too dangerous to visit.

Naturally, Himeraeus ignored him and appeared in his bedroom late one night. Demetrius was mortified and begged him to leave immediately. As usual, to no avail. Himeraeus was in the mood to drink, and he insisted Demetrius share a jug of wine with him. For once, they did not argue about the Macedonians. Instead, they took turns reading passages from Menander's new play, *The Girl from Samos*, and they laughed uproariously.

When Himeraeus, seriously drunk, finally stood up to leave, Demetrius urged him to be careful. But he scoffed and left the house bellowing an old Athenian freedom song. *This land is your land, this land is my land, from the Pi-rae-us, to Athena's high land; from the wine dark waters, to the towering mountains, this land was made for you and me.*

Himeraeus had walked no more than a stade when he was seized by a squad of Macedonian thugs. Two days later, Antipater himself cut his throat.

For a month, Demetrius did not leave his house. He barely ate, did not bathe, and said not a word to his servants. Some days he spent hours sharpening his knife and fantasizing about plunging it through Antipater's heart. On others he was overwhelmed with shame and tore at his cheeks, his dirty fingernails scratching deep, and his only thought was that he should have gone with his brother to Sunion. Most nights he wandered around the house, either moaning or screaming. Whether with rage or grief neither he nor the servants he awakened could tell.

One morning he woke up and realized he had been dreaming. All he could retrieve was a glimpse of a woman with black curly hair, but this was enough to tell him that for the first time in weeks he had slept deeply. His legs, whose twitching had been tormenting him, were finally calm, and he was able to lie still. The morning was cool, the light was fine, and he did not want to get up. He wanted to think, and for the first time since Himeraeus' murder was able to do so clearly.

His city had been battered and, he gradually convinced himself, the only way it could get back on its feet was to cooperate with the Macedonians. Further resistance and there would be a bloodbath. He knew his position would be fiercely denounced. Antipater's cruelty and his crackdown on free speech had outraged most Athenians. Still, he was sure that above all else what Athens needed was the time to regain its strength and return to itself, and this meant its citizens would have to swallow their pride, postpone their revenge, and work with their conquerors.

So strongly did he believe this that he vowed to leave the Lyceum. He would become a political man himself.

In the first hour of the first day of negotiations, Antipater, bald with hawk eyes, announced that Macedonian troops would be garrisoned in Athens. When he added that this demand was non-negotiable, three of the seven members of the delegation—Hippias, Lysis, and Eryximachus—threatened to resign on the spot. Having foreign soldiers camped on their soil was intolerable. Even the great leader hadn't dared do that. The room began to rumble and so Phocion stood up and asked for a brief adjournment so his team could meet. Antipater looked at him with disgust, but after his lieutenant whispered something in his ear, he nodded and granted the Athenians a half-hour.

The delegation retreated to an empty room. Red in the face and breathing hard, Hippias began to shout before the others had even sat down around the table. "I don't know what you think we're going to accomplish here, Phocion, because we've got nothing to discuss with these bastards! Macedonian soldiers in Athens! And us feeding them! Impossible!"

Phocion, over eighty years old, gestured toward the table. "Hippias, please, sit down, take some water," he said. With an exaggerated display of reluctance Hippias did so, and the rest of the team followed suit.

"I agree," Phocion began. "The thought of Macedonians on our land is insufferable."

"Then what the hell are we waiting for?" Hippias interrupted. "Let's tell them to go fuck themselves before they insult us even more!"

Everyone in the room except Demetrius began to speak at once, but Phocion quieted them when he raised his still strong voice and said, "Gentlemen! Enough! We must continue talking with the Macedonians. You know what they did to Thebes when it revolted. They could do the same to us here."

For a moment there was silence, but then Hippias shot back. "Damn it, Phocion, I don't get it. You say you agree with me, but then you say we should keep talking to these lying shits. Which is it?"

"Both," Phocion said calmly. "Of course I don't want a foreign army in our city, but the truth is right now we're too weak to resist. If we don't negotiate, Antipater will do whatever he pleases, and we won't be able to stop him. Remember, Athens gave us a mandate. To get the best deal possible. And this means our job is to preserve as much of our freedom as we can."

"How in god's name can we be free with their soldiers marching on our streets?"

Surprising himself as much as the others, Demetrius, the youngest member of the delegation, spoke up. "What if we never saw them?" he asked, his voice nearly cracking.

Hippias looked annoyed. "What the fuck do you mean?"

"The Munychia Hill in the Piraeus," he replied. The idea had just come to him, and he didn't know from where.

"What about it?"

"What if the Macedonians were garrisoned there? They'd be miles from the city center. What if we agree to maintain their troops—build them barracks and keep them stocked with food—but on the condition that they stay in the Piraeus?"

"They'd still be on our soil," Hippias said, although this time he was not shouting.

"True, but they'd be nowhere near the Acropolis, the theatres, or the schools. That would be our terrain. And as long as we don't meddle in foreign policy the Assembly could continue to meet."

"But they'd have control of the harbor," Lysis, a wealthy merchant, said.

"Yes and no," Demetrius replied. "Antipater has no shipbuilders. He'll need ours. In exchange for helping them maintain a fleet, we'll demand the right to issue berthing permits and collect taxes on imports."

"But he'll want his cut," Lysis said.

"Of course he will," Demetrius said softly, as if he were talking to a child. "But it's a price worth paying. If we make this deal with Antipater, our ships will have access to every port the Macedonians control. And Greeks will flock here like never before. We may have lost the war but we're still the most interesting city in the world. We'll thrive, but only if we cooperate. If we leave here without a treaty, there'll be nothing but misery and poverty."

"But if there are Macedonians on the Munychia, they'll have their eyes on everything we do," Lysis said timidly.

"True. But as long as the harbor is open and the docks are functioning, they'll leave us alone everywhere else. And, as I said, we can demand it be us, not them, who issue berthing permits for foreign ships and collect taxes on imports. This is how we will rebuild! So, as painful as it may be, I propose we resume the meeting and offer the Munychia to Antipater. I think he'll go for it. At least let's give it a try and see what he says."

The other six Athenians were astonished. With his thin shoulders, thoughtful eyes, and carefully groomed beard, Demetrius looked more like a scholar than a *politikos*, and yet in only a few minutes, he had established himself as a man to be taken seriously. Demades moved that the Athenians offer the Macedonians the Munychia and ask for control of the city center, the reopening of the Assembly, and the right to issue berthing permits and collect taxes. The delegation voted unanimously in favor. When they returned to the negotiation Antipater, just as Demetrius had predicted, accepted the deal.

After Antipater died, his son Cassander succeeded him. Once again Demetrius was appointed to the delegation charged with negotiating a pact with the city's new Macedonian ruler. This time, however, he was its head.

Cassander was a short man, very good looking with an open boyish face, sparkling blue eyes, full lips, and smooth blonde hair, but beneath the soft surface simmered ruthless ambition. Demetrius sensed this right away but was nonetheless hopeful that he could work with such a man. After all, Cassander had studied with Aristotle when the Master was living in Macedonia. Two philosophers talking face-to-face—surely, he thought, reason would prevail.

At first, he was not disappointed. Cassander was respectful, and he pledged to continue most of his father's policies. Macedonian troops would remain confined to the Munychia Hill in the Piraeus and Athenians would retain control of their local affairs. In return, he had only one demand: the agitators, Hagnonides and Demophilus, both of whom had served with Himeraeus in the Athenian resistance movement, must be surrendered to him immediately. Demetrius froze. He knew if he agreed, Cassander would execute the two men on the spot. And yet, the deal was nearly done, and on balance, it was a good one for his city. He shuddered, but he reminded himself his job was to serve Athens, not himself, and sacrificing two hot-heads in exchange for freedom from Macedonian interference made nothing but sense. He moved they accept the proposal. As usual, the other members of the delegation followed his lead.

"Excellent!" Cassander gestured to a guard who placed a papyrus scroll and a stylus in front of Demetrius. He tried to read the document, but what he saw was an unintelligible blur. Still, he pretended to study it. After a long moment he gave up and signed.

As the Athenians were slowly shuffling out of the room, Cassander blurted out, "Demetrius!" His voice was jovial. "There's one more item on the agenda. The rest of you can leave," he said with a dismissive wave of his hand. "But you, my friend, need to stay."

Demetrius looked at him in disbelief.

When only the two of them were left in the room, Cassander began. "As you know, I spend most of my time in Macedonia or on the road, and I need someone here in Athens to be my, shall we say, personal representative. I think I'll call him the Overseer. He'll have a great deal of authority in the city. Of course, he'll have to answer to the commander in the Munychia, but this will be Nicanor, and he's a reasonable man. Aristotle tutored us both when he was teaching in Macedonia, and then Nicanor married his daughter."

Cassander looked terribly pleased with himself, which shocked Demetrius back into his senses. "What exactly will this Overseer do?" he asked.

"In my absence, he will be in charge," Cassander replied.

"A dictator, handpicked by you?"

Cassander's eyes flared. "Dictator? No, no, no, not at all!" he protested. "Your Assembly will still make its own laws, your courts will still have their juries."

"But this Overseer will have, what, veto power over their decisions?"

"Only if he wants to exercise it."

"Or only if you order him to do so?"

Cassander sighed. "You don't get it, do you Demetrius? I'll be far away, and even if I wanted to, I wouldn't able to get involved in the daily doings of this city of yours. By and large you Athenians will govern yourselves, and the Overseer, well, he will oversee."

"By and large?" Demetrius asked.

A mischievous grin appeared on Cassander's full lips. "Of course, there may be occasions when—how do I say it?—my input may be needed. But I assure you they will be few and far between. No, Athens will remain the democracy it has always been."

Even though it will be subordinated to yet another Macedonian thug, Demetrius thought. "But Cassander," he said, swallowing the bile rising in his throat, "you must realize this Overseer of yours . . ."

"He's not mine, Demetrius! He's yours! He will be an Athenian, I promise."

"Everything will change if this Overseer has veto power over the rulings of the Assembly and the courts! The city will be governed by a man, not the law."

Utterly calm, his mind was as clear and focused as it ever had been. A few minutes earlier, Cassander had ordered him to execute two citizens without a trial. Now he wanted to violate the core principle of Athenian democracy. If he wasn't stopped now there would be no limit to Macedonian oppression. His eyes burning, he was on the verge of protest when Cassander beat him to the punch. "And guess who the Overseer is going to be."

"Who?" he replied, and immediately reprimanded himself for having done so.

"Why *you*, of course."

"Me?" Demetrius said, his shock genuine.

Cassander nodded triumphantly. "My father thought highly of you. He said you did a good job of managing your team. So congratulations, my friend, the job is yours!"

Just as he had once wanted to plunge a sword through Antipater's heart, he now felt the urge to leap across the table and throttle Cassander. Himeraeus had been right all along. The Macedonians were barbarians who only understood the language of force. And yet, he thought, nothing was going to stop Cassander from imposing an Overseer on Athens. After all, he hadn't budged when it came to Hagnonides and Demophilus. Demetrius cringed when he realized that, as badly as he wanted to, it would be irresponsible for him to storm out. His mandate was to serve the city, not himself, and this meant he had to make sure the position of Overseer, however repulsive, was filled by the best man possible, someone with finesse, patience, a quick mind and a persuasive voice who could keep the Macedonians at bay. Then it hit him: didn't he, more than anyone he knew, have precisely those qualities? And perhaps Cassander wasn't wrong and Nicanor actually was a reasonable man with whom he could do business. After all, he too had studied with Aristotle.

"I'm going to need some time to consider your proposition," he said.

"I'm sorry, my friend, but time is the one thing I do not have. I leave tomorrow, and I have a dozen more meetings scheduled for today. I need your answer now."

Cassander's irritation was on the surface, but Demetrius did not reply. On balance, the deal with the Macedonian was a good one for Athens. And there was no reason, he thought, why the Overseer had to be a dictator, not if the man occupying the office was genuinely committed to the common good. He could stand above the fray and make suggestions rather than issue commands. He could persuade his fellow citizens, not force them. Careful not to disclose the hope growing inside him, he sucked in his cheeks to tighten his face.

Cassander interrupted his thoughts. "You know, Demetrius, while I won't go so far as to say we're kindred spirits, we both did study with Aristotle, didn't we? And doesn't this mean neither of us has any illusions?"

Demetrius had no idea what he was talking about.

"When you become Overseer, you'll be the most powerful non-Macedonian in Athens, and Athens will flourish."

"And become the crown jewel of your empire."

He nearly slapped himself after saying this, but to his astonishment Cassander jumped up from his chair and exclaimed, "Exactly! It's win-win!

And it's you, my friend, who can make it happen. If you do as good a job as I think you will, your subjects will worship you, and I'll be grateful."

After ten years of uninterrupted rule, the scales tipped against Cassander. His bitter rival, Demetrios, son of Antigonus, captured Athens by mustering the support of its pro-democracy faction, most of them poor. The people, Demetrios proclaimed, would regain their rightful share of power, and the hateful office of the Overseer would be abolished forever. He was welcomed with shouts of joy.

Demetrius was placed under house arrest. At first, he went numb with shock and could not get out of bed. He knew he had detractors, but he had no inkling of the enormous antipathy that had built up during his decade in power. During the first three days following his namesake's victory, mobs demolished 359 of the 360 bronze statues that had been erected in his honor. Most they melted down and made into chamber pots. They left one standing in the Acropolis, but it was there only for teenagers to deface with their graffiti.

During the first few days of his confinement, he slept a great deal. He was surprised he no longer needed hefty doses of wine to do so. His energy gradually increased, and within a week, he was able to stay awake from morning to night. Instead of feeling dejected, an unexpected calm descended upon him. After years of relentless political maneuvering, he could finally drop all pretense and relax. He no longer had to submit to the whims of yet another Macedonian thug or listen to a wealthy Athenian merchant beg him for exclusive rights to a coveted trade route. He could dispense with the ironic mask he had worn for so long.

He read, mostly Plato, and concluded Socrates had been right. A truly just man cannot possibly survive in the political world.

He stopped drinking and put himself on a strict exercise regimen: thirty push-ups, fifty sit-ups, three times a day. For the first time since he had been a student in the Lyceum, he did some writing.

After a month, Demetrios informed him he had decided to spare his life. He would, however, be expelled from Athens and sent to Thebes. At first this made Demetrius sad, but he was confident that, as long as he had food and water, and the leisure to read and write, he would be fine.

◇◇◇◇

After Cassander unexpectedly died, Demetrius had no one left in the Macedonian elite to protect him in Greece, and so when Ptolemy, ruler of Egypt and Cassander's former ally, invited him to come to Alexandria, he accepted immediately. There, Ptolemy promised him, he would help build the greatest library the world had ever seen.

For nearly twenty years, far and away the happiest of his life, this is precisely what he did.

And then he mucked it up, totally. Once again he became involved in politics. Ptolemy's great hope was to spawn a dynasty that would rule Egypt for centuries, but even though he was old, he had yet to name a successor. One of his sons was Philadelphus, whose mother Berenice was Ptolemy's favorite wife. Another was Keraunus, whose mother was Eurydice, Cassander's sister. Demetrius had tutored this boy for years and admired his intelligence, courage, and innate sense of decency. He was not only philosophical, he cared deeply about the city and its people. Demetrius was confident that with him in charge Alexandria would supplant Athens as the cultural center of the Greek world. Not only would the library flourish, but so too would the lives of ordinary citizens. Even the Egyptians, for unlike his father, Keraunos didn't hate dark-skinned people.

As if he had forgotten every lesson he had learned during his career as a *politikos*, Demetrius openly expressed his views. Sure enough, when Ptolemy finally died, and his will was read, Philadelphus was named as his successor. His first act as the new pharaoh was to send Demetrius into the desert until he decided what to do with him.

His head clearing, he picked up the water jug and resumed his short trek to the shed. Its door was small, and he had to crouch in order to walk through it. He placed the jug next to the other empties and then reached down to the floor to hoist a full one. It was heavy but he had no trouble lifting it with one hand, and he felt a spasm of pride. He was seventy years old, gaunt but still fit. Given how little he had eaten for the past two years, he didn't understand how this was possible. Perhaps, he wondered, it was because of his long nightly walks and how much he slept.

At that moment, he saw it. A coiled snake, asleep, nestled against a bulging sack of lentils. In his shock, he dropped the jug, and this time it shattered. Water poured out and was immediately absorbed by the sand, but a barrage of clay fragments struck the snake and brought it to life. As

it began slowly to unfurl, Demetrius knew it was an asp. He had never actually seen one, but images of it had been common in Alexandria. He was
transfixed by the creature. Gray scales, black stripes, it lifted its head and
looked at him with cruel, protruding eyes. Its forked tongue flickered.
He knew he should leave immediately, but he told himself the snake was
too sluggish to strike. He vaguely recalled hearing that the asp actually
feared human beings. He hadn't seen another living creature for weeks,
and so he took two steps towards it to have a better view. What he didn't
know was the snake would feel threatened by his approach. Now fully
alert, it lifted the top third of its body, expanded its neck to form a hood
and opened its jaws. Demetrius was transfixed. "Poor venomous fool,"
he said out loud. He was puzzled by his unexpected choice of words. The
snake struck his right hand with the suddenness of an arrow, and its bite
was hot as fire. Strangely, however, the pain dissipated almost immediately as his hand, then his whole arm, went numb. He remembered this
was the double-edge of the asp. Its poison was the most deadly and the
most gentle, for it kills by inducing sleep. An irony, he thought, worthy
of Heraclitus.

In a daze, he staggered out of the shed and into the hateful light of
the Egyptian sun. His legs were heavy, his breathing shallow. The hut was
only a short distance away, and he resolved to reach it and then lie down
on his mat. He wondered what would happen to his corpse after he died.
His skin would break open, his insides would come out, the birds would
devour his organs. But were there even any birds in the desert? He had
never seen one. Would the scorpions feast on him as well? And what
would happen to his bones when his flesh was gone? Would they, like the
rest of him, become sand? Or would they, bleached white, remain intact?
It would be nice, he thought, if he could ask his friend Theophrastus, who
had once told him that a dead animal was a contradiction in terms.

22

Dromo and the Life of Trees

(*circa 320–240 BCE*)

Walk in the forest,
discover wonders great and small.[205]

THE FIRST THING THE new man did was cut down the stand of pines in the northwest corner. Lyco wants to build a library there, and these days what Lyco wants, he gets. And what he tells the chief groundskeeper to do, he does. He may have a nice voice, but listen to what Lyco says, and you'll know he's downright mean. He couldn't push me around, though, not when I was in charge. I'd been on the job too long, and I was appointed by Strato himself. In his will, he not only gave me freedom—I'd been his slave for all the eighteen years he was head of the Lyceum—he made me chief groundskeeper.[206] And he said I could live in the cabin facing the grove in the northwest corner until the day I died. Which is coming soon.

I watched them kill my trees. It'd been a decent morning, which means I had enough energy to get out of bed and sit on the porch. From there I could see the long saw tearing through their trunks, one by one, and then a dozen slaves pulling the rope and dragging them down. As they were falling, each tree seemed to pause, like it wanted to look around one last time, but when it hit the ground, it exploded. Branches, needles, dirt, stones went flying. Probably animals too. When the dust settled, they hacked it to pieces.

It was a nice grove, a little forest really, and when the sun dipped behind it, my porch was protected by its shade. For years, Diocles, Diophantus, Abus, and I used to sit there before dinner. We had our ritual. When work was over, we would stroll through Theophrastus' old garden in the northeast corner—even Lyco won't dare touch that. We'd talk and pick a few weeds. Then we'd amble over to my porch, where we'd sit with a cup of wine and enjoy the light and shadows, the birds singing, the smell of the pines. Porch time, we called it, and during the warm months, it's where we'd be. Best part of the day. Best part of my life.

Now there's a hole, the sky is bigger, the hills closer, the wind blows harder, and the sun bakes my porch till dark.

Each killing sent shivers through my spine. I didn't blame the slaves, of course. But the trees! My god, they were older than any man will ever be. By my reckoning, some had been there two hundred years, and they cut them down like it was nothing.

Sheltering grove, sacred to Apollo, I always thought you'd comfort me in my old age, and I know you tried. But they killed you, and soon they'll put a library on top of your grave. And none of the books in that library will tell the story.

Damn that Lyco! He picked the best spot on the whole campus. He brags that when scholars come to the Lyceum they'll enjoy the setting sun while they're studying or having a seminar. Fool doesn't realize with the trees gone it'll be hot as blazes.

I wonder what Strato would have done. He was a good man. Never worked me too hard, and he made sure I was educated enough to read. Still, he probably would have got rid of the grove too. Because when it came to nature, all he really cared about was particles, size, figure, weight, motion, velocity, words I never understood.

And Theophrastus? He wrote about trees, but he didn't love them. As far I can tell, he mostly made lists. I once tried to read his chapter on leaves.[207] Round and angular, broad and narrow, spiny and fleshy—it went on and on. Give the man credit, he worked hard, but his book left me cold, that's for sure.

And Aristotle, of blessed memory? I'm guessing he'd have done the same, and you know why? Because his first love was animals. He didn't care much for plants, thought they were undeveloped because they didn't have sense organs. You know, eyes, ears, noses, and such.

And of course he thought only animals could talk to each other. But, damn, was he ever wrong.

Let me tell you a story. One day I found a swarm of brown beetles on one of my pines. I'd never seen the likes of them before. Who knows, maybe they came up from Sicily. They were nasty creatures, hungry as the dickens, and they had already chewed through big chunks of bark. I tried sweeping them away with a broom, but there were too many, and even when I knocked them off, they came right back. I was feeling awfully bad. A break in a tree's bark hurts it like a wound on an animal's skin. Anyway, I stood there staring at those beetles for a good long time, not knowing what to do next. And then, you'll never guess what happened. The whole swarm just moved on to the next tree! I couldn't figure out why because there was still plenty of bark on the first tree for them to eat. So I clipped a piece of the bark and bit into it myself. It tasted terrible, real bitter. Then I walked way over to the other side of the grove and bit into another piece of bark. It tasted clean. So here's what I thought. When the beetles attacked it, the first tree sent out some sort of poison to protect itself. Can you believe it? But it gets better. The beetles didn't stay long on the second tree either, and for the same reason. Its bark tasted terrible. So they moved to a third, and then a fourth, and the amount of time they stayed on each tree got shorter and shorter. Finally, they just gave up and flew away. Back to Sicily, I suppose. I couldn't figure out what was going on. So I tasted the bark of a dozen or so trees from all over the grove. By then every one was tasting bitter, even those that hadn't seen a bug. And you know why? Because they'd been warned, and they'd spit their poison before the beetles arrived! I don't know how they did it, but trust me, that's what happened. So what I'm saying is, trees can talk to each other. Just like animals.

All you gotta do is think about it a little bit, and you'll see what I'm saying. You know how wicked hot it gets here in Attica? Imagine a tree standing all by itself. The sun would bake the ground around it, the tree would always be thirsty, and it would grow up weak and skinny. But put a bunch of trees together in a grove, and they work together to create their own little community. Trees know how to store water, and then they breathe it out through their leaves, which is why it's moist and cool in a forest. When they're living together, trees grow big and strong and can get really old. They're social creatures. Just like us.

When I was a kid, way before Strato became my master, I belonged to a merchant who travelled all over Greece. One day, late summer it was,

we were somewhere in the western Peloponnese and he decided to visit
the Pholoë oak forest. Thank god he took me with him because what I
saw was amazing. It was raining acorns! More like a hailstorm, so many
were falling and the noise was loud. Like a battlefield, I suppose. I wish
we'd been wearing helmets because we couldn't stay long. Anyway, that
night, I didn't sleep a wink. I couldn't get those acorns out of my mind.
The next morning I asked a local slave what the hell was going on. He
said it's called a masting, and it happens every few years. The oaks drop
a huge number of acorns. But no one knows when it will happen or why
some years there's hardly an acorn at all. It took me a while, but I finally
came up with the answer. You see, a bunch of animals—deer, squirrels,
foxes, boar—eat acorns, and this means only a few survive and grow up
to become trees. So the oaks keep the number of their acorns low for
several years in a row. Of course, the animals eat pretty much all of them,
but because there aren't that many to begin with the number of animals
goes down too. And then, boom!, one year thousands of acorns come
raining down from the trees and the animals can't eat them all. More than
a few get the chance to become saplings.

Don't tell me trees aren't smart!

Yeah, it's a damn shame Aristotle didn't pay more attention to trees.
Still, he was the best philosopher who ever lived, and you know why?
Because he loved living things, and he knew nothing in this world is more
beautiful, no matter if animal or plant. Every one of its parts has a job to
do, and they all work together to keep the whole alive. Don't matter what
they are, they all do the same thing. They bring in stuff from the outside
and change it into themselves. We breathe air, fish drink water, trees take
in sun. And the miracle is, even with change going on every second, a living thing stays itself. It stays intact. Until, of course, it runs out of energy
and can't do the work any more. Then it falls apart.

It was Aristotle's favorite word, you know. *Energeia*, being-at-work,
and no matter if it's fish or a tree, it tells you what it means to be alive.

So what I'm saying is trees and animals, they got a lot in common.
But there's one big difference. You know how if you cut off one of your
own fingers with a saw or chop it off with an axe, it can't come back to
life? It's not like that with trees. Take a cutting from a tree and plant it in
good soil and, by god, it grows into another tree. And you know why?
Because the life source of a tree is spread out everywhere. There's root
or stalk in every one of its parts. Now with animals, their life source is
concentrated in one place. The heart. It's like the king of the body and

every other part is its slave. You know how it goes. Tell your hand to move and unless you're damn near dead it's gonna move. Trees, they don't work that way. They don't have a king. The whole thing is in charge of itself.[208]

I thank god every day Strato had me educated, because that let me read Aristotle. But Aristotle, well, I gotta say it, he didn't put enough time into trees. He thought animals were hands down the best thing in the world. In fact, I'd say he thought the whole world was like one big animal. And you know what that means, right? Just like animals have hearts, which are in charge of the body, everywhere Aristotle looked, whether it was the sky or music or politics, he kept seeing the same thing over and over again. Ruler and ruled, higher and lower, better and worse. And so when he got to studying people he was sure some were supposed to give orders and others do nothing but obey. As good a man as he was, Aristotle thought slavery was just fine.[209] But I know in my bones that's not right. Because I was a slave. And I know for sure the students at the Lyceum were no better than me. And yet I ended up a piece of property belonging to another man.

Don't get me wrong, I had a good life. Especially my years with Strato. He gave me a nice place to live and had me educated enough to read, and as long as I got all my work done, he let me do as I pleased. He didn't care when me and my friends sat on the porch and drank wine even though it was still light out. He could've kept us working till dark, but he never did. In fact, I think he liked seeing us on the porch, even though we were slaves. He used to wave when he walked by.

Yeah, I had it good. Still, being bought and sold takes the sap out of a man. Too bad Aristotle didn't see it that way. A tree man could never abide the thought of slavery.

None of it matters now. I'm falling apart. I'm leaking, and I'm cold all the time. My hands used to be busy, and I could run like a deer, but now there's not much to me but these old bones. If I had the energy, I'd laugh because it reminds me of Strato. When he was dying—and I was at his bedside every minute during those days—he became so skinny he didn't feel a thing.[210] He just lay there with a blank look on his face. Thank god, that's not happening to me.

I still have my good days, though. In fact, I had one yesterday. Diocles' grandson, a real nice kid, took me for a ride in the mule cart. He drove it over to my house, lifted me from my chair on the porch, and put me in a little bed he made for me in the back. When he was sure I was settled, he took me for a ride through the forest. What a blessing to be with the trees in the fall! Air was cool and crisp. Leaves on the road, like a carpet, and leaves floating on the surface of the pond. Sun hanging low in the sky, light slashing through the reds, yellows, and browns. And I got to see an old friend. A big oak, its branches thick as trees. The giving tree is what I call her. Like she wants to take care of the whole world.

Add it all up, and it don't come out bad. And truth be told, I'm not even much angry at Lyco any more. He's just a little man who needs to feel big about himself. He wants the Lyceum to be the most famous school in Greece, and he's always busy raising money to build a new library or buy fancy furniture. You get down to it, all he cares about is what other people think of him. He seems to be paying a price, though. Poor bastard, I'm told he's suffering real bad from gout.[211]

Damn, people are smart, aren't they! They figured out how to make the saw, and now its teeth cut through a tree in minutes. They take what they want and destroy what stands in their way, and they build, build, build, always wanting more. No doubt the most amazing of animals! We got ships powering through the sea, plows wearing down the earth, nets catching birds, all kinds of medicine. Development, progress, technology, I don't know what to call it. But I do know this. It don't mean shit to a tree.

23

Epicurus in the Tub

(341–270)

Farewell, and remember my teachings.
Such were Epicurus' dying words to his friends.
He sat in warm bath, downed unmixed wine,
And straightaway quaffed chill Hades. (DL, X.16)

FAITHFULLY HEEDING HIS TEACHER's command, Hermarchus held a memorial on the anniversary of Epicurus' death. The featured speakers were Herodotus, Pythocles, and Menoeceus. Each read the letters Epicurus had sent them in which he summarized his teachings. The gathering, which was held in The Garden, was modest and no more than forty philosophers were there. Most were loyal Epicureans who were living with their circle of friends in communes modelled on the Master's own. They had come to Athens simply to enjoy being reminded of the ideas by which they guided their lives. Some, though, belonged to other schools and came out of curiosity. And one, as we shall see, came to cause trouble.[212]

When Menoeceus finished the third and final reading, Hermarchus opened the floor to questions. The first to stand was Idomeneus, a strikingly handsome older man. As he explained to the audience, he too wished to share a short letter Epicurus had sent him.

Passing a delightful day, which will also be the last of my life, I
write you this note. Dysentery and an inability to urinate have
occasioned the worst possible sufferings. But a counterweight to
all this is the joy in my heart when I remember our conversations.
In light of how admirably you, from childhood, have stood by me
and by philosophy, I beseech you to keep watch over Metrodorus'
children, who are now my wards.

"I have done my best to fulfill his wishes," Idomeneus intoned impassively, "and I assure you Metrodorus' children will be well cared for." He returned to his seat.

Almost everyone in the audience nodded and smiled.

The next to stand was Amynomachus, short and wiry with a full beard and sparkling eyes. He asked Pythocles about Epicurus' hypothesis that thunderbolts are caused when winds are compressed into a cloud and then violently ignited. "While this explanation is certainly plausible," he said, "might it not be the case that fire is compressed into the cloud and is then ignited by the wind?"

"Yes, my friend, of course that is possible," Pythocles said placidly. "Any explanation that relies solely on the mechanical interaction of atoms, is logically consistent, and does not run afoul of ordinary observation is in principle plausible. The most important point to remember is that in explaining a celestial phenomenon you must make no reference to divine intervention. Myths have no place in our science, for they breed superstition, which in turn leads not only to ignorance but to fear and anxiety. And the worst anxiety of all arises through the belief that the celestial bodies have volition."

The audience, murmuring its assent, sounded like the purr of a cat nestled comfortably on a warm and familiar lap.

"Thank you," Amynimachus said.

Hermarchus then pointed to Polyaenus, a tall skinny man. His question was directed at Menoeceus. "In the letter you read," he said, "Epicurus stated that human beings possess freedom of choice and are thus responsible for their own actions. But how is this possible if all phenomena can be explained in terms of atomic motion? Would this not include human behavior? And, if so, would it not follow that our actions are determined rather than free?"

A self-satisfied smile appeared on Menoeceus' face, as it did on the faces of most members of the audience. He explained that, however splendid a summary it was, Epicurus' letter did omit a crucial feature of his theory. "At certain moments, atoms, as they are being borne by their own weight straight down through the void, veer slightly from their linear paths. If they did not have this tendency they would fall like raindrops, in parallel lines, and collisions between them would never occur. As a result, there would be no entanglements, and the natural beings we see around us would never appear. Since natural beings manifestly do appear, it follows that atoms must do more than move in straight lines. Their trajectories must shift spontaneously. They must swerve. Injecting this measure of indeterminacy into the theory was Epicurus' greatest advance over Democritean atomism, for it opens up the conceptual space in which human freedom is possible."

Polyaenus was about to ask a follow-up question, but Menoeceus would not allow it. "Remember," he said in his most professorial voice, "philosophy begins with observations, and to these it must remain faithful. A theory that contradicts the phenomena—and I need only utter the name *Parmenides* and you will know what I mean—is *prima facie* untenable. And that we are the authors of our own actions is the most basic observation we can make about ourselves. For example," he said as he raised his right arm, "should I decide it best to do so, I can scratch my head. And so, my friends, permit me to deliberate whether this would be a proper course of action."

Menoeceus closed his eyes and pretended to look thoughtful. Then he opened them, nodded decisively, and proceeded to scratch his head for a long moment. When he was done, he spread his arms wide as if to embrace the entire audience.

There were a few appreciative chuckles.

"Understand, my friends," he continued, "there is no doubt whatsoever we experience ourselves as free agents. Determinism, whether of the Democritean or Stoic variety, thus fails the first test of good science. It stands at odds with the phenomena."

The audience applauded softly.

"Thank you," said Polyaenus and returned to his seat.

Hermarchus signalled to another man, thick and powerfully built. Mys, a slave Epicurus had educated and then manumitted in his will, stood up. His question was directed at Herodotus. "You said the soul is composed of ultra-fine atoms dispersed throughout the entire body . . ."

"*Epicurus* said," Herodotus interrupted. "I did no more than read his words."

"Yes, yes, of course, I'm sorry, I apologize," Mys stuttered. He took a deep breath. When he had collected himself he continued. "In his letter to you, Epicurus wrote the soul is composed of ultra-fine atoms which is why it is capable of generating thoughts and feelings with such ease. But it is possible that its constituent atoms are not, in and of themselves, responsible for the powers of the soul and that, instead, their form of entanglement is what makes the soul unique?"

"Unique is not the word I would use," Herodotus, exuding equanimity, droned. "Furthermore, your question is not germane. As long as you steadfastly reject the conception of soul as an immaterial substance that can exist without the body you will be safe," he said in his most reassuring voice. "For the belief that the soul lives on after death fuels the fears non-philosophers have of an afterlife in which they will be subject to punishment and reward. But this is an absolute impossibility. For after death, when the soul-atoms have scattered, there is no sensation whatsoever and therefore neither pain nor pleasure. As such, death is nothing to be feared. And since the fear of death is the source of all our worries, eliminating it is the golden key that unlocks the door to a stress-free life. So, my friend, repeat after me," he said commandingly. "Death is nothing to us."[213]

"Death is nothing to us," Mys dutifully replied, as did most of the audience.

Suddenly a short squat man, his face concealed by a black scarf, jumped out of his seat and ran to the podium where he shoved Herodotus, who tumbled to the ground. "Death is nothing to us!" he roared. "What a crock!" He tore off his scarf off and tossed it aside. The crowd, recognizing his pockmarked face, gasped. It was Timocrates, the apostate.

"Listen to me, you self-satisfied morons, if you actually believe this shit you're in worse shape than even I imagined. Because if death means nothing to you, then neither does life. For they go hand-in-hand, and if you take away one, you take away the other. And so if you really believe the only two things that exist are atoms and the void, then everything— your family, your city, friends, enemies, love, hate, sex, sickness, death— becomes the same, and nothing is special, and nothing matters, and nothing's worth caring about. Epicurus convinced you that if you take this shit seriously you'll be happy. But his kind of happiness is disgusting. It turns you into babies sucking at their momma's teats."

Herodotus, who was still on the ground, was startled by the image.

"I ought to know, goddamn it, I ought to know, because I spent years studying in this place until I couldn't take it any more. My brother, Metrodorus, he stayed, and if he hadn't died young, he'd have been the one to succeed Epicurus, not Hermarchus."

Knowing this was true, Hermarchus winced. Almost immediately, however, he resumed smiling.

"I tell you one thing, though. My brother's death meant nothing to Epicurus, even though he always said Metrodorus was his most devoted student and closest friend. The man didn't shed a single tear, and of course he didn't give him a funeral, and you know why? Because he didn't give a shit about him, and you know why? Because he didn't give a shit about anyone. Atoms and the void, his whole world. You pinheads love to talk about how good he was to his parents, how gentle he was to his slaves, how much he cared about his friends, but the truth is he didn't have friends, not real ones anyway. How could he? The only thing he cared about was feeling good, which for him meant living peacefully, without stress or fear or anxiety. But, damn it, don't you see? If you really love somebody, you're going to feel stress and lots of it. If they get sick, you get scared, if they move away you miss them, and if they die, you cry. Did you hear me? If they die, *you cry!* And cry is what you *should* do because it's what being a friend is all about. Becoming vulnerable. But Epicurus, he wanted no part of it. Oh sure, he went around yapping about how great friendship was. You remember his line, don't you? *Friendship dances around the world, proclaiming to us all to wake up and congratulate one another.* What a crock! He didn't care about Metrodorus one bit because if he had he would have given him a funeral and cried. No, he didn't about care anybody else, just his own precious self."

Choking on his anger, he began to cough.

Herodotus, still on the ground, wondered what caused Timocrates' atoms to have gotten so thoroughly out of whack. He tried to concentrate his mind on this question, but as if of its own volition, it kept coming back to the image of his mother's teat.

When he finally ceased coughing, Timocrates resumed his tirade. "When Metrodorus died, I wept for two days straight. And you know why? Because I loved him. But I hated what he had become. You people ruined my brother! When he was a kid, he was smart and funny and sweet and kind, and even though he was younger than me, I used to love playing with him. And then you turned him into a self-absorbed prune who walked around this god-forsaken Garden muttering to himself!"

His arm trembling, Timocrates pointed at Idomeneus. "And where did Epicurus get off thinking he had the right to hand over Metrodorus' children to you?"

Idomeneus smiled.

"Don't you understand, you little piece of snot, they're my flesh-and-blood. They belong to *me!* His daughter Danaë is my niece, and even though he named his son Epicurus, the kid is still my nephew, and when I get custody of him—which, I promise you, I will—I'm going to change his name to Athenaeus, which was our father's name, and make sure he never goes near this place again. I'm going to raise those kids to be human beings not ghosts."

The prospect of a lawsuit made Hermarchus grit his teeth. With a tilt of his head, he signalled to Mys it was time to take action. Mys understood. Stepping over Herodotus, he walked to the speaker's platform and with his massive hand took Timocrates by the arm and tried to yank him away. Timocrates slapped him across the face. Rather than becoming angry, Mys became even more determined. He grabbed Timocrates' wrists and pulled hard. Then he spun him around, wrapped him in a bear hug, lifted him off the ground and began to carry him to the door. Timocrates was kicking his feet and sputtering in rage. "Drunk as a skunk, that's what he was! He died in a tub—in a tub!—which is where all you assholes belong! I hate this Garden, and I hate all of you, and I'm going to get my kids back before you brainwash them like you did to Metrodorus! You hear me? I'm gonna get my kids back! So you'd better watch out, you motherfuckers, you haven't seen the last of me, not yet."[214]

Endnotes

1. For the Greek text of Diogenes Laertius, I have used *Lives of Eminent Philoso-phers*, edited by Jeffrey Henderson. I have consulted two translations: one by Hicks (in the Henderson edition), the other by Mensch, which is titled *Lives of the Eminent Philosophers*. In either quoting from or referring to Diogenes Laer-tius, I will use the abbreviation "DL" followed by the book and section numbers. In a direct quotation, I will indicate which of the two translations I am citing.
    A less formal translation of the title of Diogenes Laertius' book, which in Greek is *Biōn kai Gnōmōn tōn Philosophiai Eudokimēsantōn* is suggested by D. S. Hutchinson, "Lives and Sayings of Famous Philosophers" (Introduction to *The Epicurus Reader*, xv). My own title follows Hutchinson. According to Miller, "experts have tentatively concluded that [DL] lived in the first half of the third century AD" (Miller, *Lives of the Eminent Philosphers*, x).
2. Diogenes divides Greek philosophy into two "parallel but distinct traditions, which flourished in two different regions of ancient Greece, one in Ionia in the East, the other in Italy and Sicily in the West. Accordingly, the 'Ionian suc-cession' occupies one part of the work (Books 2 to 7), while the 'Italian suc-cession' takes up another (Books 8 to 10)" (Laks, "Diogenes Laertius and the Pre-Socratics," 589). I take my bearings from, but do not rigidly adhere to, the order of DL's biographies.
3. Long, "Introduction," xix.
4. Brennan, *Stoic Life*, 17.
5. Brennan, *Stoic Life*, 18.
6. DL VIII.69, Mensch translation.
7. DL IX.26–28.
8. Rowland, "Raphael's Eminent Philosophers," in Miller, *Lives of the Eminent Phi-losophers*, 561. Hölderlin's unfinished poem, "The Death of Empedocles," was written (in three versions) around 1800. Arnold's "Empedocles on Etna" was published in 1852. Marcel Schwob's *Imaginary Lives* was originally published in 1896.
9. As DL states in I.63, he wrote a book titled *Pammetros* in which "I discourse about all the illustrious dead in all meters and rhythms in the form of epigrams and lyrics."
10. See Chitwood, *Death by Philosophy*; Grau, "How to Kill a Philosopher."
11. Dudley, *History of Cynicism*, 8.
12. The relevant text in DL is VI.21.

13.   Geraldine Brooks attributes this remark to Styron in her review of *Hamnet* in the *New York Times Book Review* (July 19, 2020), 1.

14.   The Thales material is in DL I.22–41. Anaximander's and Anaximenes' (minimal) biographical sketches are in DL II.1–5. Many of the dates I give of a famous philosopher's life are approximate. Some, such as these three, are close to being guesses. They are all BCE. Note that DL claims that "philosophy started with Anaximander," even though he also states that "Anaximander was a pupil of Thales" (DL I.13). DL thinks of Thales as more of a sage than a philosopher.

15.   In many of his chapters, DL composes an epitaph for his dead philosopher. I will use these as epigraphs for most of my own chapters. Unless otherwise indicated, I will cite Mensch's translation.

16.   See Aristotle, *On the Heavens*, 294a10–295b25.

17.   "He is said to have been the first to demonstrate that a circle is bisected by its diameter. . . . There is good evidence that Thales predicted a solar eclipse which took place on May 28, 585 BC." Heath, *History of Greek Mathematics*, 130, 137. For more on the eclipse see Herodotus, *Histories*, I.74.

18.   See Aristotle's *Metaphysics*, I.4; DL I.27.

19.   "Anaximander was called the 'successor and pupil' of Thales by Theophrastus." Kirk et al., *Presocratic Philosophers*, 101. Also see Roochnik, *Retrieving the Ancients*, 17–24.

20.   Plato tells a somewhat different version of this story at *Theaetetus* 174a.

21.   Aristotle, *Politics* 1259a10–20; DL I.27.

22.   The *archon* was the chief magistrate in Athens.

23.   The story of Aphrodite's birth is told in Hesiod's *Theogony*, 176–206.

24.   The DL stories about Solon are found in I.45–67.

25.   In what follows I am probably exaggerating how bad Pisistratus was. In fact, Herodotus states that as tyrant he "governed the city in an orderly and excellent manner" (I.59), while in DL I.53, we are told that after he assumed power he continued to abide by Solon's laws. At I.67, DL includes a letter from Solon to Pisistratus in which he calls him the "best of tyrants."

26.   The Greek of "end of his life" is *teleutē tou biou*: I.30. So much of this story, and of Aristotle's reading of it in Book I.10 of his *Nicomachean Ethics*, hinges on the ambiguity of the word *telos*. It is best translated as "end," which can mean both "cessation" as well as "goal" or "purpose."

27.   *Odyssey* IV.254. This is Fitzgerald's translation.

28.   DL I.62. I follow Hicks here.

29.   See Riedweg, *Pythagoras*, 2.

30.   DL VIII.11. For Pythagoras' belief in the transmigration of souls, see DL VIII.36.

31.   Reported in "Iamblichus' Life of Pythagoras." See Guthrie, *Pythagorean Sourcebook*, 36–40.

32.   There are no surviving writings by Pythagoras. This is from the later Pythagorean, Philolaus. It is fragment B6 in Diels and Kranz, *Fragmente*. Hereafter all citations from this work will be indicated simply by DK and the fragment number. Here I am following McKirahan's translation in Curd, *Presocratics Reader*, 88.

33.   Pythagoras' supposed teachers are named at DL VIII.2–3.

34.   DL VIII.10.

35.   See Plato's *Republic*, 617b.

36.   See Aristotle's *Metaphysics*, 987b12.

37.   DL VIII.25.

38. Philolaus, DK B4. Galileo famously declared that book of nature was written in mathematical characters.

39. DL VIII.14. See the "affinity argument" in Plato's *Phaedo*, 78b–84b.

40. Ovid, *Metamorphoses*, XV.80–90.

41. DL VIII.39 and 24. I follow Mensch in the latter.

42. DL VIII.9, 24, 14.

43. DL IX.1–14 is the basis of many of the stories in this chapter.

44. DK B121.

45. The Heraclitean fragments from DK cited below are, in the order they appear, 73, 34, 10, 8, 60, 123, 13, 4, 97, 37.

46. See Aristotle *Nicomachean Ethics*, 1176a7.

47. DK B52. The Greek here for "child playing" is the alliterative *pais paizōn*. Fragments below are DK B64, B53, B124, B57, B121.

48. DK B36.

49. DK B66.

50. Nietzsche, *Philosophy in the Tragic Age of the Greeks*, 52.

51. DK B62.

52. I wrote this epigraph myself.

53. DK B1.1–5, 24–30. I follow, with some modifications, the Wheelwright's translation in his *The Presocratics*. Zeno is described both as Parmenides' student and his "beloved" (*paidika*) at DL IX.25. The word *doxa* is often translated as "belief" or "opinion," but it can also have a broader meaning: "appearance" or "the way things seem to be."

54. DL IX.21

55. The ancient Greek city of Elea was located near what is now the town of Ascea, which is in southwestern Italy.

56. DK B3.

57. DK B13.

58. "The same conjunction of the high and low which, in the living being, Nature naively expresses when it combines the organ of its highly fulfillment, the organ of generation, with the organ of urination." Hegel, *Phenomenology of Spirit*, 210.

59. I rely here on Huggett, "Zeno's Paradoxes." DL mentions Zeno's "Achilles" at IX.29.

60. DL IX. 26.

61. Sotion, who apparently flourished around 200 BCE, was a Greek biographer, and an importance source for DL. My use of him here is an obvious anachronism. Anaxagoras stories can be found in DL II.13–19.

62. See Plato, *Apology* 18c.

63. For this speech I cobbled together DK fragments B1, B4, B6, B12, B13, B17.

64. DK B3.

65. For centuries what we now call "natural science" was called "natural philosophy." DL uses this phrase (*tēn physikēn philosophian*) at II.16.

66. See DK B18 and B22, as well as DL II.17 for these sorts of physical explanations.

67. For my story of Socrates and Archelaus, I drew on Plato's *Phaedo*, 96b–98d.

68. DL uses the word *paidika*, usually meaning the younger and passive partner of a pederastic relationship at II.19.

69. See Thucydides, II.47–53 for a vivid, and harrowing, description of the plague. In his mention of Pericles' death in II.65, DL does not attribute Pericles' death to the plague. Samons says that Pericles "lost his sons . . . to the horrible disease" and "perhaps" died "from complications brought on by the plague." Samons, *Pericles and the Conquest of History*, 166, 178.

70. For Anaximenes, see DL II.6.

71. See Samons, *Pericles and the Conquest of History*, 192–95, for Pericles' relationship with Anaxagoras.

72. The DL source material for the stories in this chapter is VIII.56–75. Chitwood, *Death by Philosophy*, 58, mentions the distance to Etna and argues that Empedocles could not possibly have walked there.

73. Pausanias was Empedocles' *eromenos*, euphemized by Hicks as "bosom-friend" in VIII.60. Mensch's "beloved" is better. At VIII.61, DL says Pausanias was a doctor. I've turned him into a *hausfrau*.

74. "Wind-stayer" is from Hicks. Mensch goes with "Wind-Checker."

75. This Empedoclean material comes from DK B6, B8, B17, B96. Also see DL XIII.76.

76. Matthew Arnold, in his "Empedocles on Etna," has his character Callicles say this: "... 'twas no miracle! / Pantheia, for I know her kinsmen well, / Was subject to these trances from a girl. / Empedocles would say so, did he deign; / But he still lets the people, whom he scorns, / Gape and cry wizard at him, if they list." In Arnold's telling, one reason Empedocles commits suicide is because he is exhausted by just this sort of social pressure. People thought he was a healer.

77. Hicks' translation of *paides akolouthoi* as "a train of boy attendants" seems better than Mensch's "retinue of slaves." My "boy band" is, obviously, a stretch.

78. DK B111 and B112. The translations are those of McKirahan in Curd, *Presocratics Reader*.

79. The phrase "Pausanias paused" (*Pausaniou de pausamenou*) is found in Plato's *Symposium* 185c. Plato's Pausanias is not the same as the one appearing in DL's story.

80. I have altered Mensch's translation of DL's epitaph in order to connect it more intelligibly to the story that follows.

81. DL IX.43.

82. A key word for Democritus is *euthymia*, often translated as "good cheer." See DL IX.45 as well as DK B189 and B191.

83. The Greek *deisidaimonia*, "fear of the gods," is found at DL IX.45.

84. Chitwood, *Death by Philosophy*, 139 fleshes out Democritus' views on respiration by discussing DK 68a106 as well several remarks Aristotle makes about him at *De Anima* 406b and *On Respiration* 471b.

85. DL IX.34. See also Herodotus VII.109 and VIII.120.

86. DL IX.35.

87. Most of this material about Egypt comes from Herodotus II.

88. The Greek *geometria* literally means "earth/land measurement." In Book I.3 of the *Metaphysics*, Aristotle attributes the origin of the mathematical sciences to the Egyptian priests who, he says, had leisure.

89. The Greeks regularly identified Egypt as the oldest of cultures. In Plato's *Timaeus* 22b, it is stated that to the Egyptian the Greek is but a child.

90. For a contemporary explanation of this procedure, see http://math.buffalo.eduamad/AncientAfrica/mad_ancient_egypt_geometry.html#moscow10.

91. See Herodotus III.20 and II.29.

92. See Thucydides I.137.

93. See Herodotus III.38 and III.100–101.

94. *Maya* refers to the Hindu concept of the phenomenal or sensible world as an illusion.

95. In the opening scene of Plato's *Phaedo* why Socrates' execution was delayed is explained.

96.   The stories about Socrates at Potideia come from Alcibiades in Plato's *Sympo-sium*. The night at Cephalus' house refers to the *Republic*. The "crazy party" at Agathon's is also from the *Symposium*.

97.   See *Crito* 45c and 52b. Except for military service, Socrates never left Athens. See *Crito* 51b for the "persuade or obey" principle.

98.   Plato's *Apology of Socrates* 36d; DL II.42: Socrates proposed that his punishment be lodging in the Prytaneum, the "town hall" of ancient Athens.

99.   See Plato's *Apology* 24b, 36b, 36d, 30e.

100.   See Aristophanes' *Lysistrata* (1093–1094). Thucydides tells us much about Al-cibiades' advocating the invasion of Syracuse (VI.15–18), the profanation of the herms (VI.27–28), his flight to Sparta and betrayal of Athens (VI.61 and 74).

101.   DL II.23.

102.   Plato's *Symposium* 216e: Alcibiades says that Socrates "is ironic and plays with human beings." At 217b Alcibiades asks Socrates to interrupt him if anything he says is not true. Socrates does not interrupt.

103.   These stories are based on Plato's *Euthyphro* 5a, where Socrates says he wishes to become Euthyphro's pupil; the second half of Book I of Plato's *Republic*, which depicts Socrates' extended refutation of Thrasymachus; and DL II.62.

104.   After hearing Socrates' magnificent "palinode" and praise of Eros, Phaedrus, rather than asking any questions, only wants to bring the conversation back to what interests him: Lysias. See Plato's *Phaedrus* 257c.

105.   After hearing Socrates' "theory of recollection," which is both remarkably rich and manifestly problematic, Meno too fails to ask a single question. Instead, he rather stupidly reiterates his lead question: Can virtue be taught? See Plato's *Meno* 86c.

106.   Late in the *Gorgias*, Callicles becomes exhausted with Socrates' incessant ques-tioning and falls silent. Socrates is left to complete the dialogue on his own. See *Gorgias* 505d.

107.   Plato goes to great lengths in his *Theaetetus* to paint a picture of the eponymous character. He became a significant mathematician whose work is likely reflected in Euclid's *Elements*.

108.   See *Phaedo* 116d for Socrates' description of the guard.

109.   DL describes Socrates as *autarkēs*, "self-sufficient," at II.24.

110.   See *Phaedrus* 274c–276c.

111.   The phrase an "education for Greece" comes from Perciles' "Funeral Oration" in Book II of Thucydides.

112.   DL II.37

113.   Plato's *Phaedo* 60b: Xanthippe, who has spent the night with Socrates in his jail cell, says to him "Oh Socrates, this is the last time you and your friends will converse." Far from seeming like the legendary shrew, here she seems most concerned about her husband and his happiness. In one of his more poignant remarks, Socrates, at Plato's *Lysis* 22e–212a, says that he has a strong "love for the possession of friends" but in fact does not have any.

114.   Consider the story of Socrates' abstention from the Leon of Salamis affair as re-lated in Plato's *Apology* 32c–d. Critias figures prominently in Plato's *Charmides*, as does Charmides himself. At II.29, DL says Socrates encourages Charmides to go into politics.

115.   DL says Socrates was the first to "converse about human life" (*peri biou*)" (II.20), rather than nature or Being.

116.   Erinna is fictional. These words come from Hilary Mantel's *Bring Up the Bodies*, 331.

117. Socrates' dream is recounted in the *Phaedo* 60e–61b. What I render as "art" is the Greek word *mysikē*, whose meaning is much broader than our "music."

118. Socrates lays into Homer especially in Books II and III of Plato's *Republic*.

119. The line is from I. B. Singer, *Collected Stories*, viii.

120. Xenophon in his *Apology of Socrates* (6–7) puts these words into his mouth: "if I just let the years go on and on, I know the ravages of old age will surely come upon me. My vision and hearing will get worse, learning will become more difficult for me, and I will start to forget what I had always known. And if I am aware of my deteriorating condition I will hate myself. How, then, could I live with any pleasure at all? Perhaps the god in his graciousness will not only protect me by ending my life at the right time, but also in the easiest way."

121. The "Equal Itself," one of Plato's Forms, appears at 74a of the *Phaedo*; "Tallness Itself" at 100d–e.

122. This is not one of DL's epitaphs, but it is a line he gives to Aristippus when he is putting on a dress. I use the Hicks translation.

123. Plato has Phaedo, the narrator of his *Phaedo*, report that Plato was not present in the prison cell on the day Socrates was executed because "I think, he was ill" (59c). The "I think" (*oimai*) is telling.

124. See *Phaedo* 64d.

125. In his description of himself as a "midwife" in Plato's *Theaetetus* (151b), Socrates explains that when he encounters someone who does not seem "pregnant" with philosophical possibility, he sends them off to Prodicus, a noted Sophist. DL II.65 states that Aristippus was the "first of the followers of Socrates to charge a fee," a practice associated with the Sophists. Plato, Xenophon (*Memorabilia* I.2.60), and DL all agree that Socrates himself never accepted payment.

126. Socrates describes himself as a "gadfly" at *Apology* 30e. Aristodemus is described at *Symposium* 173a.

127. The story of how the friendship between Aeschines and Aristippus began is told at DL II.83. That of Laïs and Aristippus is found at DL II.74. The Cyrenaic school of Hedonism, founded by Aristippus, puts its emphasis on "particular pleasures" experienced bodily and in the moment. See DL II.30 for the phrase "about life" (*peri biou*), which is attributed to Socrates. The DL source of the stories in this chapter come from II.66–88. Dionysius I (432–357 BCE) was the ruler of the Greek city Syracuse, which is in Sicily.

128. See Plato's *Apology* 38a.

129. See Xenophon's *Memorabilia* Book II.i.11 for Aristippus' identification of freedom (*eleutheria*) with happiness (*eudaimonia*). See II.i.13 for Aristippus' statement that he is a "stranger (*xenos*) everywhere."

130. DL's biography of Stilpo is found in II.113–20. In it we read that he had a "profligate daughter" who was married to a man named Simmias and did not "play by the rules" (II.114). That Stilpo forgave her is suggested by his rejoinder to someone who says that his daughter brought him shame: "No more than I brought her honor" (II.114), Stilpo replied. Note also that one of the dialogues DL attributes to him is titled "To His Daughter" (II.120). That Aristippus had a daughter named Arete is stated at DL II.72.

131. This is the title of a book written by Martha Nussbaum.

132. This epigraph is drawn from DL VI.77–79. Note that "cynic" is derived from the Greek *kyōn*, "dog." The source of the Diogenes stories in this chapter is DL VI.20–79.

133. According to Aristotle's *Metaphysics* 1024b, Antisthenes denied the possibility of contradiction, and perhaps of falsehood. He argued that there was only one

predicate for each subject. Aristotle suggests he was trying to extend Eleatic logic (1043b18) and to explore the limits of definition. Stories that touch on Antisthenes in this chapter are based on DL VI.1–15.

134. In IV.46 DL actually says that it was Bion whose mother was a prostitute and father a fishmonger. This transfer is warranted by a remark Dudley makes: "there is an essentially Cynic spirit in the surviving fragments of [Bion's] writings" (*History of Cynicism*, 62).

135. See DL VI.12. The equality of men and women is also a central theme of Plato's *Republic*, especially Book V.

136. In DL V.37 Theophrastus is said to have been "ever ready to do a kindness" (Hicks translation).

137. For DL on Crates, Metrocles, Hipparchia, and Metrocles, see VI.85–101.

138. This epigraph is cobbled together from a line by Euripides DL quotes at IX.73 and a sentence I have composed.

139. Philista is identified as Pyrrho's sister at DL IX.66 where she is said to have lived in a "pious relationship" with him. The stories in this chapter are based on material in DL IX.65–107.

140. DL II.24–25.

141. According to Wikipedia, https://en.wikipedia.org/wiki/Antigonus_II_Gonatas, Antigonus became the Macedonian king in 277 BCE. Pyrrho died in 270 BCE. If nothing else, Philista's tirade, fabricated by me, is chronologically plausible.

142. The "modes" are basic argument patterns deployed by the skeptic to suspend judgment. They can be found in Sextus Empiricus, *Selections from the Major Writings*, 31–129. Also see Annas and Barnes, *Modes of Scepticism*.

143. Everhard Flintoff argues that since many of Pyrrho's teachings are similar to those found in India at the time of his putative visit, it is reasonable to infer that he learned much there. He states, for example, that "what is most striking [in Indian thought and Diogenes' description of Pyrrho] is that in both philosophies antinomial argument is used to produce a transformation inside human consciousness in which the world as usually experienced is suddenly seen as somehow unreal, as what the Indians call *maya*. A cessation of all conceptualization (*epochē*) takes place which leads on to a cessation of all speech (*aphasia*) which leads in turn to a cessation of all troubledness (*ataraxia, nirvana, moksa*)" (Flintoff, "Pyrrho and India," 94).

144. I largely follow Hicks here.

145. DL VII.176. On Zeno's death see DL VII.28 See Grau, "How to Kill a Philosopher," 360, on the topic of Stoic suicide.

146. These two sayings are from Epictetus' *Handbook* (#19 and #5). My putting Epictetus' words into Cleanthes' mouth is justified by a remark Brennan makes: "Epictetus was not a great theoretical innovator, and indeed I do not believe there is anything of philosophical substance in his works that we would not have found in Chrysippus' work. But the records of his conversations bring Stoicism to life better than any other writings do" (Brennan, *Stoic Life*, 11).

147. Stories are from DL VII.16, 69, 174, 177, 184, 168, 170, 37, 171.

148. DL VII.177. I follow Mensch closely here. Brennan says the following about the Stoic's conception of belief: "the Sage's beliefs are not opinions; they are all episodes of knowing something" (*Stoic Life*, 99).

149. VII.182. As Brennan puts it, Chrysippus "is one of the greatest thinkers of all time" (*Stoic Life*, 10). By contrast, "Cleanthes was not a genius. But he won admirers through the simplicity of his life, his capacity for hard work, and his gentle decency" (*Stoic Life*, 12).

150.   This version of DL's epitaph is mostly from Hicks. DL is likely referencing *Republic* IX, where Socrates says that the "ideal" city he has just created "in speech" may not exist on earth, but it does in "the heavens" (592b). An earlier version of this story appeared in Clemente, *misReading Plato*, 253–76.

151.   The only mention DL makes of Artemis (III.42) is that she was a slave Plato manumitted in his will.

152.   DL tells his Plato stories in III.1–46. At III.47 he shifts to an account of his "doctrines." Strikingly, he explains why by directly addressing an unnamed reader: it is because "you are rightly fond of Plato and eager to examine his philosophical doctrines" (Mensch translation). Because of his use of the feminine participle *zētousē* at III.47 it seems he is addressing a woman.

153.   Socrates offers this sort of description of smell at *Republic* 584b.

154.   See Grau, "How to Kill a Philosopher," 365.

155.   This is a simplified version of the division found in Plato's *Sophist* 219a–221b.

156.   See *Sophist* 227a–b. Translation is my own.

157.   See Plato's *Ion* 533d–534c.

158.   According to Alice Riginos, Olympiodorus' story is a "late Neoplatonic biography" (*Anecdotes Concerning the Life and Writings of Plato*, 24). My inclusion of it here is thus anachronistic. It is possible, however, that Olympidorus' story originated in Socrates' dream of the swan recounted in DL III.5, and which I here attribute to Plato himself. The swan, Riginos reminds us, is "Apollo's sacred bird." I follow Mensch's translation here.

159.   DL III.2. The Greek here is difficult to unravel. My colleague, Steve Scully, suggests this: "rather than meaning that he did not succeed in forcing her (unlikely meaning here because of the *kai*), it means that he raped his wife (and, we can presume, that he impregnated her) but that he did not 'succeed' in 'winning her.' Then, following Apollo's advice, he stayed away from her until she gave birth."

160.   See Plato's *Seventh Letter*, 327b.

161.   See Plato's *Republic* 592b.

162.   I allude to Nussbaum, *Fragility of Goodness*, chapter 8.

163.   See *Apology* 32a and *Republic* 496d.

164.   Aristotle will have an answer for her. See his *On Memory* 450b.

165.   Xenophon says much the same in his *Memorabilia*.

166.   See Plato's *Apology* 38a.

167.   The description of Meno and the swarm of virtues is found at *Meno* 72a. The bench escapade is reported at *Charmides* 155c. In the *Euthydemus*, Socrates converses with two ridiculous sophists.

168.   See Plato's *Phaedrus* 274e–276a.

169.   Plato's *Second Letter*, 314c.

170.   DL reports that Plato was not on good terms with both Xenophon and Aristippus.

171.   See Aristotle's *Parts of Animals* 683a20.

172.   See DL IV.16.

173.   Plato's *Laws* 803c.

174.   Plato's *Symposium* 202e.

175.   Plato's *Timaeus* 37d.

176.   Of course, I had to make this one up.

177.   DL III.46.

178.   According to DL IV.1, Speussipus was "irascible and liable to be dominated by pleasures" (Mensch translation). Also, he threw his favorite dog into a well.

179.   See Plato's *Theaetetus*, 147d–148a.

180. My depiction of Speusippus may well be terribly unfair. In DL IV.1, for example, we read that he adhered faithfully to Plato's views. On the other hand, other sources, particularly Aristotle, report that he rejected Plato's theory of Forms. See, for example, *Metaphysics* VII.2.1028b21 and XII.8.1072b31.

181. That Plato was buried in the Academy is stated in DL III.41.

182. The "divided-line" can be found at Plato's *Republic* 509d–511d. The relationship between mathematical objects and Forms is, I think, the most intractable of all the many problems this famous passage generates.

183. See DL IV.3. The description here makes it seem as if Speusippus suffered a stroke.

184. The notion of the tripartite soul is presented by Socrates in Plato's *Republic* 435c–445e. For Lastheneia's comments on *eros*, see Plato's *Symposium* 207–d.

185. See Plato's *Phaedo* 67e.

186. The stories in this chapter have been drawn from DL IV.8–19.

187. "Master of those who know" is from Dante's *Inferno*, canto 4. The epigraph is a modification of Heidegger's statement in his lectures of 1924 (published as *Grundegriffe der aristotelischen Philosophie*): "As for him [Aristotle] as a person, our only interest is that he was born at a certain time, that he worked, and that he died" (*Gesamtausgabe* 18:5). Thanks to my colleague Dan Dahlstrom for this information. That Menander was a student of Theophrastus is stated at DL V.36.

188. Herpyllis seems to have become Aristotle's partner after the death of his wife Pythias: see DL V.12. In his will, reported at DL V.16, Aristotle asks that his bones be placed aside those of Pythias. At DL V.13, he stipulates that because of how good she had been to him, Herpyllis should be well provided for. Nicanor was Aristotle's nephew. At DL V.36, Theophrastus is described as "a man of remarkable intelligence and industry" who "was ever ready to do a kindness" (Hicks). That Aristotle died at age sixty-three by "disease" is stated at DL V.10. Oddly, DL tells no story about his death.

189. Aristotle's *Historia Animalium* II.13. The bits about eyelids and teeth come (verbatim) from Peck's translation of Aristotle's *Parts of Animals* II.13 and III.1.

190. See Aristotle's *Politics* 1253a10.

191. In fact, the Greeks, as far as I know, would not have used the term "lesbian" to refer to same-sex relationships between women.

192. See Ierodiakonou, "Theophrastus."

193. The descriptions of the sponger and the penny pincher come from Theophrastus' *Characters*, chapters 9 and 10. About this book, which he translated, Ruston says the following: "the comedy of the fourth century"—of which Menander is the prime example—"brought stock characters to the fore: the flattering parasite, the greedy or mistrustful old man, the shameless pimp" (Ruston, *Theophrastus' Characters*, 16).

194. Theophrastus discusses the garrulous in chapter 7, the grouch in chapter 15, the obnoxius in chapter 11 and the superstitious in chapter 16 of *Characters*.

195. See Theophrastus' *Enquiry into Plants*, III.9.

196. DL V.16.

197. That Nicomachus was Aristotle's son is mentioned at DL VIII.88. There is a suggestion, but no explicit statement, that Herpyllis was his mother at DL V.12. Apparently, Aristotle had a daughter as well.

198. The details on Herpyllus are meager. In his will, Aristotle stipulated that she should be well taken care of on account of the "steady affection" (DL V.13) she has shown him.

199. Theophrastus, *Enquiry into Plants*, I.1.

200. See Aristotle, *Parts of Animals*, II.17.

201. DL V.75–85 is the biographical sketch of Demetrius. Historians disagree about his legacy and the role he played in the Library of Alexandria. O'Sullivan's *The Regime of Demetrius of Phalerum in Athens, 317–307*, is the most comprehensive and persuasive work I know on his life.

202. See Xenophon's *Memorabilia* II.i.13.

203. See Aristotle's *Politics* VII and *Nicomachean Ethics* X.7

204. This battle took place in 338 BCE, and effectively ended Athens' independence.

205. The only mention of Dromo is in V.63 where DL says he was a slave who was manumitted in Strato's will. My depiction of him, especially the stories he tells about trees, are drawn from Wohlleben, *Hidden Life of Trees*.

206. DL reports that Strato succeeded Theophrastus as head of the Lyceum, and occupied the position 286–268 BCE. Lyco followed Strato and lived from 299–225 BCE.

207. See Theophrastus' *On Plants*, I.x.

208. See Aristotle's *On Length of Life*, 467a6–30; Theophrastus' *Enquiry into Plants* 1.1.4. I owe this train of thought to the work of Sara Brill; in particular, Brill, *On the Concept of Shared Life*.

209. In fact, Aristotle's views on slavery are complicated. In *Politics* I, he draws a crucial distinction between a "natural" and a "conventional" slave. The latter is taken in war and is unjustly enslaved.

210. DL V.3.

211. DL V.68.

212. The epigraph is from Mensch with modifications. That Hermarchus was Epicurus' successor is stated at DL X.13. At X.120 it is stated that The Garden should not draw a crowd. For information on The Garden itself, see Wycherley, "Garden of Epicurus," 73–77.

213. I cite Mensch's translation of Epicurus' to Idomeneus (X.22). Epicurus explains thunderbolts at DL X.101–4. The swerve is best known to us through Lucretius' *On the Nature of Things*, II.216–50. We read about Mys at DL X.33 and about the soul at DL X.63. The saying, "death is nothing to us," can be found at DL X.124 and 139.

214. The brothers Timocrates and Metrodous came from Lampsacus to study with Epicurus. The former quit The Garden, and is said by DL (X.6) to have spread malicious slander about him, while the latter became Epicurus' best friend and most loyal follower. In Philodemus' *On Frank Criticism*, we find this: "Timocrates said that he both loved his brother as no one else did and hated him as no one else" (123).

Bibliography

Annas, Julia, and Jonathan Barnes. *The Modes of Scepticism*. Cambridge: Cambridge University Press, 1985.

Aristotle. *Opera*. Oxford: Clarendon, 2006.

Brennan, Tad. *The Stoic Life*. Oxford: Clarendon, 2005.

Brill, Sara. *Aristotle on the Concept of Shared Life*. Oxford: Oxford University Press, 2020.

Chitwood, Ana. *Death by Philosophy: The Biographic Tradition in the Life and Death of the Archaic Philosophers*. Ann Arbor: University of Michigan Press, 2004.

Clemente, Matthew. *misReading Plato*. London: Routledge, 2022.

Curd, Patricia, ed. *A Presocratics Reader*. Translated by Richard D. McKirahan Jr. Indianapolis: Hackett, 1996.

Diels, Hermann, and Walther Kranz. *Die Fragmente der Vorsokratiker*. Berlin: Weidmannsche, 1964.

Diogenes Laertius. *Lives of Eminent Philosophers*. Translated by R. D. Hicks. Edited by Jeffrey Henderson. Cambridge: Harvard University Press, 2006.

———. *Lives of the Eminent Philosophers*. Translated by Pamela Mensch. Edited by James Miller. Oxford: Oxford University Press, 2018.

Dudley, Donald. *A History of Cynicism*. Hildesheim, Germany: Olms, 1967.

Epictetus. *The Handbook*. Translated by Nicholas White. Indianapolis: Hackett, 1983.

Flintoff, Everhard. "Pyrrho and India." *Phronesis* 25 (1980) 91–103.

Grau, Sergi. "How to Kill a Philosopher: The Narrating of Ancient Greek Philosophers' Deaths in Relation to Their Way of Living." *Ancient Philosophy* 30 (2010) 347–82.

Guthrie, Kenneth. *The Pythagorean Sourcebook*. Grand Rapids: Phanes, 1987.

Heath, Thomas. *A History of Greek Mathematics*. New York: Dover, 1981.

Hegel, G. W. F. *The Phenomenology of Spirit*. Translated by A. V. Miller. Oxford: Clarendon, 1977.

Herodotus. *The Histories*. Translated by Andrea Purvis. New York: Random House, 2009.

Homer. *Odyssey*. Translated by Robert Fitzgerald. New York: Farrar, Straus, and Giroux, 1998.

Huggett, Nick. "Zeno's Paradoxes." *Stanford Encyclopedia of Philosophy*, 2019. https://plato.stanford.edu/archives/win2019/entries/paradox-zeno/.

Hutchinson, D. S. Introduction to *The Epicurus Reader*. Translated and edited by Brad Inwood and L. P. Gerson. Indianapolis: Hackett, 1994.

Ierodiakonou, Katerina. "Theophrastus." *Stanford Encyclopedia of Philosophy*, 2016. https://plato.stanford.edu/archives/sum2016/entries/theophrastus/.

Kirk, G. S., et al. *The Presocratic Philosophers: A Critical History with a Selection of Texts*. 2nd ed. Cambridge: Cambridge University Press, 1983.

Laks, André. "Diogenes Laertius and the Pre-Socratics." In *Lives of the Eminent Philosophers*, edited by James Miller, 588–91. Oxford: Oxford University Press, 2018.

Long, Herbert. "Introduction." In *Lives of Eminent Philosophers*, edited by Jeffrey Henderson, xv–xxvi. Cambridge: Harvard University Press, 2006.

Lucretius. *On the Nature of Things*. Translated by Martin Smith. Indianapolis: Hackett, 2001.

Mantel, Hilary. *Bring Up the Bodies*. New York: Picador, 2013.

Nietzsche, Friedrich. *Philosophy in the Tragic Age of the Greeks*. Translated by Marianne Cowan. Chicago: Regnery Gateway, 1962.

Nussbaum, Martha. *The Fragility of Goodness*. Cambridge: Cambridge University Press, 1986.

O'Sullivan, Lara. *The Regime of Demetrius of Phalerum in Athens, 317–307: A Philosopher in Politics*. Leiden: Brill, 2009.

Ovid. *Metamorphoses*. Translated by A. D. Meville. Oxford: Oxford University Press, 1987.

Philodemus. *On Frank Criticism*. Translated by David Konstan. Atlanta: Scholars, 2007.

Plato. *Opera*. Oxford: Clarendon, 1995.

Riedweg, Christop. *Pythagoras: His Life, Teaching, and Influence*. Ithaca, NY: Cornell University Press, 2002.

Riginos, Alice. *The Anecdotes Concerning the Life and Writings of Plato*. Leiden: Brill, 1976.

Roochnik, David. *Retrieving the Ancients: An Introduction to Ancient Greek Philosophy*. London: Wiley, 2023.

Rowland, Ingrid. "Raphael's Eminent Philosophers." In *Lives of the Eminent Philosophers*, edited by James Miller, 554–60. Oxford: Oxford University Press, 2018.

Samons, Loren. *Pericles and the Conquest of History*. Cambridge: Cambridge University Press, 2016.

Schwob, Marcel. *Imaginary Lives*. Translated by Chris Clarke. Cambridge: Wakefield, 2018.

Sextus Empiricus. *Selections from the Major Writings*. Translated by Sanford Etheridge. Indianapolis: Hackett, 1985.

Singer, I. B. *The Collected Stories*. New York: Farrar, Straus, and Giroux, 1982.

Theophrastus. *Characters*. Translated by Jeffery Ruston. Cambridge: Harvard University Press, 2002.

Thucydides. *History of the Peloponnesian War*. Translated by Rex Warner. New York: Penguin, 1972.

Wohlleben, Peter. *The Hidden Life of Trees*. Translated by Jane Billinghurst. Vancouver: Greystone, 2016.

Wright, M. R. *The Presocratics*. Bristol: Bristol Classical, 1985.

Wycherley, R. E. "The Garden of Epicurus." *Phoenix* 13 (1959) 73–77.

Xenophon. *Memorabilia, Oeconomicus, Symposium, Apology*. Translated by E. C. Marchant and O. J. Todd. Cambridge: Harvard University Press, 2013.

www.ingramcontent.com/pod-product-compliance
Lightning Source LLC
Chambersburg PA
CBHW030106030726
47498CB00007B/2276